THE SCENT OF DEATH

Recent Titles by Betty Rowlands from Severn House

ALPHA, BETA, GAMMA . . . DEAD
COPYCAT
DEADLY OBSESSION
DEATH AT DEARLY MANOR
DIRTY WORK
A FOOL THERE WAS
A HIVE OF BEES
AN INCONSIDERATE DEATH
MISS MINCHIN DIES
PARTY TO MURDER
THE SCENT OF DEATH
SMOKESCREEN
TOUCH ME NOT
UNNATURAL WASTAGE

THE SCENT OF DEATH

Betty Rowlands

This first world edition published 2014
in Great Britain and in the USA by
SEVERN HOUSE PUBLISHERS LTD of
19 Cedar Road, Sutton, Surrey, England, SM2 5DA.

British Library Cataloguing in Publication Data

Rowlands, Betty author.
  The scent of death. – (A Sukey Reynolds mystery)
  1. Reynolds, Sukey (Fictitious character)–Fiction.
  2. Murder–Investigation–Fiction. 3. Policewomen–Great
  Britain–Fiction. 4. Detective and mystery stories.
  I. Title II. Series
  823.9'14-dc23

ISBN-13: 978-0-7278-8391-9 (cased)

All Severn House titles are printed on acid-free paper.

Severn House Publishers support the Forest Stewardship Council™ [FSC™],
the leading international forest certification organisation. All our titles that
are printed on FSC certified paper carry the FSC logo.

MIX
Paper from
responsible sources
FSC
www.fsc.org   FSC® C013056

Typeset by Palimpsest Book Production Ltd.,
Falkirk, Stirlingshire, Scotland.
Printed and bound in Great Britain by
TJ International, Padstow, Cornwall.

PROLOGUE

'Are we all here?' Justin Freeman glanced round the room at the group of music lovers who were settling down after dinner to enjoy a programme of music in the Orchard Room at Dallington Manor, where his annual musical house party was in full swing.

Eric, who made it his business to check numbers, raised a hand. 'All except Lance,' he said in his high-pitched, slightly querulous voice.

Justin frowned. 'That's odd, he's usually here first.' There were nods of agreement all round. Lance Rainbird did not usually stay for social chit-chat over the after-dinner coffee.

'He said something about going out for a spot of air,' someone in the back row volunteered.

'Well, it is a lovely evening,' his neighbour agreed. 'And you can see the stars; that's the advantage of this place, it's quite a distance from a town so there isn't much in the way of light pollution.'

'I'm not putting the evening's programme on hold to wait for Lance,' Justin announced with a rare touch of impatience. 'Let's hope he has the grace to slide in quietly when he comes in from his stargazing. Right, we're going to listen to Mozart's Fortieth Symphony this evening. This is a particularly good example of a work composed in the sonata form. May I take it you all understand what that means? Not sure?' he went on, noting one or two doubtful expressions. 'Right, well it's very simple really. Let's take the first movement. We start with the first or principal subject.' He pressed a key on the CD player beside him and played the opening of the first movement. Hands moved and bodies swayed gently in time with the familiar music until he pressed the pause button and said, 'Now listen to the next or bridge section, leading to the introduction of the second . . .' He broke off as the door was flung open and the hotel manager appeared in an obvious state of agitation.

'I do apologize for bursting in like this, Mr Freeman.' He sounded breathless, as if he'd been running. 'There's been an accident. It's Mr Rainbird . . . one of my staff found him in the lake. We've pulled him out and someone's giving him the kiss of life, but I think . . . I do hope I'm wrong . . . but I'm afraid he might be dead.'

'Good heavens,' Justin exclaimed. 'Have you sent for an ambulance?'

'Oh yes of course. They're on their way . . . ah, I think I can hear the siren.' He turned and rushed out with Justin at his heels, leaving the assembled guests exchanging horrified glances.

ONE

'What's your take on classical music, Sukey?' DS Vicky Armstrong returned to her desk, but did not sit down. 'Classical music?' DC Sukey Reynolds cast a slightly puzzled look at her recently promoted friend. 'What's this about? Are you doing a crossword puzzle or something?'

'No, this is serious. We've just been given an assignment by DI Rathbone. It's at a place called Dallington Manor, a country house hotel a few miles the other side of Clevedon. They've got some kind of music festival going on there. A man's body's been fished out of the lake.' Vicky consulted the printout in her hand. 'A chap called Rainbird.'

'Is that all we know?'

'It seems the woman who spotted the man rushed back to the hotel and informed the manager, who told one of his staff to call for an ambulance and then rushed down to the lake with another of his staff who's trained in first aid. They managed to fish the man out of the water and did their best to revive him, but when the paramedics arrived they said he was dead and called us. They're waiting for a doctor. DI Rathbone has been notified and he's told us to get there ASAP.'

Sukey gave a resigned sigh. 'What's the betting the floater had too much to drink and lost his balance?'

Vicky shrugged. 'That's probably why Sir farmed it off on us so that he could leave on time.' She glanced at the clock. 'Another half an hour and we'd have been off duty.'

'It could be worse,' said Sukey. 'At least it isn't too far.'

Vicky grimaced. 'Typical of you, always ready to look on the bright side. I've just called Chris to say expect me when he sees me and he isn't best pleased. He's trying out a new recipe and he wants my opinion, says it won't take kindly to being kept hot.' Vicky's partner was a chef at an exclusive hotel on the outskirts of Bristol.

'Are uniformed at the scene?'

'On their way and I've booked us a car, so let's go.'

During the drive Vicky shared with Sukey the information she had obtained about Dallington Manor from their website. 'It sounds quite exclusive – only thirty-five bedrooms, all en suite of course, and the entire building's smoke-free. Secluded setting, beautiful grounds. They have facilities for conferences and wedding receptions – they erect a marquee for the receptions. Conferences are held in the main building – that's the one the victim was attending.'

'You said something about classical music,' said Sukey.

Vicky grinned. 'That's how Sir described it. Perhaps it's a sort of posh Woodstock; anyway, that's all we know at the moment. I'll have to get more info from the organizer.' She glanced once more at the printout. 'Justin Freeman. Does the name mean anything to you?'

'Not a thing,' said Sukey. 'I hope there isn't a reception being held at the same time; there could be up to seventy people at the festival – or conference, or whatever it's called – and if there's a reception as well it could mean hundreds of people milling about.' She heaved a sigh. 'Think of all the statements to be taken. Ah, here we are.'

The entrance to Dallington Manor was through an impressive pair of wrought-iron gates and along a winding drive that climbed a gentle slope. Two police cars were already there, parked alongside an ambulance. Sukey parked, they got out and Vicky spoke to one of the paramedics.

'The doctor's just arrived,' she said. 'He's down there with the police.' She pointed to a grassy slope to where glimpses of water could be seen between some trees with overhanging branches. Several people, including uniformed officers with powerful flashlights, could be seen close to a figure lying on the ground a few feet from the edge of the water. A man with a stethoscope was bending over him.

'Right,' said Vicky, 'we'd better go down and have a word.'

'Careful,' the paramedic warned, 'the grass is a bit slippery after all the rain.'

'Thank goodness it's cleared up,' Sukey remarked as they made their way down the slope. She glanced at the sky. 'It's a beautiful night. Just look at all the stars.'

As they approached, one of the officers, Sergeant Drury, came forward. He raised a hand in greeting and said, 'Hi Vicky, good to see you. Congratulations on your promotion.'

'Thank you,' said Vicky. 'You know Sukey, don't you?'

'Of course,' said Drury, 'we've worked together before. When are you going for promotion, Sukey?'

'I'm thinking about it,' she said. She glanced beyond him. 'What's the story?'

'He's a man aged about forty something, identified as Lance Rainbird. He'd been attending a music event organized by Justin Freeman, musicologist and part-time conductor. He had dinner with the rest of the participants but instead of staying for coffee and a chat he said he was going outside for some air before the evening programme. The receptionist noticed him go past her desk on the way to the front door, and so far as we know she was the last person to see him alive. Ah, the doctor seems to have finished; let's go and have a word.'

'I reckon he's been dead not much longer than an hour,' said the doctor as he put his stethoscope in his bag and stood up. 'Drowning appears to be the cause of death, but there's not enough light here to do a proper examination. I'll have a closer look when we get him to the morgue. I'll be in touch.'

'Many thanks, Doc,' said Drury. He turned back to the two detectives. 'We received the call a little after nine. The evening session had just begun; Rainbird's absence had been noted and someone mentioned that he'd gone outside for some air so the organizer began without him. They'd hardly got started when the hotel manager rushed in with the news that Rainbird had been found in the lake; he and a member of his staff had pulled him out, one of them was trying artificial respiration and an ambulance had been called. Freeman went dashing out with him, telling the others to wait till he got back.' Drury consulted his notebook. 'We got here about nine twenty; the paramedics were already here and said they were pretty sure the man was dead. The doctor on duty happened to live locally and arrived a few minutes later. I guess you'll want to have a look round before they take him to the morgue.'

They stood for a few moments in silence, looking down at the dead man. His eyes stared blankly through half-open lids;

it seemed to Sukey that they held a vague expression of bewilderment, as if he was trying to make sense of what had happened to him. Traces of duckweed clung grotesquely to his forehead and the side of his face; a froth of bubbles clung to the mouth, only partially wiped away during the efforts at resuscitation.

'Who found him?' asked Sukey.

'A hotel employee, a young woman called Rosie. He was lying face down in the water and she went back to the house in a state of panic, screaming for help.'

'We'll let the paramedics take him away and then we'd better contain the scene until we can establish exactly what happened,' said Vicky. 'Will your chaps see to that, Rob?'

'Sure,' said Drury.

'We'll go in and get some statements.' They followed the directions to reception. A tall man with receding grey hair and a neatly trimmed beard was at the desk talking to a uniformed police constable whom neither Vicky nor Sukey had met before. He moved forward to greet them.

'PC Bond,' he said, adding with a wry smile, 'James Bond. And there are no prizes for guessing why I'm known as double-oh-seven.'

Sukey gave a sympathetic chuckle but Vicky remained straight-faced. 'DS Armstrong and DC Reynolds,' she said briskly with a questioning glance at the man beside him.

'This is Mr Justin Freeman,' Bond went on. 'He's the organizer of the event Mr Rainbird was attending. All the other participants are waiting in the Orchard Room, which is where they were assembled when the news of the tragedy reached them.'

'I thought that was the best thing to do,' said Freeman, who had not spoken during the introductions. 'Forgive me, but I don't understand why members of the CID should be here. Surely this is nothing but a dreadful accident.'

'There's no need for alarm,' said Vicky. 'It's normal for the CID to be informed in any case of an unexpected death and we have no reason at this stage to assume there's anything suspicious about what happened to Mr Rainbird.' Freeman appeared reassured, but he pulled a handkerchief from his pocket and wiped his fingers. 'Perhaps you could go and see them,' Vicky went on, 'tell them we're here and say we shall need to take some details from them.'

'Is it OK to let them leave the Orchard Room?'

'Provided they don't leave the building.'

'They'll be relieved at that. My guess is quite a few will be heading for the bar. I could do with a drink myself.'

'That's fine.'

Vicky turned to the receptionist, a woman of about thirty with straight, neatly cut hair, wearing a blue blazer with a DM monogram on the pocket. 'We need to speak to the person who found the body. Is there a private room we can use?'

'Of course.' She raised the counter and beckoned them to go behind the desk. 'The girl who found Mr Rainbird is already waiting in the manager's office. The manager's wife is with her; they're both pretty upset and Mr Chapman has given them a nip of brandy to calm them down.' She opened a door and ushered them into a room with a desk, a computer and two filing cabinets. A young woman was seated in front of the desk and an older woman sat beside her, holding one of her hands. She stood up when the detectives entered, but without releasing the younger woman's hand. 'This is Mrs Chapman, our manager's wife,' said the receptionist. 'These ladies are from the police and they'd like a word with Rosie.'

'Thank you, Maxine,' said Mrs Chapman, a good-looking woman of about forty. Like Rosie, she was trembling; her eyes were wet and her voice was unsteady. 'I'm Lily Chapman,' she explained. 'I'm afraid we're both very upset – especially Rosie, of course, as she's the one who actually found him . . . that is to say –' at this point she drew a deep breath before saying – 'found Mr Rainbird.'

'It's understandable that you're upset,' said Vicky. 'It's a dreadful thing to have happened and we'll try to make this as easy as possible for you.'

'Thank you. Would you like to sit down? I can ask Maxine to fetch some chairs for you.'

'No thank you, we're fine,' said Vicky. She looked down at the younger woman, whom Sukey judged to be in her mid-twenties. Her eyes were red and swollen and she clutched a handful of damp tissues, but appeared fairly calm. 'Are you OK to answer a few questions, Rosie?' She nodded. 'We understand you're the one who first saw Mr Rainbird's body in the water and came back to raise the alarm.'

'I didn't realize it was Mr Rainbird,' said Rosie. 'I just saw a shape in the water and when I looked I could see it was a man. I couldn't see his face but he was very still and I . . .' Her voice threatened to break but she controlled it with an effort and went on, 'I think I must have screamed; anyway, I ran back into the house and asked for help and a couple of people ran out and . . . you said "Mr Rainbird's *body*". He really is dead, then?' She looked up at Lily Chapman, who bit her lip and nodded. She too appeared not far from tears.

'I'm afraid so,' said Vicky. 'Would you mind telling us what you were doing by the lake?'

Rosie jumped as if she had been stung. 'I was just out for a stroll. Surely you don't think that I . . .?'

'I didn't say that,' Vicky interrupted with a hint of impatience. 'Would you mind answering the question?'

'But I hardly knew the gentleman . . . why would I . . .?' She appeared on the point of breaking down and Lily Chapman patted her shoulder and shot a slightly reproachful glance at Vicky.

'Please, don't distress yourself,' said Sukey gently. 'We're just trying to find out what happened, and we simply want to know if you saw anything – anything at all that attracted your attention and made you walk towards the lake.'

Rosie shook her head. 'No, I saw nothing unusual. I often take a stroll down there after I've had my evening meal.'

'What time would that be?'

'The kitchen staff give us our meal about eight o'clock, after the guests have been served, so I suppose it was soon after half past eight – maybe a quarter to nine.'

'You didn't hear anything, like a shout, for example, or the sound of anyone running?'

'No.'

'Was there anyone else around?'

'I didn't see anyone.'

Sukey glanced at Vicky, who nodded and said, 'Well, thank you, Rosie, that will be all for now.'

They went back to reception, where Maxine was sitting at

the computer. Sukey noticed that her hands were shaking; evidently she too was affected by what had happened. 'Most of the guests are in the bar,' she said, 'but a few have gone down to the lake to try and view the scene of the crime. Morbid curiosity I suppose.'

'I assure you, there's no suggestion of foul play,' Vicky snapped.

'Sorry, just a figure of speech,' said Maxine. Her tone was civil but Sukey sensed that she found Vicky's manner irritating. 'Anyway, your officers have been shooing them away.'

'Quite right too.' Vicky was about to speak again when her phone rang. She took it from her pocket and moved away, spoke briefly and then beckoned to Sukey.

'That was the doctor,' she said in a low voice. 'He's at the morgue . . . says Rainbird suffered a blow to the back of the head before falling into the water.'

'So we might have a murder on our hands,' said Sukey.

For the first time since their arrival at the hotel, Vicky's face showed a trace of amusement. 'That'd spoil DI Rathbone's weekend, wouldn't it?'

TWO

Vicky called DI Rathbone and gave him the news. After a brief conversation she said, 'Right, Guv, see you shortly.' She winked at Sukey as she ended the call. 'He's not best pleased!' she said gleefully.

'I take it he's joining us here.' Sukey glanced at her watch. 'It's gone eleven. I'm surprised he didn't tell us to go through the formalities and say we'd all be back here first thing in the morning.'

'It so happens he was having a drink with DCI Leach when I called, so he could hardly get out of it. My guess is it'll just be a token appearance, to make it known that there's a senior officer in charge.' She frowned suddenly. 'I wonder why he feels he has to show up here now. When he was a mere sergeant he'd have taken charge at this stage and given out team orders, reporting directly to Mr Leach when he needed instructions how to proceed. Oh well,' she went on with a shrug, 'he'd had years of experience as a sergeant – maybe I'm too recently promoted to be allowed to handle this on my own.'

'Or Sir is conscious of his own status,' said Sukey. 'Don't you think we ought to tell the manager and Mr Freeman that he's on his way?'

'Yes, of course. You speak to the manager and I'll go and find Mr Freeman. We'll need statements from all the staff and the people attending the conference; we'll have to see what Sir says, but I don't think they'll take kindly to being questioned at this hour. Some of them may have already gone to their rooms. And ask Sergeant Drury to set up a round-the-clock guard on what is now a murder scene.'

'Will do.' Sukey had a brief word with Maxine before going back to the lakeside. When she returned, Vicky was already in conversation with the manager, a stocky man in his fifties with florid features.

'I've told Mr Freeman and Mr Chapman of the latest development,' she said. 'Mr Freeman has full details of everyone at the conference; he's gone to his room to collect the list and Mr Chapman will have it photocopied for us.'

'That'll be a great help,' said Sukey.

Moments later Freeman appeared and handed a folder to Vicky who passed it to Chapman.

'I'll get Maxine to photocopy these for you right away,' the manager promised. 'I'll be with you in a moment.'

'I thought you'd like to have a copy of this weekend's programme,' said Freeman. He gave a folder to Vicky. 'There are notes about the works we'll be listening to and it also includes the timetable and some background information about our courses in general.'

'Thank you,' said Vicky. 'Please sit down, Mr Freeman,' she went on, indicating a circle of armchairs in front of an open grate, on which the remains of a log fire were still glowing. 'This must have come as a great shock.'

Freeman made a helpless gesture with his hands. 'I just can't believe there's a murderer in our group.'

'Let's not jump to conclusions,' said Vicky. 'At the moment we're treating this as an unexplained death.'

'I don't understand. What's the—?'

'Never mind that now!' Vicky interrupted. 'We need to ask you some questions.'

Seeing that Freeman was beginning to show signs of agitation and that Vicky's patience was wearing thin, Sukey hastily intervened. 'I'm afraid we're not allowed to reveal any further information at this stage,' she explained. 'It's against the rules.'

He shrugged. 'OK. I suppose you have to follow procedure.'

'I've just spoken to Detective Inspector Rathbone, who will take charge of this case from now on,' Vicky resumed. 'He'll be with us shortly, so meanwhile perhaps you'd tell us something about this event you're running. How would you describe it?'

'It's one of a number I organize during the year for music lovers. I call them musical weekends, but this one is rather special. It lasts a bit longer than most of the others and we end with a party on the last night.'

'You're a music teacher?'

'I lectured in music at Branwell College until my retirement five years ago. It was then that I started organizing these events.'

'So you've been running them for five years?' Freeman nodded. 'Are they always held at Dallington Manor?'

'No, at various locations, but we always come here for the March one.'

'What about the people who attend? Are they the same ones each time?'

'Oh no, they tend to vary according to what's on the programme and how far they have to travel to the venue. We do have what you might call a nucleus of regular attendees.'

'Was Mr Rainbird one of them?'

'Oh yes, very much so.'

'How did he get on with the other people in the party?'

Freeman thought for a moment before speaking. 'Well enough I suppose, but I wouldn't describe him as a social animal – a bit of an oddball in some ways. He was very knowledgeable about music and always ready to talk about it or anything connected with it. I'm afraid he tended to flaunt his expertise and experience and some people were made to feel a bit – well, almost like novices you might say. He sometimes brought the score of a work such as a symphony or a piano concerto with him and I noticed him moving his hands as if he was conducting the piece. Some people may have found that distracting but it didn't bother me – I just looked the other way. He also had a habit of waffling on at length about a particular work we were studying and how he'd heard better performances by this or that orchestra or soloist.'

'You must have found that irritating.'

'Not particularly. He was entitled to his opinion.'

'Would you describe him as a heavy drinker?'

'On the contrary – I've never seen him drink anything stronger than mineral water or fruit juice.'

'You mentioned "performances". Do I take it you sometimes arrange live performances?'

'Occasionally. Most of the time I use CDs from my extensive collection and play them on my own audio equipment. I do sometimes invite a friend – a professional pianist or a singer for example – to give a solo recital, but that would be impossible with orchestral works.'

'Yes, I can understand that,' Sukey remarked. 'I can't imagine there are many among your venues with a concert hall on the premises.'

'Actually, some of our programmes do include a visit to a live concert or opera.'

Chapman returned with the folder, which he gave back to Freeman. 'I've copied everything,' he said, handing some sheets of paper to Vicky before sitting down with the others. 'Thank you, Doug,' he added as a waiter appeared with a tray. 'I thought you might appreciate some coffee.'

'That's super, thank you very much,' said Vicky.

At that moment they heard the sound of a car; moments later the door was flung open and Rathbone entered and strode towards them. 'Who's in charge here?' he demanded with a touch of aggression. Then he caught sight of the cafetière and his expression brightened. 'Well, that's a good start.' He took the cup that Sukey hastily filled for him and sat down while introductions were made. 'Right, Sergeant, let's have your report.'

He drank his coffee and listened carefully while Vicky recounted the sequence of events leading up to the doctor's call from the morgue. 'Sergeant Drury is containing the scene, the deceased's room has been secured and Mr Freeman has given us a list of the names of everyone in his group. We haven't taken statements from any of them yet.'

'No point in making a start on that tonight, so long as everyone knows they have to stay in the hotel until we've spoken to them,' said Rathbone.

'I have made that clear to all the guests, Guv, and there have been no objections,' said Vicky. 'Most of the staff have already gone home, but Mr Chapman has all their details and in any case they'll be back on duty in the morning. The staff that are still here are resident. Mr Freeman has been telling us something about the programme of musical events that he organizes during the year, of which this weekend forms a part,' she continued. 'He mentioned that Mr Rainbird was . . . something of a loner in the group, would you say, sir?'

'That's one way of putting it,' Freeman said with a faint smile. 'What I meant was that he wasn't exactly flavour of the month with some of the others because he had rather a high opinion of himself and his musical knowledge. As I said, he liked to give the impression that his knowledge was superior to that of the *hoi polloi*, but I never heard him say anything exactly humiliating to any one individual – it was just the kind of impression he gave. But it's true he always came and left alone and never to my knowledge was particularly close to other members of the party, even those he'd met a number of times before.'

'I see.' Rathbone took another mouthful of coffee. 'Have you ever witnessed any serious unpleasantness between him and any other person?'

Freeman shook his head. 'Not really. I have overheard people muttering about what a big-head he is – was – and occasionally someone would challenge him on a particular point during a coffee break, but nothing untoward.'

'Well, thank you, Mr Freeman. Vicky and Sukey, I take it you've been noting all this?' After they obediently said, 'Yes, Guv,' Rathbone turned to Chapman. 'When did you learn of the accident to Mr Rainbird, sir?'

'It was around nine o'clock when Rosie – she works with our receptionist, Maxine – came rushing into the hotel in a state of near hysterics. I left her with Maxine and called Ben, one of my staff who has had first-aid training, and we hurried down to the lake.' Chapman went on to recount the sequence of events that Vicky and Sukey had learned of during their initial enquiries.

'What do you know about the victim?'

'He's stayed here with Mr Freeman's group on a number of occasions, but I know nothing about him personally.'

'Has he ever caused any kind of trouble or upset any of your staff?'

'Not that I'm aware of – he's certainly never complained to me or my wife, and no member of the staff has complained about him to me.'

'I see. Well, thank you for your time gentlemen. I propose to leave it there for tonight. We'll have to get statements from everyone tomorrow. A small team of uniformed officers will be on duty all night and I'd appreciate it if you'd allow them to use the hotel facilities when necessary.'

'Of course. Maybe they'd welcome a hot drink or snack?'

'I'm sure they would. Thank you – and thank you for the coffee.'

As the detectives returned to their respective cars, Rathbone said, 'I'll see you at eight thirty sharp in my office tomorrow. Yes, I'm prepared for it to turn out to be an accidental death,' he went on without allowing Vicky or Sukey an opportunity to speak, 'but I'm not taking any chances.' He got into his car, slammed the door and drove off, leaving the two exchanging resigned glances.

'You know what,' said Vicky as she buckled on her seat belt, 'I reckon he'd like it to be a really tricky murder case so that when he gets a result he'll notch up a whole rack of Brownie points.'

'Don't you mean when *we* get a result?' said Sukey.

For the first time that evening, Vicky gave a spontaneous laugh. 'You could well be right. It'll be interesting to see how he handles it.'

* * *

When Sukey reached home she found a message on her answering service. It was from Harry Matthews, whom Vicky referred to as her partner but Sukey always said, 'I prefer "significant other" – it sounds less permanent.' She knew almost by heart before she opened it what he would say: 'Are you OK? You were supposed to be home by half past ten and it's gone eleven thirty. Your mobile's switched off. What's going on? Call me as soon as you get this, never mind how late. Love you.'

Sukey pressed the answer button. 'Sorry, love, I should have warned you,' she said as soon as he came on the line. 'Vicky and I were ordered to respond to a request for police presence at an unexpected death at a hotel about twenty miles away.'

'Ordered by the uppity DI Rathbone, I suppose. No chance of *him* attending of course.'

Despite her weariness, Sukey could not restrain a chuckle. 'He had to turn out in the end – what appeared to be an accidental death might turn out to be suspicious.'

'Sounds interesting!' Harry was the senior crime reporter for the local newspaper and she could visualize his expression becoming suddenly alert. 'You'll keep me posted, won't you – subject to the usual restrictions, of course.'

She decided to ignore the last remark. 'He wants us on duty at eight thirty *sharp* tomorrow morning.'

'But tomorrow's Sunday,' Harry protested.

'I know, but it happens to be our turn for weekend duty – remember?'

'Sorry, I've been away covering a trial in Birmingham and I clean forgot. Have you had anything to eat?'

'Not a lot. I'm going to have a quick snack and then bed.'

'Well mind you have a good breakfast tomorrow. Keep in touch, love you.'

'Love you too,' she said softly as the sound of a kiss came over the wire.

When Sukey checked in at headquarters the following morning she had a brief word with the staff in CID to ask if any further messages from Dallington Manor had come in before going straight to DI Rathbone's office. Two other detective constables,

Tim Pringle and Mike Haskins, were already there and Vicky joined them a few moments later.

'I've spoken to the manager and told him I'm sending a team of detectives to continue with our enquiries,' Rathbone began. 'Freeman and his lot are having breakfast and their morning session begins at nine thirty. Vicky, I want you and Sukey to have a thorough check on the area where the accident happened. Things that got missed last night might be visible in daylight. Have a further talk with Freeman and see if he can identify any of the members of his group who might possibly have crossed swords with Rainbird and if so I want you two to talk to them. Mike and Tim, you will begin by taking statements from people Freeman feels are less likely to have done so. I know this sounds a bit hit and miss,' he went on, 'but until we get some idea of the general ambience within the group we're unlikely to spot anything that looks like a lead. Any questions?'

'What will you be doing, Guv?' asked Vicky slyly.

'I do have several other cases to keep a check on,' he replied sharply, 'and please bear in mind that this is officially being treated as an unexplained death at the moment. If any of the press show up you tell them nothing.' The final remark was intended to be for the whole team, but Sukey's relationship with Harry was well known and she was aware that it was addressed principally at her.

When the team arrived at the hotel they found Chapman at reception talking to Freeman. After Vicky had introduced Tim and Mike, Freeman said, 'Mr Chapman has very kindly set aside some rooms where you can take statements, as requested by Inspector Rathbone.'

'That's excellent, thank you very much,' said Vicky. She outlined Rathbone's instructions for the conduct of the interviews. 'I believe your programme begins in twenty minutes or so and we don't want to disrupt it any more than necessary. It would be very helpful if you could identify a few people from the list of attendees who you feel might have had disagreements with Mr Rainbird.'

Freeman glanced through the list for a few moments before saying, 'There are a few that come to mind.' He put a tick against several names. 'Eric Bowen, Hugh Pearson and Charlotte Lang – she's in a wheelchair and brings her carer Millie with her. Poor Millie; Charlotte's a bit of a bully – if anything goes wrong it's always Millie's fault, but she takes it without a murmur. And there's a couple; Trixie – short for Beatrix – and Stan Day. They've been regulars since I started the business. And then there's Romeo.'

'Romeo who?' asked Sukey.

'Search me. I heard him busking in a shopping centre two or three years ago and I could hardly believe what I was hearing. He's got a remarkable voice and when he'd finished singing the bird catcher's song from *The Magic Flute* – unaccompanied except for a set of pan pipes – I asked him where he'd trained, but he insisted it was a natural voice and he'd worked on it by himself. I found it hard to believe, but that was all he'd say. He looks like a gypsy and he just turns up at these events from time to time and asks me if it's OK to give one or two solo performances during the free afternoon for anyone who cares to stay and listen. He lives in an old motor caravan and he's grateful for the few quid I give him to entertain the older, less active members of the party who tend to stay in the hotel instead of going out shopping or sightseeing. Some of the regulars say this weekend wouldn't be the same without him. Needless to say, Lance wasn't impressed. He stayed once to hear him – out of curiosity I suppose – but walked out in the middle of a song.'

'That was a bit rude.'

'That's Lance for you.'

'Which is the free afternoon?'

'Today, as it happens.'

'You describe this event as your annual musical house party,' said Vicky. 'How long does it go on?'

'It started at five o'clock Friday afternoon and ends after breakfast on Tuesday morning.'

'I don't recall seeing Romeo's name on the list,' said Vicky.

'That's because he's not staying the whole time. He'll do his act and then move on. I noticed his van parked in a lay-by about half a mile down the road. He hasn't made contact with me yet, but I've no doubt he will. He knows I'm here.'

'How does he know?'

'He's got a mobile – he can pick up emails on that and anyway he knows we come here at the same time every year.'

'What can you tell us about these people?' asked Sukey.

'I'd rather you formed your own opinion.'

'OK,' said Vicky. 'DC Reynolds and I will start with the names you've ticked and DCs Pringle and Haskins will work through the remaining names in the order they're listed. If you'd be kind enough to get them started, DC Reynolds and I will go and have a word with the officers guarding the area by the lake and we'll contact you again as soon as we get back.'

'By the way,' said Sukey, 'did you stay after dinner and chat to the group over coffee until it was time to start the evening session?'

'I stayed for a few minutes and then I went up to the Orchard Room to set up the recordings for the evening session.'

'So you were up there on your own for perhaps ten minutes or so?'

'I suppose so. Is it important?'

'Did you happen to look out of the window?'

'What would have been the point? The curtains were drawn and anyway it was dark outside.'

'If you had happened to glance through the window you might have seen something or someone out there, that's all,' said Vicky. 'We have to check every detail.'

He nodded. 'I quite understand. I'm afraid I didn't see anything at all that might help. May I take it we can carry on with our morning programme?'

'Yes, of course. We'll try to keep interruptions to the minimum. Thank you very much for your cooperation.'

Freeman gave a little bow. 'My pleasure, Sergeant,' he said.

'So Rainbird wasn't a drinker,' said Vicky as they made their way down to the lake.

'Which means he's unlikely to have fallen into the lake without some assistance,' said Sukey.

'Exactly.'

THREE

S ergeant Drury and PC Bond were the officers on duty by
the lake.

'Morning, Rob, morning, double oh seven,' said Vicky.
'Anything to report?'

'Not a thing,' replied Drury. 'I sent the night watchmen home
as soon as we arrived this morning. I take it you want to examine
the area again in daylight?'

'That's right. To be honest, I don't hold out a lot of hope of
finding much in the way of a lead – there have been too many
people milling around so identifying individual shoe prints
would be a nightmare, especially as it rained again during the
night.'

'You never know, we might get lucky,' said Sukey.

'Always the optimist,' said Vicky. 'Right,' she continued,
pointing, 'as I recall, the victim was lying on his back about
there when we arrived, about four feet from the edge of the water
and parallel to it. The paramedics had withdrawn to about here,'
she moved a short distance to her left, 'and the doctor was squat-
ting down examining the body with his back to us. Several
woodies were standing a short distance away with flashlights
focused on the scene of operations. Does that sound right to
you?'

Sukey nodded. 'Yes, I think so.'

'Anything you want to add?'

'From where we're standing I believe he was lying with his
head to the left,' Sukey said after a moment's thought. 'Not that
it makes much difference that I can think of at the moment.'

'We have to record every little detail,' said Vicky. 'As there
wasn't any suggestion of a suspicious death at that stage there
weren't any CSIs here to search for clues or take pictures.' She
ducked under the tape with Sukey behind her. 'Now, as Sergeant
Drury said, the surrounding area has been pretty churned up but
we'd better go over it with a toothcomb. I think we agreed he

was lying about here,' she indicated with a gesture, 'so we'll start at the water's edge and search backwards. I'll take the side where his head was and you take his feet.'

They put on plastic gloves, squatted down and began a minute search of every square inch of ground, poking gently with their fingers among trampled blades of wet grass. After a few minutes Sukey gave a little exclamation. 'Found something?' said Vicky.

'A cigarette butt, only half smoked.' She picked it up and held it out on her outstretched palm. The two of them peered at it for a moment.

'No lipstick, so it was probably smoked by a man,' said Vicky. 'I wonder why it wasn't finished. Maybe it was Rainbird, strolling down towards the water with a lighted cigarette in one hand. Perhaps he stumbled and fell, hitting his head on one of those and suffering concussion.' She indicated a row of rocks of varying sizes lining the edge of the lake. 'Remember what we were thinking yesterday?'

'The wound was on the back of his head,' Sukey pointed out. She put the cigarette butt in an evidence bag, labelled and sealed it. 'If he'd tripped while he was strolling down towards the water, which seems the most likely, wouldn't he have hit his forehead?'

'Unless he sort of spun round after tripping and fell backwards,' said Vicky. 'No,' she went on before Sukey had a chance to speak, 'that doesn't sound very likely.'

'Let's assume someone else was the smoker,' said Sukey. 'Perhaps he was already there waiting for Rainbird. He lit a cigarette, took a few puffs, Rainbird arrived and they had a conversation.'

'Which turned into an argument,' said Vicky, taking up the theme. 'Rainbird said something which infuriated the smoker, who lost his temper, threw down his cigarette and felled Rainbird with a lump of rock. That would mean Rainbird turned away, perhaps intending to go back to the house, in which case the smoker could have attacked him from behind.'

'And then chucked his body into the lake,' said Sukey. 'It sounds feasible – except those rocks look quite firmly set in the earth.'

'Let's see if we can shift any of them.' Vicky went to the water's edge, took hold of the nearest rock and attempted to lift it. 'Can't move that one,' she said. 'I'll try another. Ah, this one's loose . . . but I can't lift it. You're the fitness freak; you have a go.'

Sukey bent down, grasped the rock and managed to raise it a few inches. 'It's loose all right, but it's too heavy for me to pick up,' she said after a moment's effort. 'It'd take a really strong person, probably a man, and he'd have to be tall enough to strike a heavy blow to the head unless the victim was quite a bit shorter than himself – or bending down. Was Rainbird about average height, would you say?'

Vicky shrugged. 'As far as I can remember, but that's the sort of information we'll need from the doctor. And of course this is all conjecture – the rock might have come loose for an entirely different reason. Just the same . . .' She took an evidence bag from her pocket. 'Could you roll it on to one side so I can get a sample of whatever's clinging to the underside? With luck it might match something in the wound on his head.'

'I'll have a go.' Sukey bent down again and managed to turn the rock sufficiently for Vicky to take her sample. 'Despite what Freeman said,' she went on when she had recovered her breath, 'it's possible that it happened as we suggested: Rainbird fell into the water unaided because he was a secret drinker and was a bit unsteady on his feet. So it could be accidental death after all.'

'Well, the death will have been reported to the coroner, who will almost certainly order a PM,' said Vicky. 'We can't do much more here until we have the results. Now we'd better start talking to some of the people on Freeman's list.'

They returned to the hotel and spoke to the manager. 'Do you know how Mr Rainbird met his death?' he asked anxiously.

'We've made several observations, sir,' said Vicky, 'but I'm afraid there will have to be a post-mortem, which we hope will yield enough information for us to establish the exact cause of death. That could take up to a week, possibly longer. You may be able to help us on one point; have you noticed any of Mr Freeman's group smoking?'

Chapman shook his head. 'We operate a complete no smoking policy throughout the hotel,' he said. 'A person wishing to smoke is at liberty to do so anywhere in the grounds, but they are requested to dispose of their cigarette stubs in receptacles provided outside the entrance before returning indoors.'

'Thank you,' said Vicky. She turned to Sukey. 'Let's have a look at this list; who shall we speak to first?'

'What time do they have their coffee break?' asked Sukey.

Vicky consulted the programme. 'Ten forty-five.'

'Why don't we make a start then, rather than interrupt the first session?'

'That's not for nearly half an hour. What do you suggest we do meantime?'

'We've been assuming Rainbird fell into the water at the point where he was fished out, but aren't we told never to assume anything without confirmation?'

'You aren't suggesting he was attacked somewhere else and then carried down to the water before being chucked in?' Vicky's tone was incredulous. 'Why on earth would the killer do that? If, as seems probable, this was an unpremeditated murder, surely he'd want to get the job done and get the hell out of it as quickly as possible. There was always a chance of being spotted.'

'I know it sounds far fetched,' Sukey admitted. 'I just have a hunch that we've been taking too much for granted.'

'You and your famous hunches!' Vicky sighed. 'Oh well, it'll help to pass the time, I suppose.'

'It's quite a big lake and there are plenty of trees around,' said Sukey as they walked back. 'Parts of it may not be visible from the hotel. Suppose he was chucked in a short distance from where he was found? No, that wouldn't work, there's no current so he's unlikely to have drifted. You're probably right; we'd be wasting our time. Shall we go back indoors?'

'No, let's press on. I know I make fun of your hunches, but more often than not you come up with the goods.'

They began a slow, anticlockwise walk along the water's edge, carefully scanning the ground for possible clues. A small flotilla of ducks swam to meet them, obviously hoping for food. Presently they came to a tall golden cypress a few metres away to their right; the foliage reached almost to the ground, but part had been cut away to make a small space where a seat had been placed, facing the water.

'That's a nice sheltered spot to sit and have a smoke and watch the ducks,' said Vicky. 'And the swans,' she added as a couple went gliding past.

'Or to meet someone . . .' Sukey added.

'Or lie in wait for someone . . .'

'Let's take a closer look.'

They spent several minutes searching the ground. Using pocket magnifiers and flashlights they went over every inch of the wooden seat in the hope of finding traces of hair or fabric that might suggest someone had sat there recently, but they drew a blank. 'Not a sausage,' said Vicky. 'No dog-end or ash either, so the smoker didn't sit and light up here.' She glanced at her watch. 'Let's give ourselves another five minutes and then go back. I could use a coffee.'

A short distance further along they came to a large pile of recently hewn timber. 'That came from a pretty hefty tree,' Vicky commented. 'One of those chunks of wood would make a lethal weapon in the wrong hands. Let's take a closer look.'

'It's plain to see how they got here.' Sukey pointed to traces of tractor wheels. 'They dumped their load and then the driver and probably his mate went round checking that there was still plenty of space between the pile of logs and the edge of the water.'

Vicky nodded. 'To leave plenty of room for walkers, I guess. It's a huge lake; it'd take quite a while to walk right round. Hence the strategically placed seats – there's another one over there. Anyway, let's go back; it's coffee time for the music lovers.'

The group was just leaving the Orchard Room and heading across the entrance hall to the library, where a waiter was pouring coffee and tea and offering a choice of biscuits. Freeman spotted them and beckoned; when they had been served they sat down in a window seat beside him. 'Have you had a good morning?' asked Vicky.

'Very good indeed,' he said. 'I think everyone enjoyed it.'

'It sounds like it,' said Sukey, who had been listening to the enthusiastic comments from the participants as they enjoyed their refreshments.

'Thank you for not interrupting us,' Freeman added. 'They were all a bit jumpy at first and took a while to settle, so that was really appreciated. Have you made any progress?'

'We've made certain observations, which we shall of course pass on to DI Rathbone,' said Vicky. 'Perhaps now would be a good time to start interviewing the people in your group. You specifically mentioned a few who you thought might have had more to do with Rainbird than the others, but declined to give any details as to why you had picked them out. We might as well start with them.' She took her copy of the list from her pocket. 'Eric Bowen. Would you mind pointing him out to us?'

'He's over there, chatting to Millie.'

'Charlotte's carer?'

'That's right.'

'So where's Charlotte?'

'She's probably in the disabled toilet which is just through there, round the corner.' Freeman indicated a door on the far side of the room. 'She doesn't like Millie standing outside while she's in there – I don't know why, maybe she suspects she'll have her ear to the door, she does tend to be a bit paranoid in some ways – so Millie has to leave her chair outside to indicate that it's occupied and she sends her a text when she's ready. Eccentric, but that's Charlotte for you.'

'So Millie enjoys a few moments' freedom once in a while,' Vicky said drily. 'I hope she makes the most of them.'

Watching them, Sukey suspected that Millie would have preferred to drink her coffee in peace instead of listening to Eric's non-stop critique of the morning's choice of music, interspersed with additional comments. 'He seems to have a lot to say for himself,' she remarked. 'Is he always that talkative?'

Freeman laughed. 'He isn't known as Eric the Loquacious for nothing,' he said. 'Let me introduce you.'

'There's no need for that, we can introduce ourselves thank you.'

Eric Bowen and Millie Chandler were seated at a small table close to the door. As Vicky and Sukey approached he was declaiming the superiority of Alfred Brendel's interpretation of Schubert's piano music over that of the pianist whose performance of the piano sonata in D they had just heard. He appeared not to notice that Millie – who, Sukey thought, appeared totally bemused by this display of erudition – had risen from her seat in response to a message on her mobile and was already going out of the room by the time they reached the table.

'This table is well tucked away so we might as well talk here rather than waste time finding one of the rooms Chapman has set aside for us,' said Vicky. She reached for an extra chair and she and Sukey sat down facing Bowen.

'*Do* sit down,' he said. He had a slightly high-pitched voice and his tone had a sarcastic edge. 'I suppose you want to ask a lot of routine questions. Justin said you want to speak to everyone about Lance Rainbird's death. I can't imagine why; surely it was an accident.'

'Until we know exactly how he came to be in the water,' said Vicky, 'his death is being treated as unexplained.'

'Is "unexplained" a euphemism for "suspicious"?'

'Perhaps you'd allow us to ask the questions.'

The sharpness of her tone had a somewhat deflating effect on Bowen, who shrugged and said, 'Of course. Fire away.'

'Most of the windows in the Orchard Room face south over the lake,' Vicky began. 'Before the start of the evening session, did you happen to look out of any of them?'

'Of course not; the curtains were drawn. It was dark out there.'

'You might have lifted one of the curtains to take a quick look outside for some reason.'

'Well, I didn't.'

'All right. Now, Mr Bowen, how well did you know Mr Rainbird?'

'Not well at all and I didn't particularly want to. You had to respect his knowledge of music of course; he really knew his stuff – and never missed a chance to show it off.'

'Do we take it you didn't like him very much?'

For the first time, Bowen's plump features creased in a faint smile. 'Let's just say he wasn't the sort of person I could warm to,' he said, adding hastily, 'but I didn't have a particular grudge against him and as far as I know nobody else did either. He just didn't – how can I put it – encourage or inspire familiarity. He was a regular visitor to Justin's events and always took an active part in discussions – too active for some people – but if he had enemies I don't recall seeing anything to suggest it.'

'How many of Mr Freeman's events have you attended since your first encounter with Mr Rainbird?' asked Sukey.

Bowen appeared taken aback by the question. 'I really couldn't say,' he said after a few moments' thought. 'Half a dozen, perhaps – I don't go to all of them of course – but I can't recall whether Lance was at all the ones I attended. I keep all the programmes for reference,' he went on, 'so if you think it's important I can check when I get home; something in one of them might trigger a recollection of him being particularly obnoxious with his superior wisdom.'

'Thank you,' said Vicky. 'We'll bear your offer in mind.'

'By the way,' said Sukey, 'do you have a view of the lake from your bedroom window?'

'No, my room's at the side of the hotel, facing north.'

'So you have a view of the car park.'

He nodded. 'Part of it. There are some spaces at the front of the building as well, but I can't see them. What of it?'

'Just checking.'

'Is that it, then?'

'For the time being,' said Vicky.

They returned to the corner where Freeman was draining his coffee cup. Sukey had the impression that although they had been well out of earshot while talking to Bowen, he had been keeping a close watch on them from his window seat. 'How did that go?' he asked as they approached.

'I think there's time to speak to one more before your next session begins,' said Vicky. She consulted the list. 'Is Mr Hugh Pearson still here?'

Freeman stood up and glanced round the room. Most of the people had already drunk their coffee and left, apart from a few who were still standing around chatting. 'That's Hugh, over there.' He indicated a tall, bespectacled man wearing a bulky knitted sweater who was hovering on his own by the door and had been casting slightly anxious glances in their direction. Sukey suspected that, like Freeman, he had been observing the conversation with

Eric Bowen. 'If you don't need me any more for the time being I'd like to get back to the Orchard Room.'

'That's fine,' said Vicky. 'Thanks for your help.' She invited Pearson to join them saying, 'I'm DS Armstrong and this is DC Reynolds. We're having a word with all the members of your group, so perhaps you can spare us a few minutes before the next part of your programme?'

'Yes, of course,' he said.

By now the room was empty and they sat on the cushioned window seat, with Pearson between them. He appeared to be slightly on edge and in an attempt to put him at his ease Sukey said, 'I've been admiring your pullover – Aran, isn't it? Did your wife knit it for you?'

The remark did not appear to give him any particular pleasure. 'Yes, that's right,' he said offhandedly. 'I understand you're here on account of Mr Rainbird's death,' he went on without giving her a chance to offer a further comment, 'but I don't see how I can help you. All I know is what everyone else knows – he went outside saying he needed some fresh air and one of the staff found him floating in the lake. Surely it must have been an accident – unless Eric Bowen offered answers to some questions you haven't thought of asking.'

'What makes you say that?' asked Vicky.

'He's a bit of a big-head and loves to show off his knowledge about music – and more or less any other topic that comes up,' said Pearson. 'Lance seemed to know almost as much about music as Justin – it was always an obsession with Eric to try and score points off him. In fact, I've noticed that he's a touch obsessive about a lot of things, especially security. My room is close to his and he practically shakes the door down when he comes out to make sure it's locked. I've noticed him going down to check his car every evening after dinner to make sure he's locked that as well.'

'You've all been together on these events before?'

'Oh yes, and they're always the same. My wife quite liked Lance but she can't stand Eric Bowen; during the regular disagreements between the two of them she always made a point of disagreeing with Eric and supporting Lance. She was very upset when I phoned to tell her about the accident.'

'She isn't here with you?'

'Not this time; we usually come together and her sister looks after our children when we're away, but she has flu so Julie's had to miss this one. She was really disappointed; Schubert is one of her favourite composers.'

'What a shame. Anyway, thank you, Mr Pearson. Enjoy the music.'

'That's interesting,' said Sukey after he left the room. 'I wonder why Bowen didn't mention going down to check the car.'

FOUR

'I wonder what became of Charlotte and Millie,' said Vicky as the last few members of the group swallowed the remains of their coffee and wandered out of the room. 'Surely she can't have been in the loo all this time.'

A waiter who was loading the used cups and plates of biscuits on to a trolley said, 'If you mean the lady in the wheelchair, her carer has probably taken her up in the lift. It's through there.' He indicated the door through which Millie had disappeared earlier.

'Thank you,' said Vicky. Once again she looked at the list. 'I suppose we'll have to start pulling witnesses out of their pre-lunch session now. Shall we start with Charlotte? She's one of the names Freeman ticked.'

'I suggest we leave her until teatime,' said Sukey. 'I have a feeling she might not take kindly to being interrupted; she'd probably be anxious to get the interview over and back to the music as quickly as possible.'

'You reckon we'll get more out of her if she doesn't have to miss a few bars of whatever composer they're listening to until lunchtime?'

'Something like that.'

'I think that'll be Mozart's Fortieth Symphony,' said Vicky. 'I heard someone say something about it being a classic example of sonata form – any idea what that means?'

'Vaguely – I think it's to do with the way the various movements are organized. We can ask Freeman to explain it if you think it's significant.'

Vicky shrugged. 'I don't see how it can help our investigation, but you never know – it might be worth asking. Tell you what, why don't we leave them all in peace for the time being? We could go and look for Romeo's motor caravan and have a word with him next. Didn't Freeman say he's parked in a lay-by half a mile or so down the road?'

'I think so,' said Sukey, 'but I don't recall passing a lay-by between here and the roundabout. It must be in the other direction. It's hardly worth taking the car; the sun's shining – and the walk will help get rid of some of the flab,' she added with a sly glance at Vicky's waistline.

'Touché,' Vicky sighed. 'It's Chris's cooking, especially the pasta. That's his Italian grandmother's influence of course.'

After a fifteen-minute walk they spotted the lay-by where an old blue Dormobile was parked. 'I reckon that was nearly a mile,' said Vicky. 'Anyway, it looks like Romeo is there.'

A swarthy, bearded man in green corduroy trousers and waistcoat over an open-necked shirt was sitting on a stone wall with a mammoth burger bun in one hand and a can of beer in the other. He wore gold earrings and a gold chain round his neck. 'Mornin' ladies,' he said. He raised his beer can in salute before taking a swig and wiping his mouth with the back of his hand. 'Out for a walk? Mild for early March, innit? Brought the blossom out early.' He waved the can in the direction of a blackthorn bush on the opposite side of the road, its flowers frosty white against the duck-egg blue of the sky.

'Yes, it's lovely,' said Vicky. 'Actually,' she went on, 'we came specially to see you. We'd like to ask you one or two questions, if you don't mind.' She and Sukey showed him their IDs.

He gave a knowing grin. 'I s'pose you wanna know if I saw anythin' suspicious about the goin's on at the manor.'

'What goings on?'

'Some poor sod found drowned, so I heard. Is that right?'

'Who told you that?'

'One of the reporters what was sniffin' around. The blues was chasin' 'im an' his mates away and they started askin' me a lot of questions. Couldn't tell 'em nuffin'; only got 'ere a couple of hours or so ago.'

'Mr Freeman has told us that you have a very fine voice and that you sometimes give impromptu recitals at his musical events. Is that why you're here?'

Romeo, rendered speechless for a moment by a large bite from his burger, nodded. 'Tha's right,' he said after chewing noisily for several seconds and taking copious swigs of beer. 'Sent me a text one day last week. I was expectin' it anyway; 'e comes every year about this time. The punters show up around five on Friday and leave after breakfast on Tuesday.'

'I understand you've shown up at quite a few of these events,' said Sukey. 'Have you got to know any of the attendees?'

'The what? Oh, you mean the geysers what come to these music parties. I've chatted to a few regulars; some are friendly and say nice things about the voice, but one or two are a bit toffee-nosed and look down on me 'cos I live in an old van and never 'ad much schoolin'.'

'Do you know a man called Lance Rainbird?'

Romeo guffawed. 'I'll say. One of the worst – thinks his farts sound like Schubert's serenade.' For a few seconds he was overcome by laughter at his own witticism, while Sukey and Vicky exchanged covert smiles. 'Don't suppose 'e's flavour of the month with anyone,' he said when he had controlled himself. His good humour suddenly faded. 'Don't tell me he's the stiff they pulled out of the lake?'

'We can confirm that a man's body was found in the lake,' said Vicky, 'but until he has been formally identified and the cause of death established, no details are being released.'

Romeo shrugged. 'That figures – his folks must be told first.'

'That's right.'

'So – d'you want anything else from me?'

'You obviously don't have a very high opinion of Lance Rainbird,' said Vicky. 'Is that just because he was – "toffee-nosed" I think you said – or did you dislike him personally?'

Romeo scowled. 'He said my singin' was rubbish and anyone could tell I'd 'ad no trainin'. Said as much to Mr Freeman, who was pretty sharp with 'im. What does 'e know anyway – it's not as if 'e had a string of qualifications after 'is name like Mr Freeman, is it?'

'Perhaps he was jealous because *he* couldn't sing,' suggested Sukey.

Romeo beamed. 'Maybe. Now there's a thought!' He laughed again, although less heartily, drained the can, dropped it into a bag that was on the ground at his side and pulled out another. 'Come to me recital,' he said as he pulled at the ring. 'Three o'clock this afternoon.'

'Maybe we'll do that,' said Sukey. 'Enjoy the rest of your lunch. It occurs to me,' she said to Vicky as they waved him goodbye and headed back to the hotel, 'that we don't actually know much about Freeman except what he told us. From what Romeo's just said it sounds as if – despite what he said to us – there are times when Rainbird got under his skin and he let it show.'

'You're right,' Vicky agreed, 'but by and large it's not in his interests to upset the customers – bad for business and all that. I wonder what made Rainbird think he had a right to be so critical; maybe we'll learn more about him when the woodies have spoken to his next of kin.'

'Romeo also suggested that Freeman's pretty highly qualified,' said Sukey. 'Does it give any details in the programme?'

Vicky searched through the pages. 'There's a short piece in here about him. It describes him as "a well-known lecturer in the music world and part-time amateur conductor" and he's got degrees in several American universities including a doctorate in Musical Arts, whatever that may be.'

'Sounds impressive,' Sukey commented. 'It'll be interesting to find out something about Rainbird's background when they've managed to contact his next of kin. Maybe he also had some letters after his name that Romeo doesn't know about – or Freeman doesn't know about either,' she added as an afterthought. 'I wonder – suppose he does know but for some reason or other keeps it quiet.'

'From what Eric and Hugh told us, it's not something that's generally known,' said Vicky. 'Just the same, if it's true and Freeman knows, it might have made him feel a bit defensive when Rainbird started holding forth.'

'No one's claimed that Rainbird openly challenged or disagreed with Freeman,' Sukey pointed out, 'and we've no reason to think

there was any sort of private disagreement between them. It was
in discussions with the other members of the group that he tended
to throw his weight around.' By this time they were back at the
hotel. 'It's just under half an hour to their lunch break. We can't
sit around for all that time so we'll have to interrupt. Who shall
we pull out first?'

'There are the Days – Trixie and Stan, who've been regulars
since these events began,' said Vicky. 'Why don't we start with
them? Hang on a minute, here are Tim and Mike,' she added as
the two DCs suddenly appeared and headed towards them. 'Let's
see how they've been getting on.'

The four of them sat down in front of the fire and began to
compare notes. 'We've spoken to ten so far,' Tim began, 'including
two couples who insisted on being seen together. We've been
allowing ten minutes each, including a couple of minutes to
discuss what we've learned; they all agree that Rainbird said he
was going out to get some air and none of them saw him after
that. We've got all their details and told them they can go home
if they want to, subject to your OK, Sarge.'

'They're all a bit jumpy,' said Mike, 'particularly the older
women who are here on their own. One lady said she double-
locked her bedroom door last night and then pushed an armchair
against it – and still hardly slept a wink. She can't make up her
mind whether to go home after lunch or stay the rest of the time
and get her money's worth. The others said they've no intention
of leaving before the end of the session.'

'That's fine,' said Vicky. 'Let me have your reports when
you've finished.'

'We've been having a chat with Romeo,' said Sukey. 'He's
quite a character. Couldn't help us with our enquiries, but he has
an original turn of phrase.' She repeated his comment about
Rainbird's opinion of himself and his bodily functions, much to
their enjoyment.

The four of them went upstairs. When Vicky cracked open the
door of the Orchard Room Justin was saying, 'Right, we'll now
hear the second movement.' Catching sight of Vicky he said,
'Yes sergeant, who would you like to see next?'

'Could we have Mr and Mrs Day and Mr and Mrs Harland,
please?'

Two couples stood up and followed the detectives out of the room. Sukey noticed that the Harlands made no attempt to hide their irritation at the interruption, while the Days appeared intrigued at the prospect of being interviewed by members of the CID. They presented a slightly bizarre appearance when standing side by side as Stan Day, who was on the portly side, barely came up to his very slim wife's shoulder.

'We realize this must be upsetting for you,' Vicky began when they were settled in one of the rooms Chapman had set aside for the interviews. 'We'll be as brief as possible.'

'That's perfectly all right,' said Day. 'We don't think we can be of much help as we don't remember seeing or hearing anything unusual, but we know that sometimes things that seem insignificant can be very important in an investigation.'

'I'm afraid we're both very keen on detective stories,' said Trixie Day with a self-conscious giggle.

'No need to apologize,' said Vicky. 'Now, if you wouldn't mind telling me . . .'

She began with a few routine questions; from their answers it appeared at first that neither of them had observed anything worth mentioning.

She was about to ask about previous events on which they and Rainbird had been present when Trixie said, 'One unusual thing I recall about Lance yesterday evening; he was unusually quiet over dinner.'

'That's right, love,' said Stan. 'He usually finds something in the day's programme to talk about, but he hardly said a word – seemed almost preoccupied, didn't stay for coffee, said something about needing fresh air and went out.'

'Did anyone comment?'

Stan shook his head. 'I think I heard someone make a crack about it being a change from the usual *hot* air and there were a few chuckles, but nothing significant.'

'So everyone else stayed chatting over coffee until it was time for the evening programme to begin?' said Sukey.

'Yes – except Justin of course,' said Trixie. 'He always nips up to the Orchard Room a while before the rest of us, to check his equipment. A real perfectionist is Justin.'

'Yes, he mentioned that. He told us that you've been to quite a few of these events since they began. Were you at the first one?'

'Oh yes – and so was Lance.'

'We have the impression that he sometimes irritated other people by showing off his knowledge.'

'That's one way of putting it,' said Stan. 'You could see some people getting impatient, although others were quite appreciative of something he told them about a work or a composer that they hadn't heard before.'

'Apart from exchanges of that nature while everyone else was around, have you ever heard him having a serious dispute with anyone?'

'Not enough to make them a suspect,' said Stan. He looked appalled at the thought. 'But surely you don't think he was attacked – murdered even?'

'Until we find out exactly how he came to fall into the lake we are treating his death as unexplained, which means we have to consider all possibilities,' said Vicky.

'I understand.'

'You've probably got to know Justin Freeman quite well after attending so many of his events,' said Sukey. 'Would you regard him as a friend?'

'Not exactly a friend,' said Stan. 'We like him very much and we've learned quite a bit about him through chats over coffee and at meal times. He's a widower with one son who lives with his wife and children in South Africa and he visits them every winter for a couple of months – but mostly our relationship is confined to making arrangements to attend the events that appeal to us. He confirms the booking and acknowledges the fee, makes all the arrangements and sends details of the hotel once every-thing's finalized. He's very businesslike and professional and everything usually runs like clockwork, but he's very quick to deal with any problems.'

'Not that there are many of those,' said Trixie.

'Well, thank you very much,' said Vicky. 'Do we take it that you'll be staying on until Tuesday?'

'Oh yes, of course,' said Stan. 'As far as I know, only Mrs Dacre has been talking about leaving early – but I believe she's changed her mind. Is that all for now?'

'For the time being. We hope you haven't missed too much of the music.'

The couple went back to the Orchard Room and Vicky checked the time. 'There's only another ten minutes or so left to half past,' she said. 'It's hardly worth interrupting again so why don't we go to the bar for a quickie before lunch?'

'Good idea.'

'We don't seem to have picked up anything significant so far,' said Vicky as they took their drinks to a corner table. 'Is there anything we haven't covered?'

'I suppose we should try and pinpoint the exact time Freeman left to go up to the Orchard Room to check his equipment,' said Sukey, 'but only because DI Rathbone will expect us to have logged every detail. And perhaps we should ask around to see if anyone has any idea why Rainbird was so preoccupied at dinner. About Romeo – there's something bugging me . . . something I noticed or some remark he passed . . . but I can't for the life of me remember what it was.'

'If it's important, it'll come back,' Vicky prophesied. She raised her glass. 'Cheers!'

FIVE

Sukey and Vicky were joined a few minutes later by Tim and Mike and the four sat together with their drinks in the bar lounge and studied the menu while comparing notes about the people they had interviewed during the remainder of the morning. The music lovers would shortly have their lunch in the dining room; however, a few dropped in for pre-lunch appetizers and it was noticeable that most of them stood at the counter with their drinks and even those who sat at tables made a point of avoiding the corner where the detectives were sitting. Most of the chatter was about the morning's programme and Eric's voice could be heard above the others, declaiming about the choice and quality of the music.

'A classic example of a symphony composed in the sonata

form and brilliantly performed,' he said and heads nodded in agreement. 'It's just occurred to me,' he went on, 'the investigations being carried out by our noble band of police officers –' he turned towards the far corner of the bar and waved his glass in their direction – 'could almost be compared to the way Mozart constructed the first movement of his fortieth symphony.' His voice rose in pitch and volume as he developed his idea. 'The first subject was of course Lance's disappearance, the second subject the discovery of his body and the closing theme the arrival of the boys in blue. How about that then?'

'Ooh, death in sonata form!' Trixie squeaked in excitement. 'That'd make a good title for a mystery novel, wouldn't it?' There were appreciative chuckles all round.

'I'll drink to that!' said Eric, suiting the action to the words. 'What are we all going to do this afternoon? Lots to see in Bristol – I'm told the zoo's worth a visit, and the aquarium.'

'There's a beautiful cathedral,' said Hugh, 'and a famous church. Queen Elizabeth the First said . . .'

'. . . and the art gallery and museum,' Eric broke in, evidently determined not to relinquish centre stage.

'I'm told it's a very good shopping centre too,' added Trixie, at which her husband rolled his eyes in mock dismay.

Eric finished his half pint of ale and put his glass down. 'Right, I'm for lunch,' he announced. He went out followed by the others, leaving the four detectives exchanging amused glances.

'Well, you got your explanation of sonata form, Sukey,' said Vicky. 'No need to ask Freeman. Maybe the first subject in the second movement will be the discovery of a vital clue – except that we won't recognize it straight away.'

'You mean like the something that I couldn't pinpoint after our chat with Romeo?' said Sukey. 'Perhaps we should take him up on his invitation to hear him sing this afternoon – it might ring a bell.'

'You never know,' said Vicky, brandishing the menu. 'Have we all decided what we're going to eat?'

After lunch a number of people congregated in the car park. A few couples drove off separately but others, who appeared to have agreed on their destinations, stood by their cars studying maps. Eventually several carloads drove away in convoy. Some members of the group had evidently retired to their rooms, presumably for an afternoon nap, but a few couples chose to wander round the garden before the sun lost what remained of its warmth.

'A few of the ones who've stayed behind are among those we still have to see,' said Vicky, 'but I think it would be as well to leave them to digest their lunch in peace. We could catch a few more at teatime, after Romeo has done his act.'

'Tim and I thought we'd have a walk round the lake,' said Mike. 'We've only checked a short distance on either side of the point where Rainbird's body was found and we figured it might be worth looking a bit further afield for possible clues.'

'Good idea,' said Vicky. 'Sukey and I have already been part of the way round and made a few observations, but it would be as well for the four of us to go together. We might pick up something between us that we missed.'

They set off, walking clockwise this time. Eventually they came to the pile of cut timber. 'One of those chunks would make an ideal blunt instrument,' said Tim.

'That's what we thought,' said Vicky, 'but if the attack took place here, and if Rainbird was partly concussed, we thought it was unlikely that he could stagger back to the point where his body was found, even though it is only a short distance. And if he fell in here there's no current to carry him along.'

'And if his attacker intended to kill him and realized he hadn't succeeded the first time, he'd hardly have stood by and watched; he'd have been more likely to take another swipe at him to make sure he'd finished the job.'

'That's something the result of the post-mortem should make clear,' said Mike.

They were about to walk on when Sukey said, 'Just a minute, I think I can hear something. It sounds like water trickling.' They all stood still and listened. 'It's coming from along here.' She walked back a few yards and peered through the dense foliage. 'There must be a spring. I'll just see if I can . . . oh!' She gave a sudden shriek and grabbed at an overhanging branch.

'What is it?' asked Vicky. 'Don't tell me you've found another goner.'

'I very nearly fell in,' said Sukey as she scrambled back. 'I think someone should point out to the manager that there should be a rail or something here; this part of the bank shelves quite steeply.'

The others moved forward to investigate. 'You're right,' said Mike. 'If Rainbird's attacker had struck him near the edge with one of those bits of tree trunk, he might have staggered forward a couple of paces and found himself heading down the slope and into the water before he could stop himself. Then, if he was dazed anyway, he might not have been able to struggle to the surface.'

'That still doesn't explain how his body came to be found a few feet along,' Vicky objected.

'But if he was at least semi conscious, he might have been struggling to keep afloat long enough get back to a place where he could scramble out of the water,' said Sukey. 'And look there,' she added, pointing to a leaf floating on the surface and gently drifting in the direction of the point where Rainbird's body had been found, 'there is a current, admittedly a bit weak, so the sound we can hear must be a little waterfall.'

'You're right,' said Tim, who had been investigating. 'As you suspected there's a stream gushing out from the bank and that's causing the water to move.' He picked up a couple of leaves that were lying on the ground and walked back a few paces before throwing one of them into the water. 'See what I mean? It's moving slowly in the right direction.' He retraced his steps a short distance and threw in the second leaf, which floated without moving. 'Now what current there is has petered out – and in any case it's isn't strong enough on its own to move a body – but if Rainbird remained conscious long enough and with that bit of extra help he could easily have struggled as far as the spot where he was found, passed out at that point and drowned.'

'Right, let's do a recap,' said Vicky. 'Rainbird was unusually quiet at dinner, didn't stay for coffee and went out, saying he needed fresh air.'

'From what the Days said it sounds as if he had something on his mind,' said Sukey.

'Right. Let's assume for the moment he'd arranged to meet someone by the heap of logs to discuss what ever it was and that

someone – or maybe someone else – was either waiting for him
or arrived shortly after and crept up on him.'

'Clobbered him with a heavy log and watched him stagger
down the slope into the water . . .' said Mike.

'. . . stood by with his log intending to have another go if
Rainbird tried to get back ashore . . .' continued Tim.

'. . . watched him flailing about in the water and eventually
passing out . . .' said Sukey.

'Probably hung around to make sure he didn't come to,' said
Vicky, 'and when he was sure his victim was dead or at least
soon would be, went back into the hotel – which is what I suggest
we do now. We've got a lot to think about and Romeo should
be here shortly. Let's jot down some notes and then foregather
in the lounge for his performance. We can do our detailed reports
later.'

About a dozen of the party had settled down in the lounge to
await Romeo's arrival. Most of them – including the nervous
Mrs Dacre – were elderly. Several who had heard him before
were telling the rest what a treat they had in store. Millie had
placed her employer's chair at the front and taken a seat beside
her. When the team of detectives entered, Millie was adjusting
the rug wrapped round Charlotte's knees, only to have her hands
brushed aside with the curt instruction, 'Oh do stop fussing,
woman!' Sukey noticed that Millie's expression registered a blend
of embarrassment and resignation, and sensed that there was little
love lost between the two.

Very shortly Romeo entered, to an enthusiastic round of
applause. He sang half a dozen songs, including arias from well
known operas, and ended with 'Come Back to Sorrento', accom-
panying himself on a guitar. Each number was followed by more
applause and when he announced the end of his programme there
were several requests for encores, which he smilingly refused,
excusing himself by saying, 'The old voice-box 'as 'ad enough,'
and noisily clearing his throat by way of an illustration. He sat
down and chatted with his audience; shortly afterwards the rest
of the party returned from their various excursions and tea and
cakes were served. Romeo accepted a cup of tea and a generous
slice of cake before quietly slipping out of the door, leaving the
group to compare notes on their afternoon's activities. Having

waited on Charlotte, Millie sat down to consume her own tea, but there was no conversation between them nor did Charlotte show any inclination to talk to anyone else.

'Perhaps this is as good a time as any to have a chat to those two,' said Vicky. 'And you and Tim,' she added, turning to Mike, 'might as well tick a few more names off your list.'

'Right, Sarge,' said Mike. 'The consensus so far is that no one was particularly close to Rainbird, but by and large people found him pleasant enough and they certainly respected his knowledge of music. In fact, several of the ladies spoke quite warmly about him; when it came to his arguments with Bowen they were on his side rather than Bowen's. They all noticed that he didn't wait for coffee after dinner on Friday. There was one person who said she thought it might have been a little before eight when he went out, but she couldn't be sure.'

'It seems it was only the people sitting near him who heard him say anything about going out for air,' said Tim. 'We've made a note against their names in our reports. And we've also asked everyone to let us take a DNA sample – no one's refused, although the Harlands had a grouse at missing ten minutes of music to answer a lot of pointless questions.'

Charlotte's hostile stare made it quite clear that she did not welcome the interruption. 'You'd better go take your tea somewhere else,' she snapped at Millie, who obediently stood up and moved away. 'I suppose you'll want to talk to her as well,' she went on with a note of disparagement in her voice. 'Not that she'll be of much help – she never sees further than the end of her nose. Sit down,' she added imperiously, indicating the chairs on either side of her. 'Right, what do you want to know? I didn't push him in,' she added. 'You can take it from me that I don't sit in this wretched chair for fun – I lost the use of both my legs in a car accident and all I can do is hobble a couple of paces to my bed or the toilet.'

'We can assure you that you are not a suspect, Miss Lang,' said Vicky, 'and in any case we have no reason at the moment to think there was anything suspicious about Mr Rainbird's death. What we should like to know is whether there was anything that struck you as in any way unusual from Friday dinner time until you heard the news.'

'We have often noticed,' said Sukey, 'that people like yourself who are . . . immobilized, shall we say? . . . tend to compensate by being particularly interested in what is going on around them and may notice things that more active people tend to overlook.'

This hint that Charlotte's powers of observation might be superior to that of those without her disability seemed to appeal to her vanity, and she very nearly smiled. 'Well, people often say to me, "Charlotte you don't miss much, do you?", and I think that's probably right,' she said. 'Now, you want to know if I noticed anything unusual about Friday evening. Well, Mr Rainbird joined our party at about the normal time for check-in, room allocation and so on. We were given a copy of the programme and we read through it while we were having our customary message of welcome from Mr Freeman, accompanied by cups of tea and biscuits. Mr Rainbird sat in a corner and didn't say much; that's the first thing I noticed. He's usually got plenty to say for himself, like that awful Mr Bowen; in fact the two of them sometimes have a quite lively – almost heated you might say – exchange of opinions, although I never noticed any outright hostility between them. In my opinion Mr Rainbird's knowledge was superior to that of Mr Bowen, but in any case I make a point of keeping my own counsel and avoiding the pair of them. I think Mr Freeman found them somewhat tedious, but of course he can't choose his clients and he's hardly likely to kill them, is he? As it happens, I've noticed numbers dropping slightly, but of course a lot depends on what the programme is and what else people are doing, and now he's retired I expect he finds whatever he makes out of these events a useful addition to his income.'

'I'm sure you're right,' agreed Vicky. 'Now, we understand that Mr Rainbird didn't appear to have many friends. Is that your impression of him?'

'Generally, yes, although most people respected him because he obviously knew a great deal about music – almost as much as Mr Freeman and as I said probably more than Bowen. The Pearsons often sat with him and they appeared to be on quite friendly terms. There was something about him that certain women seemed to find attractive; I think Julie Pearson was one of them and I know she always supported him when Bowen challenged him. Trixie Day was another, and so was Millie – but of course she'll simper at any man who says a word to her, even Bowen. Julie's not here this time, but I don't know why. Is she ill, do you know?'

'She's not ill, but her sister who usually looks after their children has flu,' Sukey explained.

'That must have been disappointing for both of them.'

'We're sure it was. Now, about yesterday evening, would you say Mr Rainbird was unusually quiet from the very beginning?'

'Oh yes, definitely so. The people who were sitting close to him tried several times to engage him in conversation, but he made only short, non-committal replies and they soon gave up. It was plain to see that he had something on his mind.'

'Did you notice him looking at any one individual during the meal?'

'On the contrary, he kept his head down for the whole time, and when the waiter announced that coffee was being served he hastily got to his feet and spoke for the first time, saying he didn't want coffee and was going out for air.'

'What time was this?'

'I didn't look at my watch, but coffee is usually served in the lounge at eight o'clock so it was probably a few minutes to.'

'Did you go to the lounge for coffee?' asked Sukey.

'Yes, of course. Millie took me; the others were already there and we stayed until it was time to go to the Orchard Room.'

'Did anyone besides Mr Rainbird leave before the evening programme started?'

Charlotte thought for a moment. 'I remember Mr Bowen saying he had to fetch something from his car and he'd have his coffee when he got back. Mr Freeman didn't join us until later, after he'd been to check on his equipment, but that's what he usually does.'

'Did you happen to notice what time Mr Freeman and Mr Bowen returned to have their coffee?'

Charlotte shook her head; Sukey thought she appeared slightly embarrassed, as if she had been guilty of a lapse. 'I'm afraid not. Various people came to have a chat with me and . . .'

'We don't expect you to have eyes everywhere,' said Sukey with a smile. 'As it is, you've really been very helpful.'

'I do hope so. It's a dreadful thing to have happened and whatever Mr Rainbird has done it's hard to think anyone would want to kill him.'

'You believe he was murdered, then?'

'Of course I do. It's obvious he was going to meet someone and was worried about it, possibly even afraid of that person. Find out what was troubling him and you'll find your murderer.'

'Well, thank you very much, Miss Lang,' said Vicky. 'Now we'll have a word with Millie.'

They found Millie sitting a few feet away. She was chatting to Hugh Pearson and appeared more relaxed than they had seen her previously. When they approached, Pearson stood up and said, 'I think the sleuths want to talk to you, Millie, so I'll leave you. I've so enjoyed our chat.'

'So have I,' said Millie. 'I do hope your sister in law soon recovers.'

'Thank you,' he said with a smile. Her manner became more tense as she turned to Vicky and Sukey and said, 'I don't think I can help you; I didn't do anything.'

'Don't worry, we aren't suggesting you or anyone else did anything wrong,' said Sukey. 'We'd just like to know if you noticed anything unusual from Friday evening, before Mr Rainbird's body was found, until now.'

'Well, of course, everyone was very shocked when we were told what happened to him, and we were all very surprised when the police were called. Do you think he fell in by accident?'

'We don't yet know how he came to be in the water,' said Vicky. 'Had you spoken to him at all from the time he arrived until he went outside after dinner?'

'No, but he never talks to me anyway – not that I particularly want him to. I didn't see him talking to anyone else, but I wasn't paying attention. I heard people say he went outside but I didn't see him go and I don't know why he went.'

'Well, thank you, Millie,' said Sukey. 'We apologize for interrupting your chat with Mr Pearson.'

'Oh yes, I always enjoy talking to him!' Millie suddenly became animated and her colour rose slightly. 'He's a really nice

gentleman – he misses having his wife with him. I miss her too
– we have quite a lot in common – although I don't usually have
much time for chatting.' She cast a meaningful glance across the
room to where Charlotte, showing signs of impatience, was
waiting for her. 'Miss Lang wants me; will that be all?' She
scuttled across the room without waiting for a reply.

'From what we've learned so far, which doesn't add up to much,'
said Sukey, 'it seems pretty certain that if Rainbird fell into the
water as the result of an attack, it wasn't a premeditated killing.'

'So as we figured out earlier,' Vicky replied, 'he said something
to the person he met which must have been a serious enough
threat to make it essential to put him out of the way.'

'Hang on a minute,' said Sukey, 'I've just remembered what
it was that I noticed about Romeo. I think he was lying when
he told the rat pack that he only arrived a short time ago – couple
of hours or so I thought he said – before they started asking him
questions and that was why he couldn't tell them anything. Let's
get back to his van and see what he's got to say about that.'

Through the gathering darkness they hurried along to the lay-by
where Romeo's van had been parked, but it was empty.

SIX

'He must have driven off as soon as he left the hotel,' said
Vicky. 'Anyway, what did you want to question him
about?'

'Remember he said that when the paparazzi started questioning
him about the goner who'd been fished out of the water he'd
only been here a couple of hours, so he couldn't tell them
anything.'

'That's right. What about it?'

'I've been thinking. We arrived here last night some time after
nine o'clock. Rainbird's body was still lying on the grass; the
paramedics were standing around and the doctor was examining
him. We walked towards them for a short distance and waited;
we were careful because we'd been warned the grass was wet

and slippery, but by then it had stopped raining. Presumably it had stopped by eight o'clock or Rainbird wouldn't have gone out just for a breath of air.'

'But we're pretty sure now that he'd arranged to meet someone,' Vicky pointed out, 'so he'd probably have gone anyway – but I don't see what difference it makes.'

'We know it had been raining most of the day, but it had stopped by the time we got there and it hasn't rained since. We saw Romeo before lunch today and if he was telling the truth about his time of arrival the ground under his van should have been dry – but I suddenly remembered that it was wet. I must have noticed while we were chatting, but didn't think anything of it at the time.'

'I see what you're driving at,' said Vicky. 'That means he was here some time before it stopped raining, or at least while the ground was still wet. So, is it possible that it was Romeo that Rainbird had arranged to meet? Or did he happen to see Rainbird in the water with the attacker standing there with some sort of weapon in his hand, let him know he'd been spotted and decided to try a little blackmail?'

'It's a thought, isn't it?' said Sukey. 'Perhaps the attacker wasn't willing to play ball and reacted aggressively, so Romeo decided to leave here as soon as he'd given his performance and collected his money from Freeman. I noticed Freeman handing him something that looked like an envelope when he joined the others for tea after they came back from their afternoon excursion. They shook hands and exchanged a few words and then he left.'

'You reckon he felt threatened but didn't want to let Freeman down?'

'He struck me as being a decent type and he might have felt under an obligation. Besides, he probably needed the money anyway.' They thought for a moment. Then Sukey said, 'So what should we do now?'

'I suppose we could ask Freeman if he knows where he's heading for next,' said Vicky. They went back to the hotel. Most of the group had dispersed, presumably to have a rest and then prepare for dinner, but Freeman was in reception talking to Chapman. He merely shrugged when Vicky enquired about Romeo's probable destination. 'He's not due to sing for me until my next meeting, which isn't until the beginning of May,' he said. 'As far as I know he picks up other engagements on an ad hoc basis, but I don't normally hear from him in the meantime.'

'Do you have his mobile number?'

'Yes, sure – would you like me to call him?'

'If you wouldn't mind.'

'No problem.' Freeman took out his phone, called a number, waited a few moments and shook his head. 'His phone's switched off,' he said. 'I'm sorry, I really can't help.'

'Well, thank you anyway.' Vicky moved a short distance away and took out her own phone. 'I'm giving the DI a call to put him in the picture,' she told Sukey. 'Stand by – he may want to talk to you as well.' After a few moments she switched off and said, 'He wants us both back at his office right away.'

'What about Mike and Tim?'

'He said we should update them and leave them to catch up with as many on their list as they can,' said Sukey. 'It will be after eight by the time we've seen the DI and I doubt if he'll expect any of us to work overtime, so with luck we'll all be able to go home at a reasonable hour.'

They found Rathbone sitting in front of his computer. 'I've been trying to get hold of some info about this Romeo chap, but Google isn't much help. Did you happen to get the number of his van?'

'Of course; it's in our reports, Guv,' said Vicky.

'Which you haven't submitted yet,' he snapped.

'Give us a chance,' Vicky pleaded. 'We've been working our socks off and so have Tim and Mike. There are a lot of names to check off, DNA samples to deal with and notes to polish up.'

'All right – so give me the number now.' Vicky wrote it down and he entered it in the computer. 'All it says here is that it's a Dormobile camper van on a VW chassis, manufactured in 1979. Last registered owner was a Frederick Jones of Clapham who took it off the road eight years ago.'

'Romeo seems to live from hand to mouth, so maybe he picked it up in a scrapyard and got a mate to fix it up for him,' Sukey suggested.

'It's obvious he didn't bother to register it,' Rathbone pointed out. 'He probably couldn't afford to pay tax and insurance anyway. Maybe he moves around for short distances, parks off the road and takes a chance at being picked up by the traffic department.'

'He's obviously got away with it so far,' said Vicky. 'So where do we go from here, Guv?'

'We don't know in which direction he was heading, but if my surmise is correct he should be within a fairly short radius of the hotel. I'll get him located and stopped until we can question him.' He picked up his phone, punched in a number and gave the necessary instructions. 'And now,' he said after a protracted yawn, 'there doesn't seem much more we can do from here and it's nearly eight o'clock so we might as well go home. I'll let you know as soon as we've located him. Tell DCs Pringle and Haskins and say I'll be in touch.' He shut down the computer, stood up and put on his jacket. 'Till tomorrow then. Good night. Turn off the light before you leave.' He marched out, slamming the door behind him.

'Charming,' muttered Vicky. 'At least, the boys will be happy to see us home at a reasonable time. I'll check the car in and then call Chris to tell him to rustle up something extra tasty.'

'I'll call Harry and tell him the same,' said Sukey. 'With luck, Romeo will have gone somewhere too obscure for traffic to locate him, which would mean we'll get tomorrow off.'

'In your dreams!' said Vicky. 'We'll still be on duty and something else might turn up to keep us amused. So long for now.'

When Sukey reached home she found Harry in the kitchen and the table laid for supper. 'Something smells good.'

'Chicken *chasseur*,' he announced, giving a stir to the steaming contents of a pan. 'I made it for Dad and me during the week; we ate half and I froze the rest.'

'You're a star,' she said.

'You're only saying that because it's true.' He took her in his arms and she clung to him with her face buried in his shoulder. It suddenly dawned on her how desperately tired she was.

After a few moments he released her and said, 'Sit down and relax. We'll have some wine while the rice is cooking. I've brought this bottle of Pinot Grigio – it goes down a treat with chicken.' He filled two glasses, handed one to her and sat down beside her. 'How has your day been?'

'Tiring, interesting and frustrating,' she said. 'We began to think we were getting somewhere and then realized that someone who we think could be an important witness had left. He's not going to be easy to trace by the looks of things.'

'That wouldn't by any chance be the chap who calls himself Romeo and lives in an old Dormobile?'

'You know about him?'

'When I heard about the incident at Dallington Manor I went there early this morning to find out what was going on. A woman from the *West Country Express* mentioned she'd seen an old van parked in a lay-by and was going to have a word with the driver so I and several others went along with her. Romeo seemed perfectly willing to chat but couldn't help because he'd only just got there. Is he your missing witness?'

'We think so. DI Rathbone has put a search call out so it will be on the news in the morning – possibly tonight. He couldn't find anything on the computer about either Romeo or the van, so . . .' She broke off and put her glass down. 'I really shouldn't be telling you this, Harry. I mean, there's no reason to suppose he's done anything wrong; we just want to know if he happened to see anything.'

'But if the chap fell into the water on Friday night he couldn't have seen anything, unless . . .' He thought for a moment and then said slowly, 'Unless he was lying. Is that why your lot are so anxious to talk to him?'

'Look Harry, if he was lying he may have a perfectly innocent reason,' said Sukey. 'Don't think Vicky and I haven't been over all this till we're blue in the face, so please let's forget about it for now. I'm starving – the bar lunch was light years ago.'

They ate their meal and then relaxed in the sitting room with the rest of the wine and watched the news. The programme was almost over when a newsflash announced that there had been an accident on a country road, when a motor caravan had left the road on a sharp bend, overturned, rolled over and landed on its roof in a ditch. Emergency services were at the scene but no further details were given. The police were appealing for witnesses.

'I have a nasty feeling that it's Romeo's van,' said Sukey. 'I wonder—'

'Whether it was a genuine accident or the van had been sabotaged,' said Harry.

'I don't want to think that,' said Sukey. 'It's a very old van and I don't suppose it gets proper maintenance. Or he could have had too many beers and lost control, but that seems unlikely; all he had after giving his performance was two cups of tea and some cakes. Just the same, we were surprised that he left in such a hurry.'

Harry took her empty glass and pulled her to her feet. 'You're not to think about it any more tonight,' he said firmly. 'What you need now is sleep.' He held her close, gently stroking her hair. 'Do you want me to stay?'

'Please.'

At seven o'clock next morning Sukey's mobile phone rang. DI Rathbone was on the line. 'Romeo's pranged his van. He's dead; they haven't been able to get him out yet because the driver's door is jammed and in any case we have to get the underside of the vehicle checked to see if there's any mechanical reason why he lost control. DS Armstrong will pick you up in half an hour and I'll see the two of you at the scene in an hour.' He gave directions and ended the call.

'It is Romeo and he's dead,' said Sukey. 'I have to go. Vicky is picking me up. No time for a shower; I'll have a quick wash and get dressed.'

'I'll fix some coffee and toast for you,' said Harry, who was already wide awake and reaching for his shirt.

'Thanks love.'

Half an hour later she and Vicky were on their way to the scene of the accident. It was difficult to find, being on an unmarked country lane less than two miles from the hotel, and by the time they arrived Rathbone and DCI Leach were already there. Sukey's gorge rose at the sight of Romeo's crushed head jammed against the driver's door, the surrounding area covered in blood. She turned away, swallowing hard.

'How awful,' she said. 'What a dreadful thing to happen to the poor man.'

'Forget the sentiment,' said Rathbone brusquely.

'You are sure this is the man you wanted to interview?' said Leach.

'Quite sure, sir,' said Vicky.

'I understand from DI Rathbone that the reason you were anxious to see him is that you suspected him of lying about his time of arrival.'

'That's right, sir,' said Vicky. 'It was Sukey who spotted the fact that the ground under his van was wet, indicating that he had arrived some time during Friday night while it was still raining instead of yesterday morning as he told the paparazzi. We've been wondering why he lied about it and that's why we wanted to talk to him.'

'Do you think, sir,' Sukey said, 'that if we could contact the last known owner of the van, Frederick Jones of Clapham, he could remember what he did with it after he took it off the road? If he sold it to a scrap dealer we might be able to trace it and maybe find out who did any repairs and what he did with it after that.'

'It was a long time ago so it's a long shot, but worth a try,' said Leach. 'See to that, will you Greg? Have you spotted something?' he added, seeing that Rathbone was staring at the underside of the van.

'Look there, sir. It doesn't take an expert to see that the pipe carrying the brake fluid has come away. The question is, has it just worked loose of its own accord or has it been tampered with?'

Leach studied the pipe for a moment. 'You're right. I'll get our experts to carry out a special check. Meanwhile, this road must be kept closed. I take it diversion signs have been set up?' he said to a uniformed officer who was standing a short distance away.

The man saluted. 'Yes, sir.'

SEVEN

DCI Leach returned to his car and drove away. Before going to his own car, Rathbone said, 'Vicky, you and Sukey might as well go to the hotel and break the news to the people there. Keep a particular eye open for reactions – most of them will probably be genuine shock-horror, but if you suspect that it's a bit of play-acting on someone's part make sure you question them very closely about their movements. Then carry on working through the remaining names on your list; I've already instructed Mike and Tim to do the same. And don't forget the DNA samples,' he added with one hand on the driver's door.

'Of course we won't, Guv,' said Vicky. 'As if we would,' she added scornfully as he drove away. 'Why does he have to keep treating us like a pair of rookies?'

'He's enjoying his taste of power,' said Sukey. 'If he hadn't been a policeman he'd have made a good schoolteacher. Right, let's go back to the manor and tell everyone what's happened to Romeo. They'll obviously be full of questions, but we can shelter behind our usual excuse for not giving details.'

'It's going to be a while before we get any DNA results,' said Vicky as she clipped on her seat belt. 'So we still have no idea who smoked that cigarette. Right, you've got the directions – can you get us back to civilization?'

They reached Dallington Manor just as Freeman and his group were finishing their breakfast. Some were already on their way to the Orchard Room; Freeman was at the reception desk discussing arrangements for lunch with Chapman.

'Good morning,' said Freeman. 'I suppose you still have a few more people to interview, but you must have spoken to nearly everyone. Is something wrong?' he added, seeing their unusually serious expressions.

'I'm afraid there is,' said Vicky. 'There's been an accident to Romeo's van – it went off the road on a bend and ended up on its roof in a ditch.'

'Good heavens!' Freeman exclaimed. 'However did it happen? Is he badly hurt?'

'I'm sorry to have to tell you he's dead,' said Vicky. 'He's trapped against the driver's door and there will have to be a detailed examination of the van before we can get him out and take him to the morgue. A post-mortem will we hope reveal the exact cause of death.'

'Do you think he might have had a heart attack?' asked Chapman.

'It is of course possible,' said Sukey. 'Do you have any reason to think he might have had a health problem, Mr Freeman? Or did he perhaps hint that he had something on his mind that might have made him lose his concentration?'

Freeman shook his head. He had a bewildered expression and made vague gestures in the air, as if unable to grasp the situation. 'Far from it,' he said. 'Whenever I've seen him he's always been full of energy and *joie de vivre* – never seemed to have a care in the world.' He compressed his mouth and put his hands over his eyes. 'Poor Romeo; such a wonderful talent wasted – I can't take it in.'

'We've been instructed to inform everyone ourselves,' said Vicky. 'Perhaps you'd call your staff together, Mr Chapman, but please don't say why.'

'Yes, I'll do that right away; I'll ask them to meet you here,' said Chapman, who appeared equally shocked.

To Freeman Vicky said, 'If you don't mind delaying the start of your session by a few minutes, we'll come and speak to the members of your group as soon as we've broken the news to the staff.'

He nodded. 'That's fine with me.'

While they were speaking a few stragglers had passed them on their way to the Orchard Room. They had been speaking in low voices, but one or two cast curious glances at the group as if sensing that something unusually serious was being discussed. Freeman followed them up to the Orchard Room and Vicky and Sukey waited for the staff to assemble. In a short time Chapman appeared with Maxine and two waiters.

'Romeo wasn't a guest in the hotel so none of the domestic staff knew him and in any case they weren't on duty in the afternoon,' said Chapman 'Maxine was here and these two waiters were serving tea yesterday afternoon. They were all able to hear him sing and said how much they enjoyed it.'

'Thank you,' said Vicky. 'Please sit down everyone. I'm afraid I have some very disturbing news about Romeo. He had an accident in his van yesterday, shortly after leaving here yesterday afternoon.'

'Oh dear!' said Maxine. 'I'm sure we're all very sorry to hear that. Was he hurt?'

'I'm afraid he was pronounced dead at the scene,' said Sukey. 'What we'd like to know is, did any of you notice anything – or hear him say anything – that might make you think he had something on his mind and perhaps disturb his concentration?'

There was a short silence. The two waiters shook their heads, but after a moment Maxine said, 'I wouldn't say he had something on his mind, but he did seem anxious to get away.'

'Maybe he wanted to get wherever he was going before it got dark,' suggested one of the waiters.

'That's probably it,' said Vicky. 'Well, thank you all very much. We'll go and break the news to the guests now.'

In the Orchard Room the whole group were assembled. Before either of the detectives could say a word, Eric jumped to his feet and said 'Really, this is quite intolerable. First we have our sessions interrupted and now we have to wait your pleasure before we can even begin. Can't you save your questions until our coffee break? We realize you have a job to do but we've paid good money to attend this event and this has all been very distracting.' He glanced round for support; a few people nodded and one or two said 'Hear! Hear!' although in rather subdued voices.

Vicky stepped forward. 'You are quite right, Mr Bowen, but I have something very important to say that cannot wait,' she said. 'I know that a number of you enjoyed a performance yesterday of solo songs by a man you know as Romeo. Mr Freeman told us about his remarkable voice and how he usually comes to entertain members of his group if he happens to be in the neighbourhood.' There were nods all round and a few appreciative remarks exchanged. 'I'm sure all of you,' Vicky went on, 'especially those who, like my colleague and I, enjoyed his singing yesterday, will be very sorry to hear that shortly after he left there was a serious accident in which his van was involved.'

As expected, there was a shocked silence, followed by various exclamations of 'How dreadful!' and 'Is he badly hurt?' Eric jumped to his feet again and said, 'How did it happen? Was he in a collision? How is he?'

'Tragically, he was pronounced dead at the scene,' said Sukey. 'It appears that his van left the road and ended up on its roof in a ditch, but I'm afraid that's all we can tell you at the moment. We are of course appealing for witnesses.'

There was a barrage of questions, to all of which Vicky and Sukey gave the same response, namely, 'That's all we can tell you at present. An official statement will be issued as soon as possible.'

By this time Freeman had recovered his composure. 'Perhaps the sensible thing to do now is get on with our usual programme,' he said. 'There may be further news during the morning – if so we'll hear it when it's time for coffee.' He turned to the two detectives. 'I take it that's all right with you?'

'That's absolutely fine,' Vicky assured him. 'We still have a few people to take formal statements from concerning Mr Rainbird's death, but they can wait until your coffee break. Enjoy the music.'

'Why don't we go for a coffee?' said Sukey as they went back downstairs.

'Good idea!' said Vicky and led the way to the bar. 'So,' she went on as they settled down with large mugs of cappuccino, 'we come back to the two possibilities: one that Romeo saw the attack on Rainbird and was trying to make some money out of it, or that he killed Rainbird himself but had to stay and give his performance to avoid drawing suspicion to himself.'

'A lot will depend on what emerges from the PM and the examination of the van,' said Sukey. 'Romeo could have had some sort of health problem that even he wasn't aware of. Suppose that hit him as he was negotiating that bit of road.'

'That wouldn't account for the detached brake fluid pipe,' said Vicky.

'True. And if sabotage is suspected it would mean we're hunting a double killer.'

'Who wouldn't hesitate to kill again if he thought anyone else might have seen him.'

'You're thinking of Eric?'

Vicky nodded. 'We still haven't asked him why he didn't mention going down to his car on Friday evening. We'll tackle him about that at coffee break.'

They fell silent for a while. Then Vicky's phone rang. 'Thanks, Guv,' she said before switching off. 'I'll pass it on. They've managed to trace Rainbird's next of kin,' she said. 'Not that it's a great deal of help. He has just one brother who's living in Australia and hasn't seen him for five years. They fell out over some property they both claimed ownership of – in the end the brother, Julius, couldn't be bothered to pursue the matter further as the property was pretty run down anyway. He'd already made arrangements to settle in Oz, said the two of them were never very close, even as children, so he didn't bother to stay in touch.'

'As you say, not much help,' Sukey agreed. 'Just the same, it would be interesting to know if Lance Rainbird still owns the property and if so who will inherit. And out of interest, does anyone know what sort of education and qualifications the Rainbird brothers had?'

'Good point. I'll ask the DI if he has answers to either of those questions.' Vicky made the call. 'He can't answer the first question until they've seen Rainbird's will. He doesn't see how Rainbird's education can have the slightest effect on the case. That means,' she continued, opening her laptop, 'we'll have to find out for ourselves.'

It took only a short time to find the information they needed and they studied the screen together. They learnt that Lance and Julius Rainbird were the only children of a Millicent and Frederick Rainbird and the family home was in Surrey. Julius was the elder by three years. The father died when the boys were small and the mother, a teacher and a devout Roman Catholic, sent them to a Jesuit boarding school. Lance went to Oxford and Julius to the London School of Economics. At Oxford, Lance studied mathematics; while there he belonged to a number of music societies and regularly attended concerts and recitals. Later he took an Open University degree course in music. By profession he was a chartered accountant. Julius left the LSE after only one year and became a social worker.

'Well that answers our main question and explains why Lance felt able to chuck his weight about during the music discussion,' said Vicky.

'I wonder why he kept quiet about his music degree,' said Sukey. 'Maybe he felt that a part-time OU degree wouldn't count for much against Freeman's more impressive list of qualifications.'

'Could be,' Vicky agreed. 'He seems to have been a rather strange character all round – no close friends as far as we know, estranged from his brother and failing to mention how he came by his own musical knowledge. It's pretty obvious Freeman didn't know about it or he'd have mentioned it.'

'That's true.'

As soon as the group came down for their coffee the four detectives set about interviewing the remaining people on their respective lists. Vicky and Sukey spoke to Eric Bowen first.

'I've already told you everything I know,' he complained.

'Not quite everything,' said Vicky. 'You said quite definitely that you didn't go outside after dinner on Friday evening.'

'That's right.'

'We have a witness who says you are exceptionally careful to make sure that your car is locked overnight and in fact you are in the habit of going down to check it every evening after dinner.'

'So what's wrong with that?' said Eric. He was plainly on the defensive. 'You can't be too careful nowadays.'

'So presumably on Friday evening you carried out your normal check after dinner?' said Sukey.

'What if I did?'

'You were very insistent when we questioned you before that you went straight to the Orchard Room after dinner. Did you have a reason for not mentioning going out to check on your car?'

'I suppose I must have forgotten.'

'Or did you happen to see something – or someone – while you were out there and for some reason decided not to mention it?'

There was a silence, during which Bowen took several

mouthfuls from his coffee cup. Then he said, 'I didn't mention it because I couldn't be sure.'

'Go on,' said Vicky.

'I happened to glance across the garden and I saw a man walking down towards the lake. It was dark and I couldn't be sure, but I assumed it was Rainbird because I'd heard him say he was going out.'

'And then what happened?'

'He stopped by the water's edge and another man appeared from behind a tree on his right and they appeared to be talking. That's all I saw – I didn't really take any notice and having checked that my car was locked I went straight indoors.'

'Did you recognize the other man?'

'I told you – it was too dark to see.'

'And that's all you're prepared to say?' said Sukey.

'Yes.'

'All right,' said Vicky, 'but as we have not yet been able to establish exactly how Mr Rainbird met his death, we can't discount the possibility that someone attacked him. If someone saw what happened and the attacker was aware that he had been observed and by whom, he might feel it necessary to silence the observer. Do I make myself clear?'

Bowen looked aghast. 'Are you saying you think he was murdered, and that the murderer might kill again?'

'If he felt threatened with exposure, he might well do that,' said Sukey.

'So think it over,' said Vicky. She turned to Sukey. 'Right, let's go and ask Mr Freeman if he knew about Rainbird's OU degree, shall we?'

Freeman was surrounded by members of the group asking if he had any further news, but he waved them away, shaking his head. He still appeared unable to come to terms with the situation.

'It's like a personal loss,' he said when they approached him. 'In a way, I feel I've been his mentor. I don't suppose you've heard any more?'

'No so far,' said Vicky. 'We just wanted to have another word about Lance Rainbird. We've discovered that some time after he left Oxford he took a degree in music at the Open University.'

'Good heavens!' Freeman exclaimed in astonishment. 'I had no idea; it explains his exceptional knowledge of music – but I wonder why he never mentioned it.'

'As you yourself and everyone here who knew him have agreed, he was a loner,' said Sukey. 'He fell out with his only sibling, a brother who now lives in Australia, some time ago. It would appear that there was some kind of flaw in his personality that made it difficult for him to form relationships.'

'A form of autism, perhaps,' said Freeman. 'Poor chap, life must have been hard for him. I suppose music was his only outlet. Well, perhaps he derived some pleasure from coming to my events. I'd like to think so.'

At that moment, Vicky's phone rang. She left the room to take the call; when she returned she took Sukey aside and said, 'Guess the latest. Romeo has a brother – two brothers in fact!'

EIGHT

'We have to drop everything and get back to HQ,' Vicky told Sukey. 'One of Romeo's brothers turned up at the morgue a couple of hours ago saying he'd recognized the registration number of Romeo's van and was expecting to be able to identify him. His name is Luke Grayson; he's been told about the circumstances of the accident and is pretty upset.'

'That's understandable,' said Sukey. 'Where is he now?'

'At HQ. He was persuaded not to go to the scene of the accident and he agreed to wait until his brother could be taken out of the van and cleaned up.'

'I take it there's no doubt about this chap Luke being Romeo's brother?'

'The desk officer questioned him pretty closely. No one at HQ has met Romeo or knows anything about him except what we've given them, so they couldn't say if there's a family likeness or anything else of that nature. Just the same, they say they're reasonably sure he's telling the truth.'

'Has Sir interviewed him?'

'Are you kidding? Why d'you think he wants us back?'

Sukey chuckled. 'He enjoys having minions to do his work for him while he swigs endless cups of coffee and spends time on his computer doing research.'

'I'm to tell Freeman there's been a development in the case, but give no details,' said Vicky. 'All I'm to say is that we've been called back to HQ and we'll be in touch. You have a word with Tim and Mike, put them in the picture and say they're to carry on with their interviews but say nothing about Romeo's recently discovered next of kin.'

'Will do. They should be nearly through the interviews by now.'

'You're probably right. When they've finished they'd better ring in for further instructions.'

At first sight it was difficult to believe that Luke Grayson was related to Romeo. He had clean cut, almost patrician features, thick brown hair flecked with grey brushed back from a high forehead and steady blue eyes. When Vicky and Sukey had introduced themselves and sat down opposite him in the interview room he took a colour photograph from his pocket and passed it to them. It was evidently a family snapshot of a middle-aged man with three teenage boys, two of whom bore a strong resemblance to him. A stranger might have supposed the third to be a family friend, as his heavier build, piercing dark eyes, swarthy colouring and mass of unruly black hair were in striking contrast to the conventional appearance of the others.

'The one who looks like me is my elder brother Mark,' said Grayson. 'I'm in the middle and the one on my left – the one you know as Romeo – is our younger brother John. There were four of us to begin with but Matthew died when he was just a few weeks old. None of us ever knew him. Our parents were committed Christians – hence the choice of names.'

'Your mother isn't in the picture,' said Vicky. 'Perhaps she was taking it?'

'No, she died when John was ten. I have her picture here.' He passed another photograph across the table.

'Well, you and Mark obviously resemble your father,' said

Sukey, 'but I can't see any resemblance in John to either of your parents.'

'I should explain that our mother was Hungarian,' said Grayson. 'Our father was in the diplomatic service and she worked as a translator and interpreter in the British embassy in Budapest. They fell in love and when Dad returned to England they married and, as I said, had four sons.' There was a silence, after which Grayson took a deep breath and said, 'When John arrived, and was so utterly different in appearance from us, I can remember overhearing snatches of conversation between them. Mum kept saying "Please, you must believe me" and Dad saying "I want to believe you . . . I do believe you . . . I love you." I guess he couldn't bear to think that Mum had been unfaithful to him – and as things turned out, it was proved she hadn't. She was a good woman and a devoted wife and mother. Anyway Dad did some research into her ancestry. He discovered that two or three generations ago one of her ancestors had married a Romany gypsy and that explained it – John was a throwback. They brought him up in exactly the same way as they brought up Mark and me, but from childhood it was obvious he was going to be different in more than just appearance. He simply couldn't fit in to our conventional lifestyle; he bunked off school, looked down on us for liking pop music, saved his pocket money to buy classical music CDs and spent hours in his room listening to them. The only way in which he would conform was coming to church on Sunday, because our church was well known for its music. The quality of his voice from an early age was remarkable and he was a member of the choir – often singing solos – until his voice broke. By this time Dad had accepted that he was never going to settle down to a nine-to-five existence and offered to pay for him to have his voice professionally trained, but he would have none of it. I suppose he just relied on the training he'd had at church – our choir master had a fine tenor voice himself – and listening carefully to his recordings of top singers. After a couple of years or so he became the very fine singer you have heard and earned some sort of a living at, well, busking. Mark and I were getting on with our own lives and simply accepted things as they were, but Dad has never really been able to.'

'Is your father still alive?'

'Oh yes. He's getting on a bit now but he's still pretty good for his age.'

'Does he know about the accident?'

'Not yet. I spoke to Mark after I got to the morgue and was told I couldn't see John's body because they couldn't get him out of the van. Reading between the lines I had the impression that his face is pretty badly smashed up – is that true?'

'There's too much blood about to be able to see him clearly,' said Sukey diplomatically. 'It makes sense to wait until they've cleaned him up.'

Grayson nodded. 'I'm sure you're right. Anyway, Mark and I agreed not to say anything to Dad until . . .'

'You want to be able to tell him exactly what happened,' said Sukey. 'That's quite understandable. And as I think you've already been told, we won't know the answer to that question until we're further on with our enquiries.'

'Has Romeo – John, I mean – been keeping in touch with you?' asked Vicky.

'Oh yes, he calls us regularly on his mobile. We all live in London and if he happens to be anywhere near he makes a point of coming to see us. He puts on a fake Cockney-style accent to fit in with the image he's built for himself, but he knows it upsets Dad so he drops it when he comes home.'

'Does he come in his van?'

Grayson gave a rueful half smile. 'Oh yes, much to our embarrassment. He arrives after dark and parks it on the drive at whichever house he's visiting. We were all horrified the first time he turned up in it. Dad wanted to buy him a car and live at home, which he refused because he preferred living like a vagrant, so then the three of us offered to club together for a better quality van. He wouldn't accept anything from us – said he could cope on his own.'

'Which as you say he's been doing by busking,' said Sukey. 'We've learned that from Justin Freeman, who organized the musical event that Romeo – John, that is – has just been to. Did you know about that?'

'Oh yes, he's always kept us up to date with his movements,' said Grayson. 'We know about Freeman, of course, although we've never had occasion to contact him ourselves. John did, however, say something about this particular booking that Mark and I have agreed you should know. Mark is in Germany on business at the moment, by the way, but he'll be back on Wednesday.'

'Please go on,' said Vicky. 'John said something that you think might be significant?'

'Yes. He's mentioned a man called Rainbird who comes to Freeman's events and seems to have really got up his nose.'

'Yes, he told us about Rainbird and how he'd said something derogatory about his voice that made him very angry. What else has he said to you?'

'He rang me on Saturday morning and said he'd arrived at his latest venue and he sounded really chuffed. He said, "It looks like the bugger's bitten off more than he can chew and I might make something out of it." I asked him what he meant and he said he'd talk to me when he knew a bit more. That was the last time we spoke. When they told me what had happened to him . . . and his van . . . and how badly . . .' For the first time, Grayson appeared overcome with emotion; his voice failed and he covered his eyes with both hands. 'I can't tell you what a dreadful shock it's been,' he said when he had regained his self control. 'He was my brother and I loved him very much. We all loved him – for all his odd ways he was a good, kind man.'

'I think we all had that impression of him,' said Sukey. 'When he spoke to you on Saturday, did he explain who he was talking about and what he meant by "might make something out of it"?'

'No. All he would say was he'd tell me later. Although he didn't say who "the bugger" was I had a feeling it was Rainbird. Have you any idea who it might have been?'

'You didn't know that Rainbird was found drowned in the lake in the hotel grounds on Friday evening?'

Grayson's jaw dropped. 'Good heavens! No!' he exclaimed, evidently shocked at the news. 'Whatever happened?'

'We don't know yet,' said Vicky, 'but for the moment we're concentrating on the accident to your brother. We – DC Reynolds and I – spoke to him on Saturday morning. We found him in a lay-by a short distance from the hotel. He told us he'd arrived that morning, but we have reason to believe he arrived some time on Friday evening, so after his recital we went along to the lay-by to have a further word with him. We were surprised to find that he had already gone. Did you by any chance hear from him after about five o'clock on Saturday afternoon?'

Grayson shook his head. 'No, and I wasn't expecting to. What made you think he was, well, not speaking the truth about the time of his arrival? Could he have made a mistake?'

Sukey explained about the overnight rain and the state of the ground under Romeo's van on Saturday morning. 'We wondered why he was in such a hurry to get away, although it might have been because the light was fading and he didn't like driving in the dark. Freeman didn't know where he was going next and his mobile was switched off. The next thing we knew was that there had been this dreadful accident and we won't know how it happened until the van has been righted and your brother's body brought out. So far no other witnesses have come forward.'

There was a short silence while Grayson appeared to be mulling over what Sukey had told him. 'Perhaps,' he said, 'that by saying that Rainbird seemed to have bitten off more than he could chew John meant that he was dead. But I've no idea what he could have meant by "making something out of it" – unless he saw a chance to make some money. And that would mean he saw what happened to Rainbird and that someone else . . . my God!' he exclaimed. 'Is it possible that Rainbird was murdered and that John saw what had happened and was planning to . . .?' He broke off as if the word that came to mind was too repugnant to associate with a beloved brother.

'You think he might have been planning a spot of blackmail?' said Vicky.

'It's an ugly word, and I hate the thought of my brother stooping so low,' said Grayson. 'It isn't as if he was in need of money – as I've explained, we've all offered to support him and he's always refused any financial help.'

'Well thank you very much, Mr Grayson,' said Vicky. 'You've certainly opened up another possible line of enquiry for us.'

'You'll let me know as soon as I can see my brother?'

'Of course; in any case we shall need you or someone else from your family to identify him. Are you planning to go home now or stay somewhere local?'

'I'm going straight home. Dad will start asking questions if I'm not there at the usual time this evening.'

'Is he on his own during the day?'

'Yes, except for the "Meals on Wheels" people who bring his lunch. He doesn't venture out on his own, but he has one or two friends who take him to the pub or call in and sit with him.' Grayson sighed heavily. 'John's death is going to hit him very hard.'

As soon as he had left, the two detectives returned to the CID office, where they were told that Rathbone wanted to see them immediately. He listened carefully while they reported on the interview with Grayson and made notes on his pad. 'It's beginning to look as if there was a fatal attack on Rainbird,' he said. 'If this Romeo chap spoke to the attacker in the hope of getting some hush money out of him it's a classic motive for murder, which would suggest that the brake fluid pipe was deliberately disconnected. But if Romeo lost control of the van for another reason it could have come off in the accident, so we still have to wait for the tests to be complete. Meanwhile, we've received another piece of the jigsaw. A colleague of Rainbird has come forward, saying he has something to tell us that might shed some light on his death.'

NINE

'His name is Morgan Ashman and he's a senior partner in Ashman, Lee and Edwards, an old-established firm of accountants,' said Rathbone. 'Their head office is in the City of London and Lance Rainbird has been working for them for the past five years. According to Ashman, he was made redundant from a previous job and was lucky enough to be taken on by his firm.'

'Presumably he lives in London,' said Vicky. 'Do you want one of us to go and see him?'

'He's planning to come here tomorrow,' said Rathbone. 'He wants to see exactly where Rainbird died. He wouldn't say why

– said he'll explain when he gets here.' He sat back in his chair and chewed the end of his pen. 'Nothing in this case seems to make sense,' he grumbled. 'I think we might as well call it a day. There's nothing more we can do until we've spoken to Ashman. I'll send word to Mike and Tim and I'll see all of you tomorrow morning at eight o'clock sharp.'

'Well, the plot isn't so much thickening as curdling,' said Vicky as, after saying goodbye to Rathbone, she and Sukey went down to the car park.

'If Romeo saw something, my guess is that it was Rainbird being attacked,' said Sukey. 'Logic would suggest that he recognized the attacker and thought he might make something out of it.'

'Except that we don't know yet whether Rainbird was attacked or whether he fell into the lake by accident,' Vicky pointed out. 'We won't know that until we get the result of the PM.'

'But it does appear that there was someone else by the lake at the same time,' said Sukey. 'Eric claims to have seen them. He was pretty cagey and he seemed a bit uneasy when we warned him of possible danger, but he still didn't tell us anything useful. He claims he didn't recognize the person he saw talking to Rainbird, but he might have been lying – perhaps he too thought he might pick up some hush money.'

'Well, he's a fool if that's what his game is,' said Vicky. 'It already looks as if we may have a second murder. And don't forget this event has got until Tuesday morning to run. Time for at least one more death!' she added with a sardonic chuckle as she got into her car and clipped on her seat belt.

'Heaven forbid!' said Sukey.

Vicky rolled down her window and waved. 'See you in the morning! I'm looking forward to a cosy evening with Chris.'

'Enjoy!' said Sukey. She switched on her phone. 'I'll see what Harry's doing.'

Harry answered immediately. 'I was hoping you'd call,' he said. 'Perfect timing as well! Dad, Freddie and I are just having a drink before dinner. There's plenty for four so we'll hang on until you get here. And don't bother about dressing up. We've been playing golf so when we came home we just showered and put on jeans and sweaters.'

'Sounds lovely,' said Sukey. 'With you as soon as possible. Ciao!'

Harry and his father, retired army Major George Matthews, lived in an apartment called The Stables, which was one of a number of buildings comprising the former Sherman Estate which had some years ago been sold off and converted into individual dwellings. Sukey's own apartment was in a separate building just off Whiteladies Road and next door to The Stables. She gave a quick rat-a-tat with the heavy brass knocker in the shape of a horseshoe. Harry opened the door, gave her a quick hug and a kiss and led her into the sitting room, where a log fire crackled in the hearth and easy chairs were grouped invitingly around a low table bearing drinks and snacks. She was greeted affectionately by Harry's father and the woman he gallantly referred to as his 'lady friend', Lady Frederica Sinclair, known to her friends as Freddie. Affectionate greetings were exchanged, the hosts' drinks topped up and a drink poured for Sukey.

'It's so nice that you can join us,' said Freddie. 'George and Harry have made one of their wonderful casseroles and as you know they make enough to feed a regiment.' She raised her glass. 'Cheers!' Everyone did the same. 'Harry says you've been working today,' she went on. 'Another nice juicy murder?'

'Sukey's working on the Dallington Manor case,' said Major Matthews. 'It's no good asking her questions – all you'll get will be something on the lines of "there'll be an official statement before the next blue moon". Harry usually decides to do his own investigating. He finds something interesting, tells Sukey, she follows it up while making him swear not to tell his editor until it's officially released. That's how it works, isn't it, Harry?'

'It isn't normally quite that simple,' said Harry. 'But you must admit,' he added, turning to Sukey who had raised a quizzical eyebrow, 'that I have been known to be useful.'

'Yes – and nearly getting us both killed into the bargain,' she retorted.

'Let's not drag that up again,' Harry protested. 'It was only once, and several cases ago. And if you're sitting there on tenterhooks,' he went on, his manner becoming serious, 'I did come across something today that I thought was interesting. It concerns a recent road accident.' He sent a provocative glance in Sukey's direction, but she chose to ignore it and kept her eyes focused on her glass.

'Come now, let's not talk shop,' protested Major Matthews, but Freddie put up a hand.

'What road accident was that?' she asked. 'Has it got something to do with the case Sukey's working on? The one where a man's body was found in the lake?'

'That's the one,' said Harry. 'As far as my editor is concerned, the case is being covered by one of our juniors. The police won't know until after the PM whether it was an accident or murder – right, Sukey?' She nodded. 'But we know that another death has taken place since and the victim was recently at Dallington Manor. My gut instinct tells me there's a connection and the question is: were there two accidents or two murders? Or one murder and one accident? Or some other possible computation? Watch this space.'

'How intriguing,' said Freddie. 'You certainly work on some interesting cases, Sukey.'

'Yes, and Harry's always after advance information so he can write his story and get into print ahead of the competition,' said Sukey.

'It's called a scoop,' said Harry. 'We usually manage to come to an arrangement, don't we, love?' he added. She didn't reply, but in spite of herself she couldn't help returning his smile.

The food, as always, was delicious, the wine perfectly chosen and the dessert, contributed by Freddie, a delicate concoction of fruit, yogurt and mixed nuts. They were just enjoying some cheese when Harry's phone rang. He made an excuse and left the room; when he returned his face was serious.

'Something wrong?' said his father.

'Nothing that can't wait,' he replied.

For the rest of the evening Sukey kept a covert eye on him. Although he quickly appeared to recover his normal, cheerful mood she sensed that the call had disturbed him. Her suspicions were confirmed when, at the end of the evening, he escorted her to her door as usual, and said, 'Is it OK if I come in for a minute? Something's happened that I think you should know about.'

'I guessed something was up,' she said. 'Yes, of course, come in.'

He led the way into her kitchen but made no move to sit down. 'First of all,' he said, 'it's pretty clear there's some doubt about the cause of the accident to Romeo's van. Your people have been very cagey as usual, but the staff at Dallington Manor have been talking among themselves about it and have already heard about the problems you're having deciding whether Rainbird's death was an accident or the result of an attack. And we also know there were two people besides Rainbird down by the lake the night he died.'

'Two people?' said Sukey in astonishment. 'Where did you pick this up?'

'I have to confess I've been holding out on you,' said Harry. 'The fact is, I have a mole at Dallington Manor. One of the staff; he slipped out for a smoke that night and saw – or thought he saw – Rainbird speaking to a man. He couldn't say who it was because he'd only been on duty since tea time, and didn't recognize him among the sea of newcomers. All he said was that the chap was fairly tall and well-built.'

'What's this chap's name?' asked Sukey.

'Reg Law – he's one of the waiters.'

'I don't recognize the name,' said Sukey. 'I don't think either Vicky or I have interviewed him. I'll have to check with Mike or Tim.'

'Oh, he was interviewed all right but he must have decided not to tell your lot what he'd seen,' said Harry. 'The fact is, he rang my office and asked to speak to the senior crime reporter so the call was passed to me. He told me first what I've just told you and then went on to say he knew something else that could make a good story and offered to tell me if I'd make it worth his while.'

'Why the hell didn't you report this to us?' Sukey demanded.

'To be honest, I wasn't convinced he'd seen anything and I told him as much,' said Harry. 'He insisted he had and wanted to meet me so I suggested he call in at the office. He was a bit miffed at that said he'd think about it.'

'When was this?'

'On Saturday, the day after the body of Lance Rainbird was found.'

'Did he come back to you?'

'No. I wasn't bothered. Like I said, I didn't take him seriously anyway.'

'The phone call that came during dinner,' said Sukey. 'I have a feeling it wasn't good news.'

'You're right. The call was from one of his friends.' Harry took a deep breath. 'Reg's body was found near the lake at Dallington Manor a couple of hours ago.'

'Oh no!' Sukey sat down and put her hands over her eyes. 'You know, when Vicky and I said goodnight, she said there was plenty of time for another death. She was joking, of course, but . . .'

'There's many a true word spoken in jest,' Harry finished. 'Only this is no jest, is it?'

'What time did you get that call?'

'It was a little after ten. Keith – Reg's pal – said they were waiting for the police and a doctor.' He clapped a hand to his forehead. 'Oh my God! Maybe if I'd told you straight away he'd still be alive.'

'You mustn't blame yourself,' said Sukey. 'My guess is that his killer overheard him making that call to you and decided then and there that he had to be silenced as soon as possible. You said he'd gone down for a smoke the night Rainbird died – maybe the killer had noticed that was his habit. We'll probably be hearing from DI Rathbone ere long to tell us to go straight to Dallington Manor tomorrow. Hang on a minute, I'll check my phone. Yes, there's one missed call.' She listened for a moment then switched off. 'It's being treated as a crime scene and will be guarded by uniformed until we get there in the morning.'

'What was the cause of death?' he asked. 'Not that I expect you to tell me, even if you know.'

'As it happens, I don't know. No doubt there'll be plenty of your lot sniffing around by the time we get there.' She shook her head in bewilderment. 'The more we investigate this case the more complicated it gets. And tomorrow we have this chap Ashman, who—' she drew a sharp breath and put a hand over her mouth. 'You can just forget I said that.'

'Not a chance,' Harry teased her, 'but I'm not going to try and pump you now. You need some sleep.'

'You're right.' She leaned against him and shut her eyes. 'It's been quite a frustrating day, but this evening was a real treat.'

He put his arms round her and held her close, then kissed her gently and said, 'It was lovely for me too. Goodnight my love. Sleep well.'

A thought struck her; she pulled away from him and said, 'Harry, you will be careful won't you? We're looking for a very dangerous person who's killed at least once and won't hesitate to kill again.'

'I might say the same to you,' he said. 'I hope that pesky DI of yours won't send you into some dangerous situation on your own.'

'I'm sure he won't do anything of the kind,' she assured him.

DI Rathbone was already there when Sukey and Vicky arrived at Dallington Manor. They found him near the point where they had stopped for a while during their tour of the lake following the discovery of Rainbird's body. The area had been taped off and several uniformed officers and an ambulance driver stood by awaiting orders.

'There he is,' said Rathbone, pointing. Slumped on the wooden seat within the alcove formed by the golden cypress was the slight body of a man in a waiter's uniform of white jacket and black trousers. 'Strangled – manually – and the killer probably wore gloves. His name's Reg Law. He's worked here for about six months according to Chapman. He was found by another waiter called Keith Gunn. He's in a state of shock; we haven't interviewed him yet but apparently when he reported finding the body he was pretty incoherent. All he kept saying was that Law had told him he thought he might have done something stupid but didn't say what. He wasn't fit to go home so they found him a bed in the hotel and rang his parents to say why. They're not much more than kids, the pair of them. They're friends; they started work here at the same time. Chapman's tearing his hair out . . . talking about sending everyone home and shutting the hotel down until all this is sorted. Needless to say I've told him no one can leave without our say-so.'

Sukey and Vicky stood for a moment staring down at the victim. There were livid bruises round the slight neck and a scattering of broken blood vessels round the wide-open eyes. 'There's not much of him,' said Vicky. 'It wouldn't take a heavy-weight to throttle him.'

'Poor kid,' said Sukey. 'What do we know about him?'

'His parents are dead and he's been lodging with Gunn since the pair of them started working here. According to Doc Hanley, death was somewhere between five and eight o'clock yesterday evening. I suggest you have a good look round and see if you can pick up anything the CSIs have missed. Then we'll go indoors and carry out some more interviews. Mike and Tim are already here, by the way, but I think it best if you two talk to Gunn.'

'Right, Guv.'

TEN

Sukey and Vicky spent some minutes examining the seat and the area surrounding it, closely observed by a couple of Crime Scene Investigators, Bill and Sid, who had lit cigarettes and were smoking them by the edge of the lake a short distance away.

'It seems DI Rathbone reckons we don't do our job properly,' Bill observed, flicking ash into the water.

'It's nothing personal – he likes everything double-checked,' said Vicky.

'We've noticed he doesn't do much checking himself,' said Sid.

'Not like he did before he got his promotion,' added Bill.

'Did you find anything useful?' asked Vicky.

'A half-smoked cigarette that was probably dropped by the victim,' said Sid, 'but of course it'll have to go for DNA testing.' He ambled across and bent down, pointing. 'We found it there – and took photos. And there was a black thread that probably came from his trousers clinging to the underside of the front slat of the seat. Also recorded on photo, both items bagged up and labelled. And as you can see, the grass in front of the seat has been flattened in places.'

'No doubt you've taken pictures of that as well,' Vicky observed. Sid grunted and went back to where Bill was standing. Vicky bent down and gently took hold of one of the victim's feet and raised it a few inches. 'Look, there are traces of mud on the heel. The other one as well, as if he dug his heels quite hard into the grass – which he wouldn't have done if all he did was sit down and light up.'

'You're right,' said Sukey. 'That would suggest he was taken completely by surprise.'

'We came to the same conclusion,' said Bill.

'Not too difficult,' said Sid.

'What is this – a wind-up?' said Vicky crossly. 'Don't get on to us – we're only obeying orders.'

'Never mind them,' said Sukey. 'Let's try to visualize the action. He was sitting there, having a quiet smoke, when someone approached out of the shadows and grabbed him by the throat.'

'He dropped his cigarette and most likely grabbed hold of the attacker's wrists in an attempt to free himself . . .'

'. . . didn't have the strength to pull the hands away, but dug his heels into the ground, probably kicked out frantically at his assailant's shins, first with one foot and then with the other – or maybe both at the same time; we've no way of telling, but when he stopped kicking the assailant probably let him go.'

Vicky shook her head. 'I think he's more likely to have kept up the pressure until he was completely sure his victim was dead, and then he'd slip quietly away.' She lowered the feet to the ground and stood upright. 'I wonder if he managed to inflict some bruises on the attacker's shins before he passed out,' she said. 'On second thoughts, though, those are very light shoes – I doubt if there'd be much in the way of bruising.'

'We might find someone with mud on their trousers,' said Sukey, 'but of course, they'll have had plenty of time to brush or sponge it off. Do we know what time his friend found the body?'

'Not until quite late, judging from the time DI Rathbone called us,' said Vicky. 'Well, I don't think there's much more we can do here. They might as well take him to the morgue. I suppose we'd better check with Sir first and then perhaps Reg's pal Keith will feel up to answering a few questions. All right, guys, you've passed your test,' she added with a jaunty wave to the two CSIs. 'Enjoy your smoke but make sure you put the stubs in the box by the door.'

Bill gave a mock salute. 'Will do, Sarge.'

They found DI Rathbone sitting in reception nursing a mug of coffee. 'Freeman and his mob are still having breakfast,' he said. 'I've told him we've got to interview everyone all over again and he's not a happy bunny. I have a feeling he and Chapman are of the same mind – for two pins they'd chuck in the towel and retire to the country to raise chickens.'

'So exactly when did they hear about Law's death, Guv?' asked Sukey.

'Not right away; by the time the guy who found him had pulled himself together and come rushing into the hotel to raise the alarm they were all upstairs for their evening sing-song. That would have been some time after eight thirty. The ones who went straight to bed after the evening's programme probably didn't hear about it until this morning, either when they looked out of their windows and saw the police or when they came down to breakfast this morning. The barman told the ones who went for their usual nightcap and of course they all went rushing out like a load of ghouls in the hope of seeing the body. Did you find anything?'

'Nothing that the CSIs hadn't spotted, but we made a couple of observations that gave us some idea of how things would have looked to an observer,' said Vicky. 'We'll mention them in our reports. We're wondering if this might be a good time to talk to Law's friend – the one who found him.'

'He's been having breakfast in his room – that is, the room Chapman let him use for the night. I made it clear that he's to talk to no one else until you've seen him. Chapman's in his office – he'll show you where he's been stashed away.'

Keith Gunn was sitting in an armchair in a small bedroom on the second floor. He appeared to be a couple of years older than Law and of a sturdier build. It crossed Sukey's mind that had he been attacked he might have put up a better fight than his friend. He was clutching a mug of coffee; there was a tray on his lap bearing an empty glass that appeared to have contained fruit juice, a bowl of half-eaten cereal and some untouched toast and

marmalade. When Sukey and Vicky entered he hastily jumped
to his feet and put the tray on a table, spilling some of the coffee
over his trousers as he did so.

'Oh, silly me!' he exclaimed. He ran to fetch a towel from the
en suite shower room and dabbed at the stain. 'You'll have to
bear with me – I'm still very upset. Poor Reggie . . .' He put the
towel to his eyes. 'It was obvious he was scared of something
and I begged him to be careful. There must be a serial killer about
– is anyone safe?'

'We don't think for a moment that this was a random killing,'
said Vicky. 'We think it's possible that your friend saw the attack
on Mr Rainbird and that the attacker knew and killed him before
he could tell us. We want to find the person who killed your
friend and we need your help. Do you feel up to answering a
few questions?'

'Of course,' he said. 'I'll do anything.' Although he was
evidently still in a state of shock it was clear that he was making
a serious effort to control himself.

'Just take your time,' Vicky went on. 'Finish your coffee.'

'Oh, thank you.' He drained the mug and put it on the tray.
'I'm ready,' he said.

'Good man. First of all, we understand that when you were
telling Mr Chapman that you'd found Reggie's body you said
something about him being worried and that he told you he
"might have done something stupid". Is that right?'

'Yes.'

'When did he say that?'

'It was on Sunday, while we were setting up the tea things
for the guests. They'd had a free afternoon and were due back
about half past five.'

'Is that all he said?'

Gunn put a hand to his forehead. 'I can't remember the exact
words, but the gist of it was that he thought he'd done something
stupid and should have gone to the police instead of trying to be
clever, and then he said, "Sorry, got to go," and ended the call.
I guessed it was because the guests had started to come back for
their tea and I assumed he'd tell me later. And that was the last
time I spoke to him.' His voice trailed away and he covered his
eyes.

'All right,' said Vicky, 'we'll leave it at that for now. About yesterday evening; tell us why you were by the lake.'

'I went out for some air.'

'What time would that have been?'

'I can't tell you to the minute, but it must have been some time after half past eight. I'd been serving the after dinner coffee; most of the guests had left the dining room so I and one of the other waiters were helping to clear the table and take the used cutlery and crockery into the kitchen.'

'So having done that you went outside?' He nodded. 'Is this something you do regularly when you come off duty in the evening?'

'Not regularly. Reggie always goes – went – out for a smoke and if we were on the same shift I usually went with him, but I don't smoke.' His voice faltered and he choked back a sob. 'I can't believe he's gone.'

'Would it be fair to say that the two of you were very close?' asked Sukey.

'Yes . . . very close,' he whispered.

'So tell us about last night.'

'Last night it was warm in the hotel and as I said, I felt in the need of air. And I was concerned about him, wondering why he hadn't come back to me . . .' His voice trailed away. 'Poor dear Reggie.'

'You were concerned about what he'd said?' He nodded. 'So finding him like that must have thrown you into a state of shock. What did you do?'

'I took his hand and called his name, but he didn't answer so I thought he must have been taken ill . . . that is, I hoped that was all it was, but I think I knew straight away that he was dead. Anyway, I suppose I panicked and went rushing back to the hotel and told Mr Chapman.'

'And that really is all you can tell us?' said Vicky.

He gave a deep sigh. 'I'm afraid so.'

'Well, if you think of anything else we'll be around for a while. I guess you'd like to go home now.'

'Thank you. Oh, I do hope you find who killed him. And the other gentleman, of course.'

'We will,' said Sukey.

They went back downstairs and reported the conversation to Rathbone. 'Do you know who interviewed Law after Rainbird's death?' he asked.

'It was neither of us,' said Vicky. 'It must have been either Mike or Tim.'

'Well, find out which of them it was. From what Gunn told you it's obvious Law saw something suspicious – presumably the attack on Rainbird – but decided to use it to his own advantage rather than mentioning it to us.'

'It certainly looks that way, Guv,' said Sukey. 'Ah, there's Mike, he's just finished questioning Millie.' She signalled to DI Haskins as he was about to follow Millie upstairs. 'Just a quick word – was it you or Tim who interviewed Law after the Rainbird death?'

'I did,' said Mike. 'I wanted a chance to speak to you about him, sir.' He opened the folder he was carrying and ran a finger down a list. 'I remembered having some doubts about whether Law was holding something back or just so nervous and upset that he couldn't remember anything clearly. He admitted being outside having a smoke; said he nips out whenever he has an opportunity because of course smoking inside the hotel is forbidden. What he couldn't – or wouldn't – say was exactly where he was at the time we think the attack took place. All he would say was that he couldn't be sure because he strolled about a bit. But he was adamant that he didn't see anything suspicious.'

'It's pretty obvious he did see something, so the reason he decided not to tell us must have been so that he could screw some hush money out of someone,' said Rathbone.

'Which could only mean that he saw Rainbird being attacked – and recognized the attacker.'

'Right.'

'So there were three people out there on Friday evening: Rainbird who said he was going out for some air but who we now believe had arranged to meet someone, probably the man who attacked him, the attacker himself, and Reg Law who witnessed the attack and thought he'd try a spot of blackmail.'

'I'm wondering whether we should have another word with

Eric Bowen, sir,' said Sukey. 'When Vicky and I spoke to him after Romeo's accident he admitted that when he went down to check that his car was locked he'd seen two men talking together by the lake but didn't recognize either of them.'

'That's right,' said Vicky. 'Hugh Pearson told us how security conscious Bowen is and checked his car every evening to make sure it was locked. We asked Bowen why he hadn't mentioned this and he said he must have forgotten.'

'We warned him that if he was – or if the killer thought he was – a potential witness, then he could be in danger himself. He appeared shaken, but he didn't say any more.'

'So go and have another talk with him,' said Rathbone. 'All right,' he said to Mike, 'carry on interviewing the music lovers. I think maybe I'll have another check on the staff.'

'That means reading through the list of names while swigging yet another coffee,' Vicky whispered to Sukey as they followed Mike upstairs to the Orchard Room. 'We'd like another word with Mr Bowen,' she said to Freeman. 'It should only take a moment.'

'Bowen's not here,' said Freeman. 'He wasn't at breakfast either. Maybe he's ill.'

'I don't think so,' said Hugh Pearson. 'He had breakfast in his room – a waiter had just put a full English on a tray outside his door when I came down.'

'Thanks, we'll go and have a look,' said Sukey.

When they knocked on Bowen's door he called, 'Who is it?'

'DS Armstrong and DC Reynolds,' said Vicky. 'May we come in, please? We need to speak to you.'

'Just a moment.' There was a rattle of a chain and the door opened a fraction. Bowen peered through the crack and after a moment released the chain and opened the door. He closed it behind them, replaced the chain, and then, after a moment's thought, undid it and picked up the breakfast tray from which most of the food had been eaten. 'I wonder – would you mind?' he said nervously.

'No problem.' Sukey put the tray outside the door and closed it.

'Sit down, Mr Bowen,' said Vicky. 'We've been checking on your replies to our previous questions and it's perfectly obvious that you've been holding out on us. We warned you that any witnesses to the attack on Lance Rainbird might themselves be in danger, but you declined to say anything further. Now there's been another death – and it's obvious you're scared stiff, so we think it's time you came clean. What exactly did you see?'

'I saw two men, one of whom I'm pretty sure was Lance Rainbird although as I said it was quite dark.'

'What about the other man?'

'He was in even deeper shadow and I could only see his outline. I really have no idea who it was.'

'Was he short or tall? Fat or thin?' asked Sukey.

'Pretty tall, probably several inches taller than Rainbird, and quite well built. That really is all I can tell you. Look, it could be one of several people and I don't want to throw suspicion on an innocent person.'

'Well, as you say there are several people who might fit that description,' said Vicky. 'Just the same, what you have told us could be very useful. I suggest you go and join your group now. As long as you don't go wandering off by yourself you have nothing to fear. Enjoy the music.'

'All right, perhaps I will . . . if you're sure.'

'Quite sure.'

As the two detectives opened the door to leave a waiter was just collecting the empty tray. He hurried along the corridor ahead of them and they exchanged glances. 'He fits that description!' said Vicky. 'I'll get his name.' She ran after him and after a brief word returned to Sukey. 'Mal Carter. We'll do another check on him.'

'I've just thought of another person who fits Bowen's description,' said Sukey.

'Who's that?'

'John Grayson, aka Romeo.'

ELEVEN

'We'd better bring DI Rathbone up to date,' said Vicky. 'No prizes for guessing where we'll find him.'

'In the lounge or the bar having coffee?'

'Right.'

They were mistaken in the location only. Rathbone, coffee mug in hand, was pacing to and fro a short distance from the place where Law's body was found. 'Well?' he said as they approached.

'Bowen admitted that he had been holding out on us, Guv,' said Vicky. 'He saw someone he thinks was probably Rainbird talking to another man who approached him out of the shadows. He said he wasn't sure of the identity of either man and insisted he didn't want to incriminate an innocent person. And he's scared witless because he thinks there's a serial killer about. We think we managed to reassure him on that point.'

'Is that it?'

'We asked for a description, Guv,' said Sukey, 'but all he would say was that the second man was several inches taller than Rainbird and quite well built.'

Rathbone swallowed the last of his coffee and with the empty mug indicated the area round the seat. 'Looks like Law put up a struggle from the way the turf has been kicked about.'

'We've noted that, Guv,' said Vicky. 'It'll be in our reports.'

'So get on with them then. Not much to go on from what Bowen told you but make a list of everyone – guests and staff – who fits the description he gave.'

'Will do, Guv.'

'There is one other thing that's occurred to us, Guv,' said Sukey. 'There's another person who fits Bowen's description, and that's the man whose real name we now know is actually John Grayson.'

'You mean the singer who calls himself Romeo?' Rathbone raised his eyebrows.

'Yes, Guv.'

'You said you wanted to question him about the time he arrived on Friday and found he'd scarpered before you got to the place where he'd parked his van. What possible motive could he have had for attacking Rainbird?'

'We've absolutely no idea,' said Vicky, 'but taken together with the fact that he was in such a hurry to get away it would have been interesting to hear what he had to say. Unfortunately, of course, we'll never know. Maybe the PM on Rainbird will give us at least some of the answers.'

'It'll show the cause of death, but not necessarily whether it was murder or an accident,' Rathbone pointed out, 'and we won't know until Doc Hanley has been able to do the PM on Grayson whether the disconnected brake pipe caused the accident and if so how it came to be disconnected, or whether he died at the wheel of natural causes, or . . .' He broke off to take a call on his phone. He listened for a moment then said, 'That's great, keep me posted,' and switched off. 'That was to say the accident investigators have finished checking the underside of the van and the next stage is to get Grayson's body to the morgue. As soon as he's been cleaned up his brother can go and see him. He called me earlier to say he's already booked in at a local B & B and he'll be staying there for as long as it takes. He's told his father he's been called away on business and may have to be away for a day or two. He's arranged for a widowed aunt to stay with the old man until he gets back. As soon as we get the all clear from the morgue we're to let him know. Sukey, you'd better update him. Here's the number of the B & B.'

'I'll do that right away, sir.'

'Any theories about the brake pipe?' asked Vicky.

Rathbone shook his head moodily. 'They can't say. It's an old van, not been properly maintained . . . it could have come away any time. There's nothing to say whether it was deliberate or not, so we're none the wiser.'

'We'll get on with our reports, then,' said Vicky.

'And make a list of everyone you can think of who even remotely fits Bowen's description. I'm going to have an early lunch. Morgan Ashman is coming down by the afternoon train and I have to send a car to pick him up at the station. I want you both to be present when I talk to him.'

'I guess we might as well have an early lunch ourselves,' said Vicky, 'and then liaise with Tim and Mike about questioning the staff. Maybe we could pick up a sandwich in the bar and eat it out here – or wherever *he's* not going,' she added under her breath.

'I'd better speak to Luke Grayson first and tell him about his brother,' said Sukey. She called the number Rathbone had given her. 'Good morning. I believe you have a Mr Grayson staying with you? Could I have a word with him please? Thank you.' There was a short pause before she continued, 'Mr Grayson, I'm pleased to be able to tell you that your brother's body is on its way to the morgue. It'll be a little while before you can see him but I'll keep you posted . . . I can't be certain but it shouldn't be too long, so I suggest you have some lunch and . . . oh, that's very kind of you, thank you very much.' She ended the call and put her phone back in her pocket. 'Sorry, Sarge, you're on your own for lunch. Mr Grayson has invited me to meet him for lunch at a restaurant in Clevedon.'

'Lucky you,' said Vicky.

The restaurant was perched on a hill a short distance from Clevedon and had sweeping views across the Bristol Channel towards the coast of Wales. The day was clear and a number of yachts and dinghies were out on the water taking advantage of the brisk breeze. Grayson was waiting for Sukey in the lounge and escorted her to a table by the window. 'My landlady recommended this place so I rang straight away and booked a table,' he said. 'I hope the food lives up to the view,' he went on, handing her a menu. 'What would you like to drink? A glass of wine?'

'Just an orange juice please,' said Sukey. 'This is an unexpected treat. The bar snacks in the hotel aren't anything to write home about, although the guests say the food they're getting in the restaurant is first class.'

'You're doing me a favour,' he assured her. 'Mrs Bird who runs the guest house is very sympathetic; normally she doesn't encourage guests to sit around after breakfast, but when I explained the situation she let me sit in the lounge and read the

papers. She brought me coffee and stayed for a chat, but she's
no great conversationalist.'

'And you think I might be an improvement?'

'I'm hoping you can shed a little light on my brother's death,'
he said earnestly. 'Oh, I know that until I've done this formal
identification you're talking about you can't say for certain that
the man in the van is my brother, but—'

'Look, I saw the victim and I can assure you that it is the man
we know as Romeo. What we don't yet know is what caused the
accident and whether the accident was the cause of death.'

'You're suggesting he might have died at the wheel of a heart
attack or something? Out of the question,' he assured her. 'John
never had a day's illness in his life apart from the odd childhood
complaint. He was as strong as an ox.'

Sukey nodded. 'Yes, we do have that impression. Just the
same, there will have to be a post-mortem.'

'I suppose so.' Grayson stood up. 'I'll get our drinks. Have
you chosen what you'd like to eat?'

'I'd like the mixed grill, please.'

Towards the end of their meal Sukey's phone rang. She moved
a short distance away to take the call; when she returned she
said, 'That was a call from the morgue. We can go now. Perhaps
you'd like to follow me. After you've made the ID we'd like you
to come back to HQ and answer a few questions.'

'Of course.' Grayson signalled to the waiter and paid the bill.

At they entered the morgue Sukey shivered slightly and felt
the usual contraction in her stomach at the familiar, instantly
recognizable smell of death that hung in the atmosphere. She
watched Grayson as he approached the corpse and stood by as
the attendant lifted the sheet. They had, she thought, done an
excellent job in laying the head to one side so that only part of
the injury was visible. She saw the muscles round Grayson's
mouth tighten as he stared down for well over a minute before
nodding and saying, 'Yes, that's my brother, John Grayson, God
rest his soul,' in a barely audible whisper.

Seeing that he was on the verge of breaking down altogether,
Sukey took him by the arm and led him outside. 'Come and sit
down,' she said, half propelling him to a chair. He sank into it,
covered his face with his hands and wept quietly for a few minutes.

When he was calmer he wiped his eyes, blew his nose and said, 'I'm sorry . . . I . . . it's so dreadful, seeing him like that . . . losing him will leave a huge gap in our lives. I dread breaking it to Dad.'

'I can't tell you how sorry we all are,' said Sukey. 'He was very popular with the guests. My colleagues and I heard him sing and thought he gave a great performance. Look,' she went on as he remained silent, 'why don't we go back to reception. There's a snack bar there – I could get you a cup of tea or coffee.'

Grayson shook his head. 'No thank you. You said there are a few questions you'd like to ask me so perhaps we could do that right away. I'd like to get back home as soon as possible; I'll talk to Mark and then I'll go and see Dad. If only John had listened to us, or at least let us buy him a decent van, this would never have happened – but he'd have none of it. We even offered to pay to have his old banger thoroughly checked over to be sure it was roadworthy, but he insisted he had a mate who did it for him.'

When they arrived back at headquarters, Sukey showed Grayson into an interview room and called DI Rathbone. He joined them almost immediately. 'I won't keep you more than a few minutes, sir,' he said. 'There's just one point you might be able to help us over.'

'What's that?'

'Apart from the call your brother made referring to someone – whom we now think was probably Lance Rainbird – having "bitten off more than he can chew", has he at any other time made any particular comment about any of the other attendees at any of Justin Freeman's courses that he's been to?'

'Not that I remember,' said Grayson. 'What kind of comment do you have in mind?'

'Nothing in particular. Just take your time, sir.'

Grayson thought for a moment. 'Ah, I do remember something; he once mentioned "a couple of know-it-alls who always seem to have it in for each other" – or words to that effect.'

'Can you remember when that was?'

'Not offhand, I'm afraid. Dad might remember. He's always kept a note of John's calls and the dates and anything else he told us.'

'Would you mind asking him, sir?'

'Of course I will, but I may have to leave it for a day or two. He's going to be very distressed, but naturally he'll be anxious to find out the truth.'

'As we all are, sir. Thank you for your cooperation, and may I once again express our sincere sympathy. Have a safe journey home.'

'Thank you. You will let us know as soon as you have more information, won't you?'

'Of course we will.'

As soon as he had left, Rathbone said, 'Right, back to my office.' Vicky was already there, sitting beside a slight, bespectacled man dressed in a grey lounge suit. 'Mr Ashman, please accept my apologies for keeping you. This is Detective Constable Reynolds, another member of the team investigating the death of your colleague Mr Lance Rainbird.'

Ashman half rose from his seat and gravely shook hands with Sukey. 'As I was saying, Inspector, Lance's death has come as a great shock to me. He asked my advice when he acquired ownership of a property left jointly to him and his brother Julius by a distant relative. The property was pretty run down and Julius wanted to sell it for whatever it would fetch but Lance insisted that it could be renovated and would then fetch a much better price. They wrangled about it for months – they'd never been on very good terms anyway – but eventually Julius was offered a job in Australia so he just let Lance have it. He needed financial advice and he trusted my judgement so I arranged a bank loan for him and he had the building – quite a large Victorian house – converted into flats.'

'Do I understand that you're here as a friend rather than a professional adviser?' said Rathbone.

'That's right.'

'We can understand your concern, of course, sir, but why do you feel it necessary to see the actual place where your friend met his death?'

'It's because of something he said a couple of days before he came to Dallington Manor.'

'What was that?'

'As far as I remember, his actual words were, "I've found out that chap's a jumped-up phoney . . . I've a good mind to have it out with him".'

'Did he say who he was talking about?'

Ashman shook his head. 'No, that's the odd part. I've got a feeling he might find out he was barking up the wrong tree and didn't want to put himself in a situation where he had to admit he'd made a mistake. He was like that.'

'From our enquiries we've gained the impression that he was a . . . how shall I put it . . . a very private individual,' said Rathbone. 'One person suggested he might have what he described as "some form of autism". You have obviously had quite a close relationship with him, so . . .'

'I'm not sure I'd have used that particular expression, but as you say he didn't seem to have any close friends. He once said I was the only person he could talk to since his parents died.'

'Have you any idea what he meant by "jumped-up phoney"?' asked Sukey.

'I asked him the same question, but that was the point when he clammed up.'

Rathbone frowned. 'And that's the only reason you're here?'

'I'd like to have a word with the chap who organizes these events to see if he can help. I'm sure you've questioned everyone very thoroughly, Inspector, but I just thought that if I came down and met some of the other participants something might occur to me . . . something that perhaps Lance let drop . . . that could help you find out who killed him.'

'But surely, Mr Ashman, you've seen the latest official statement issued by the police in which we made it clear that we've not yet established exactly how your friend met his death. What makes you so sure he was murdered?'

'You might say it's what is popularly known as a "gut feeling",' said Ashman after a momentary hesitation.

'With respect, sir, we need something more substantial than that as a proof of murder. We hope the post-mortem may throw some light on the matter.'

'How long will that take?'

'We have asked for his case to be given priority, so with luck it shouldn't be more than a few days. Unfortunately there was a delay because the weekend intervened.'

'I see. Yes, that would delay matters.'

'So what exactly are you asking of us?'

'I'm not actually asking anything of you, Inspector. I'm simply letting you know, out of courtesy, that I have arranged to stay at Dallington Manor until tomorrow.'

'I see.' Rathbone stood up. 'Well, of course I have no power to prevent you, but I should make it clear that everyone – guests and staff – have been thoroughly questioned and I think it unlikely that Mr Freeman, the organizer of the course, or Mr Chapman, the hotel manager, will welcome what they may see as any further interference with their enjoyment – such as it is – of the event.'

'I assure you, Inspector, I shall be very diplomatic.'

'I hope so, sir,' said Rathbone.

TWELVE

'So he's convinced that Rainbird was murdered,' said Rathbone when Ashman had left them. 'I'm beginning to come round to that conclusion myself, but so far we haven't found anyone with a motive.' He frowned and nibbled the end of his pen for a moment before saying, 'This reference to a jumped-up phoney keeps bugging me.' He made a note on his pad. 'Right, have either of you come up with anything interesting?'

'We've noticed that the waiter who picked up Bowen's breakfast tray is another man of similar build to the guy Bowen saw,' said Vicky. 'His name's Mal Carter. He's been interviewed already, of course.'

'So talk to him again. And anyone else who fits the description.'

'That remark Romeo made during a conversation with his father about "a couple of know-it-alls who always seem to have it in for each other" must have been a reference to Rainbird and Bowen, sir,' said Sukey. 'That would mean he was present on some occasion when the two of them were there. It's hardly likely to have been during one of the music sessions, so presumably it was during a tea break while Romeo was either about to do his act or when he'd finished it. So once we know exactly when that call was made we can be reasonably sure during which of Freeman's events he particularly noticed the constant spats between those two.'

Rathbone nodded. 'Sukey, you seem to have managed to win Luke Grayson's confidence. Have a word with him and ask him to treat checking the date when Romeo made that call as urgent. Yes, I know what he said about not adding to the old man's distress, but this could be crucial.'

'I'll do my best, sir.'

'So, you two, go and update Mike and Tim and then get your heads together to pick out anyone fitting Bowen's description.'

'Will do, sir.'

'And get a move on. Time's getting short and this event ends after lunch tomorrow. They'll all be itching to go home.'

Back in the CID office Sukey called Luke Grayson. 'Is there news already?' he asked eagerly.

'I'm afraid not,' she apologized. 'I'm just calling to say that my Inspector considers it important to our enquiries that we know the dates when your brother John called and exactly what he said. You said your father logged everything in detail, with the dates, and we're wondering—'

'I understand what you're saying,' he broke in, 'but as I explained, it's going to be very upsetting for Dad so I'll have to be careful how I broach the subject.'

'We appreciate that, sir, and the last thing we want to do is add to his distress, but is it possible for you to check in his diary without his knowing – perhaps after he's gone to bed or having his afternoon nap?'

'That could be tricky. Can you give me an idea which calls you might be interested in?'

'The one about someone having bitten off more than he can chew, of course, but also a previous call in which John referred to "a couple of know-it-alls having it in for each other". We'd like to know if he gave any more details. And if you should happen to come across anything else you think relevant . . .'

There was a pause before Grayson said, 'Well, all right – if you think it's that important I'll see what I can do.'

'Thank you very much, sir. That's much appreciated.' When she returned to Rathbone's office he was at his desk. Vicky was already sitting beside him; he nodded briefly when she reported what Grayson had said and beckoned to her to join them. 'I've got something to show you,' he said. 'I've had a feeling we've been missing something so I've been running through what we know about our list of possible suspects. They're pretty thin on the ground; so far we've only got Romeo and now this waiter Mal Carter. We haven't a motive and the only thing we have to go on is that Romeo and Carter fit Bowen's admittedly vague physical description. However, it occurs to me that there's one person none of us has thought of. Any ideas?' Vicky and Sukey exchanged glances and shook their heads. 'How about Justin Freeman?'

'Freeman?' Vicky thought for a moment. 'Well, I suppose he is the right build, but I seem to recall Sukey and I more or less dismissing him out of hand on the basis that he's hardly likely to top one of his regular clients. Still,' she went on, 'I suppose he might have used the time everyone thought he was checking his equipment to meet Rainbird, bash him over the head, shove him in the water and get back in time for the evening session, but—'

'Where's the motive?' Sukey finished as Vicky broke off in apparent bewilderment.

'Which is exactly the question I asked myself,' said Rathbone. 'All we know about Freeman, apart from what we've learned from other people, is the blurb on the programme, including all his qualifications. I'm well aware,' he went on, a trifle smugly, 'that you think I do nothing but sit around drinking coffee while you do all the leg work, but it so happens I've been doing some research on Mr Freeman and I've come up with some very interesting results. Get me another coffee, please Vicky.'

Obediently she went to the machine he had installed in the corner and refilled his mug. 'Here you are, Guv,' she said as she handed it over. 'Don't keep us in suspense. What have you turned up?'

He opened a window on his computer. 'I've managed to establish,' he said, a little smugly Sukey thought, 'some of these wonderful sounding qualifications Freeman claims are phoney. The part about lecturing in Branwell College is genuine, by the way; I checked an old prospectus; it described him as a musicologist and he obviously has a very extensive musical knowledge. And it's true he has been running these events since his retirement, getting increasing numbers of punters and they're obviously satisfied as they keep coming back for more. I've also checked on a few of the professionals who've taken part in his events and they're all genuine, although none of them particularly well known. It's when we come to all these degrees from American universities that he comes unstuck.'

'You mean he invented these universities, Guv?' said Vicky, pointing to the list of degrees from American universities copied from Freeman's current prospectus, which he claimed to have been awarded.

Rathbone shook his head. 'No, he's not that stupid. The unis are genuine – it's the degrees that are phoney. A very obliging lady at one of them managed to turn up an application he made to do a course but they turned him down because he didn't have what she described as "the necessary level of musical expertise".'

'Wow!' said Sukey. 'So Lance Rainbird had found out and knew he's a phoney.'

'And was probably threatening to expose him,' Vicky speculated. 'So he got him to agree to the meeting by the lake. I suppose the idea was to get some hush money out of him; Freeman doesn't strike me as the sort to submit to blackmail and exposure would have ruined his business and made him a laughing stock.'

'So he picked up the nearest weapon – probably one of those hefty chunks of wood that we saw – and felled him with it,' said Sukey.

'That's what I'm thinking,' said Rathbone, 'and John Grayson, aka Romeo, saw what happened and thought he might put the screws on Freeman himself, which meant he had to be silenced as well.'

'You reckon Freeman tampered with the brake hose, Guv?' said Vicky.

'It would make sense. And having killed once, he had nothing to lose. And then Reg Law pops out of the woodwork with another threat and he has to be dealt with as well. So, I think it's time we had a serious chat with Justin Freeman. I'm thinking that out of consideration to all the music lovers who've already put up with a lot of disruption we'll let them have their party and leave it until tomorrow morning to nick him. That's subject to DCI Leach's approval, of course – I'll have a word with him and get back to you.' He picked up the phone and indicated with a wave of his coffee mug that they were to wait outside.

'Well, it looks as if we've got this one wrapped up at last,' said Vicky as they made their way back to the CID office.

'I'd like to think so,' said Sukey, 'but there's still something bugging me.'

'Another hunch?' teased Vicky.

'Not exactly a hunch, just an unanswered question. What do you think Romeo meant by "making something out of it"? Surely he can't have been referring to money? His family were always offering to pay for anything he needed and he always refused. And Luke I know found it hard to believe that he could stoop to blackmail.'

'Maybe he'd run up some debt that he didn't want them to know about,' suggested Vicky.

'Such as?'

'Maybe he'd lost money on the horses, or perhaps he'd started taking drugs and needed to pay off a supplier.'

Sukey shook her head. 'From my impression of John Grayson he wasn't a blackmailer or a gambler and there was absolutely no reason to think he was a junkie . . . Anyway, the PM will reveal the presence of drugs, if any.'

'That's true,' said Vicky, 'but we still don't know what Law meant by having "done something stupid".'

It had already occurred to Sukey that he might have been referring to his abortive effort to get money from Harry. She knew it was her duty to report this to Rathbone but before doing so she felt it was only fair to tell Harry, so that he could report it himself.

'Maybe things will become clearer once we've talked to Freeman,' she said. 'Ah, here comes the DI – he's got his coat on so I guess that means we can go home.'

'We nick Freeman tomorrow morning, as soon as the punters have left,' he informed them. 'Before you go home,' he added over his shoulder, 'just check on Carter, the waiter. Not that I think he can add anything to what Gunn has told us about Law, but you seem to think he's worth talking to so get on with it.'

'Yes, *sir*,' said Vicky under her breath as the door slammed behind him. She went to the office to enquire if Carter was on duty and came back with the news that he had finished his shift at five. 'So we can go home as well,' she told Sukey gleefully. 'It'll have to wait till tomorrow.'

When Sukey got back to her flat she found a message from Harry. 'I'm just calling to touch base. Any chance of seeing you this evening? Love you.'

She went to the freezer, took out a lamb hotpot, put it in the microwave to thaw out and sat down with a glass of wine before returning his call.

'Hi,' he said, 'what sort of a day have you had? Anything exciting to report?'

The subtext of the question was of course, *'anything you're willing to share with me?'* and she was careful to keep her voice level as she replied, 'No further bodies, if that's what you mean, but the pressure's mounting; Freeman's event finishes with a party this evening and they all go home after breakfast.'

'So no breakthrough yet?'

'Not exactly, but there is something you should know – or rather, something you have to do. Can you come round?'

'Try and stop me. I'll be with you in two ticks.'

'Give me half an hour while I unwind and have a bite to eat. I'm starving.'

She had just finished her food and put her plate and cutlery in the dishwasher when Harry arrived. 'So what do I have to do?' he asked without the usual preliminary hug and kiss.

'You have to tell me officially what you told me on Sunday evening.'

'About Reg Law being my mole?'

'About him claiming to have a story and trying to get money out of you for it,' she said. 'We've been talking to his friend,

Keith Gunn, who said Law had told him he thought he'd done something stupid, but he never got around to saying what it was. I believe he was talking about the call he made to you, offering to sell you a story.'

'You think he'd learned something that was dangerous to whoever killed Lance Rainbird, that the killer overheard him making that call and made sure he never lived to pass on the information?'

'I think it's possible. I haven't mentioned it because I only learned about this a couple of hours ago.'

'Well, of course, go ahead and pass it on for what it's worth,' said Harry.

'Thanks. Have a drink and tell me about your day.' She filled a glass with wine and handed it to him. 'Cheers! Tell me, has this man they've arrested for the murder of that pensioner been charged yet?'

'Not yet, but the police seem pretty sure they've got their man.' In the absence through sickness of several members of the staff at the *Bristol Express,* Harry was covering cases that would normally have been assigned to a junior reporter. 'There has been a bit of light relief, though – oddly enough it concerns a member of the staff at Dallington Manor?'

'Light relief at Dallington Manor? You must be joking.'

'No, this is serious – at least for the chap I'm about to tell you about. He has ambitions to become a journalist; he called the office one day, asked if he could speak to a crime reporter and the switchboard put him through to me. He explained that he'd been reading various crime reports in the *Express* and wanted to know if I'd be kind enough to read a piece he'd written about the case and give him my opinion. It's not the first time I've been asked something similar by a wannabe journalist and they usually turn out to be pretty useless, but this chap sounded quite young and dead keen so in a moment of weakness I said yes. Apart from feeling some sympathy with the guy, I thought there might be a faint possibility that he'd observed something that your lot had missed, but no such luck. It was just a run-of-the mill piece.'

'And is it any good?'

'Better than most, but he's obviously got a lot to learn. I was able to give him some advice and encouragement – his gratitude was quite embarrassing.'

'He'll have to grow a thicker skin if he wants to get anywhere in your business,' she commented. 'Would you mind showing it to me or have you returned it to him?'

'I returned the original, but I kept a copy. You can have it for what it's worth.' He took a folded sheet of A4 paper from his pocket and gave it to her.

'Thanks.' She scanned it briefly and was about to put it aside when she spotted the name under the text and exclaimed, 'Mal Carter wrote this!'

'The name obviously means something to you,' said Harry. 'What's his job at the hotel?'

'He's one of the waiters,' she said. 'It so happens that Vicky and I have to see him tomorrow.' She tried to sound casual, but Harry wasn't deceived.

'He's a suspect?' he asked eagerly.

'It's just a loose end that needs tying up,' she said, 'and no, that's all you're going to get out of me.' Inwardly she felt a twinge of excitement. She was finding it difficult to dismiss the feeling that despite Rathbone's confidence that he had all but solved the Dallington Manor murders there was an important piece of the puzzle missing – a piece that could widen the list of suspects even further. Could this be it?

'So you aren't going to repay me for giving you what might turn out to be a useful little crumb to add to your apparently short list of clues?'

She shook her head. 'Not a chance. Let's talk about something else.'

'If you insist.' He reached for her and said softly, 'But is there any need for conversation?'

THIRTEEN

S ukey awoke the following morning after a refreshing, dream-less sleep. With a sigh of contentment she yawned and turned over in bed, half expecting to feel Harry still lying beside her, then remembered that he had slipped away around midnight saying that he had a piece to finish in time for the early edition.

As she got out of bed and pulled on a robe she found herself humming the opening theme of Mozart's Fortieth Symphony, the one she had heard Justin Freeman introducing on the morning after the death of Lance Rainbird. *There's been all this talk about sonata form,* she found herself thinking, as she filled the kettle. *Trixie thinks 'Death in Sonata Form' would make a good title for a detective novel and Eric was banging on about first and second subjects – by which I assume he meant different tunes – and then the closing theme. I suppose the first subject would be Rainbird's death, then Romeo's and then poor young Reg. From my limited knowledge of that symphony that's too many subjects for one movement, never mind the complications in between – not sure how Eric would describe them, variations perhaps, but whatever it is, that's what we're struggling with at the moment.*

Telling herself impatiently not to waste time on irrelevancies, she ate a hasty breakfast, showered and dressed and went to her computer to bring her report up to date. As she worked, refer-ence to the hotel employee Mal Carter aroused a brief stab of optimism. Could this man, who had caught her and Vicky's attention solely because of his height and build but had now taken on a new significance in her mind, be in possession of some vital piece of information? Since reading the piece Harry had shown her she had begun to regard him not so much as a possible suspect, but rather as someone likely to be more obser-vant than many. Her increasingly close relationship with Harry had taught her that journalists always kept their eyes and ears open for extra titbits that they could add to their stories to make them more interesting. Was there perhaps a faint chance that Carter had observed something he had not thought to mention to any of the investigating officers but who might now, under careful questioning, recall to mind? If so, it could open up a new line of enquiry. *It'll have to be good to shake Rathbone off Freeman's back*, she thought as she finished her report, saved it and sent it to DCI Leach and DI Rathbone with copies to the other members of the team.

Vicky had suggested they arrive at Dallington Manor no later than eight o'clock, when whoever was in charge of the kitchen might be willing to release Carter for a few minutes to enable them to talk to him. They were in luck; almost all the guests had opted to take their breakfasts in the dining room.

'They always have breakfast together on the last morning,' he explained as he followed the detectives out of the kitchen. 'They're asked to get their luggage out of their rooms by ten o'clock and in any case I think some of them who haven't been to one of Mr Freeman's parties before like to exchange addresses with new friends, find out who is going to the next or subsequent events and so on.'

'You've worked here for some time then?' said Vicky.

'Oh yes – for several years in fact. It's the only job I've been able to get so far but my real ambition is to become a journalist. I can't afford to go to college – my father's dead and my mother only has a small pension – but I've been told there are correspondence courses.' He looked enquiringly from one to the other. 'What do you want to talk to me about?'

'It so happens we've already heard about your ambition,' said Sukey. 'A friend of mine is a journalist and one of the things I've learned about him is that he's an incorrigible people watcher. Does this apply to you?'

He gave a slightly self-conscious smile. 'Well, yes, you could say that,' he admitted. 'As a matter of fact, I'm particularly interested in being a crime reporter; I'm aware that Mr Rainbird's death still isn't being treated as murder,' he hurried on, 'but once Reg Law was killed it's pretty obvious that you – the police – are thinking on those lines.'

'As you say, we're still not sure how Mr Rainbird met his

death,' said Vicky, 'but we believe someone here has noticed more than they've told us.'

'As you know, I've already been interviewed by one of your colleagues.' His manner became defensive as he added, 'I assure you I answered his questions fully and frankly.'

'We're not suggesting for a moment that you're deliberately withholding anything,' Sukey assured him. 'We're just wondering if you might have noticed or possibly heard something that struck you as, let's say, interesting or even unusual . . . about any of the people in Mr Freeman's group.'

'Let me think now.' Carter closed his eyes for a moment, and then opened them again. 'Well of course there are the two gentlemen who seem to like showing off how much they know about music and are always arguing with each other. Everyone seemed to agree that one of them – the one who died that is – knew a lot more than the other. He certainly commanded more respect anyway and I've noticed he had a few admirers among the ladies. One or two in particular seem to hang on his every word. Now I come to think of it, he did have a very attractive voice – a romantic novelist might describe it as "mellifluous". And there's the lady in the wheelchair – or rather her companion; I think she was rather smitten as well.'

'That's interesting,' said Sukey. She recalled Hugh Pearson's remarks about his own wife and wondered how many other husbands shared his views. 'Do you happen to know the names of any of these ladies?'

'I'm afraid not,' he apologized. 'Except the companion – I know she's called Millie because her employer often summons her in a very audible voice. Most of the others chat very informally and if they use names at all it's only their first names or even nicknames.'

'By the way,' said Vicky, 'were you on duty on Friday evening – the night Mr Rainbird died?'

He shook his head. 'No, my shift finished at five o'clock. I've been on the early shift for the past couple of weeks.'

'Well, thank you, you've been very helpful,' said Sukey. 'And good luck with your journalistic career.'

'I don't see that he's been much help,' Vicky remarked as Carter went back to the kitchen.

Sukey shrugged. 'Well, it was worth a try.'

'Sir should be along any minute so we'd better get back to reception,' said Vicky.

Rathbone was there waiting for them. 'The punters will be getting ready to leave soon,' he told them. 'They'll be coming to the desk to settle their bar accounts before setting off home. Freeman will be here to speed them on their merry way –' at this point he lowered his voice although there was no one within earshot – 'and I shall quietly detain him for a minute or two after they've gone and request a word with him down at the station. He'll no doubt put on a show of reluctance – want to know why we can't have our word here and so on – but he'll have to agree in the end. He's got his own car here of course so I've brought double-oh-seven to ride shotgun with him and we'll all drive in convoy back to HQ.'

'I've just learned something that may help to throw light on Reg Law's death, Guv,' said Sukey.

'What's that?'

She briefly outlined the approach Reg Law had made to Harry Matthews. 'He didn't mention it at the time because he didn't take Law's claim seriously at first. When he heard about his death, he told me straight away.'

Rathbone thought for a moment. 'Obviously, the "something stupid" was to try and make a bit on the side instead of coming straight to us. Unfortunately for him, Freeman overheard that call. Excellent. More grist to the Freeman mill.'

'Do you want us to wait here with you, Guv?' asked Vicky.

'No, you go back to your own cars and wait. Any joy from that waiter, by the way?'

'Not really, Guv.'

He shrugged. 'As I thought. All right, see you outside.'

'He's like a wolf waiting to sink his fangs into his prey,' commented Vicky. 'You can't blame him, I suppose – it's pretty satisfying to be ninety per cent sure you've got your man.'

Seated in their respective cars, which were parked some distance away from Freeman's, Sukey and Vicky watched as the last of the party drove away. Having seen the last one off, Freeman picked up his own luggage and put it in the boot of his car. He had evidently not noticed PC James Bond sitting in the front passenger seat, but as he reached for the handle of the driver's door, Rathbone quietly approached him from behind and put a hand on his arm. He swung round in evident surprise, listened as Rathbone spoke to him and then shook his head and lifted both hands in what looked like a gesture of refusal before making another attempt to open the door. Rathbone gripped his wrist and he made an unsuccessful effort to shake himself free. There were two or three minutes of altercation before Freeman ceased arguing, got into the car and switched on the ignition. At a signal from Rathbone and before Freeman moved forward, first Vicky and then Sukey pulled out and headed for the exit. Freeman followed and with Rathbone bringing up the rear the party travelled in convoy to the police headquarters.

Once in the interview room and before Rathbone had a chance to say a word, Freeman said, 'I can't for the life of me understand why this couldn't have been sorted out before we left the hotel. You're supposed to be out hunting for a killer, not wasting my time with questions you could have asked earlier. I need to get home – I've got things to see to – and what the hell are you switching that thing on for?' he went on as Rathbone, ignoring the outburst, went through the formalities of starting the recording and settling down opposite Freeman with Vicky and Sukey on either side of him.

'Mr Freeman,' Rathbone began, 'you are here because we believe you can help us in our enquiries into the death of Lance Rainbird and the subsequent deaths of John Grayson and Reginald Law. If you wish to call your solicitor you are free to do so – or we can arrange for you to be advised by the duty solicitor.'

'Why the hell should I need a solicitor?' demanded Freeman, 'and how can I help you with your enquiries when I've already told you all I know?'

'Mr Freeman,' said Rathbone, 'you are on record –' here the detective opened a file that lay on the table in front of him – 'as saying that the last time you saw Mr Rainbird alive was when he left the dining room on Friday evening at around eight o'clock saying that he was going out for some fresh air.'

'That's correct,' said Freeman. 'But why—?'

'You further stated,' Rathbone continued, 'that you went up

to the Orchard Room some ten or fifteen minutes before the evening programme was due to start, on the pretext of checking your equipment.'

'It wasn't a pretext, it's something I do as a matter of routine,' said Freeman. 'Anyone will tell you.'

'Ah yes, routine. Of course. So naturally no one doubted for a moment that your reason for leaving the dining room before everyone else on this occasion was the usual one.'

'Which it was!' As if to drive the point home, Freeman slapped the table with an open palm. Sukey noticed that he had long, powerful looking fingers and she had a fleeting vision of them clamped round Law's throat.

'Mr Freeman,' said Rathbone, 'we have taken a statement from a witness who claims to have seen you speaking to Mr Rainbird close to the lake, shortly after he left to go outside.'

Freeman appeared startled and hesitated for a moment before saying hurriedly, 'I can't think what witness you have in mind, but I can only repeat that I went straight up to the Orchard Room after drinking my after dinner coffee, so whoever it was obviously mistook me for someone else. Surely you aren't suggesting that I was the one who attacked Lance Rainbird? If that's what this is about, you're barking up the wrong tree. All right, he could be a pain in the backside at times but that's hardly a motive for murder unless you're looking for some kind of psychopath, which I assure you I'm not. And if that's all you have in the way of evidence against me . . .' He half rose in his chair, but Rathbone raised a hand.

'As to motive,' he said, 'I was coming to that. You say Rainbird could be "a pain in the backside at times" – could that be on account of his extensive knowledge of music?'

'Not so much his knowledge – as I've already told you, I'm well aware of that and I respect it – so much as his way of letting us all know about it. Eric Bowen's just the same; neither of them is a qualified musician, not—'

'Not with a string of degrees like you, for example?'

'Well, yes.'

'So it will surprise you to learn that Lance Rainbird held a degree in music from the Open University?'

Freeman's jaw dropped. 'I had no idea. He was obviously

a real lover of music with a very wide knowledge, but . . . what a
strange chap . . . to keep it a secret. You'd have thought . . .'

'He'd want to boast about it, to let everyone know.' Freeman
nodded. 'It was a surprise to us,' Rathbone continued, 'but we
have reason to believe that this was typical behaviour on his part.
From the string of qualifications you claim here –' at this point
Rathbone picked up a copy of Freeman's prospectus – 'you obviously have no such inhibitions.'

'That's not boasting, it's all about PR. People who are being
asked to spend their time and part with their money need some
sort of guarantee that they're going to get value for it.'

'Ah yes, and this impressive string of letters is their assurance
that you are a suitably qualified person to help them to a greater
understanding of music and get more enjoyment out of it?'

'Of course.'

'Maybe they wouldn't be so impressed if they knew that you
were never actually awarded those degrees.'

The effect on Freeman was striking. It almost seemed to Sukey
as if he had become physically smaller. He put a hand to his
mouth and his eyes widened in mingled astonishment and dismay.
'How in the world did you find out?' he asked.

'It wasn't difficult,' said Rathbone drily. 'We have our methods.'

Freeman made a little gesture of despair. 'I needed something
more than my existing CV to get this business off the ground. I
did a lot of searching on the Internet and I found these American
universities offering distance learning courses. I thought I could
do that while I was approaching retirement and it would be
something extra to put on my prospectus.'

'As it happened you didn't qualify for any of the courses, but
you claimed the qualifications anyway, thinking no one would
ever find out.'

'I knew it was a risk but I took a chance on no one taking the
trouble to check.'

'But Rainbird did, and he was trying to blackmail you, wasn't
he?'

Freeman sat bolt upright and his jaw dropped. 'What in the
world gave you that idea?'

To Sukey, the man's look of bewilderment appeared genuine,
but evidently Rathbone was not impressed. He leaned forward

and said, 'I put it to you that Lance Rainbird told you he had discovered that you were not entitled to the qualifications you claim on your prospectus and wanted money to keep quiet. You weren't prepared to submit to blackmail so you lured him into the garden at a time when no one else would be around and—'

'No!' Freeman leapt to his feet and the uniformed officer standing behind him moved forward and firmly pressed him back on to his chair. 'This is crazy . . . you've got it all wrong,' he continued. 'It wasn't like that – he just . . .' As if realizing that he had been on the point of giving himself away, he broke off and pressed his lips firmly together.

'All right, it wasn't like that,' Rathbone continued. He waited for a moment before saying quietly, 'So tell us how it was, then.'

'I'm not saying another word without my solicitor's advice.'

'That's your right, sir. Would you like us to arrange for a duty solicitor to advise you, or . . .?'

'I'll call my own, if you don't mind.'

After Freeman made his call he said, 'My solicitor has an appointment with a client in an hour's time. He will be here at three o'clock.'

'Very well. If you would like to have some lunch this officer will arrange for your choice of food from the canteen to be brought here while you await your solicitor's arrival.'

Freeman's solicitor, whom he introduced as Dennis Nugent, was about the same build as his client, but he had a leaner, paler face and his steady, direct gaze as he took his place beside his client reminded Sukey of DCI Leach. Once the formalities were over he said briskly, 'Inspector Rathbone, I am sure we can clear this matter up very quickly. My client admits that he has made certain misleading claims on his prospectus – claims that he assures me will not appear on the new edition which will be printed shortly. He does, however, categorically deny that Mr Rainbird informed him that he knew of the deception or asked for money – or made any other demands – as a price for his silence.'

'To make sure you are fully in the picture, Mr Nugent,' said Rathbone, 'I'll ask Detective Sergeant Armstrong to inform you of the relevant question and your client's answer.'

Reading from her notes, Vicky began, 'DI Rathbone said to

Mr Freeman, "You lured him into the garden at a time when no one else would be around", at which point the witness jumped to his feet and said, "You've got it all wrong . . . it wasn't like that, he just" – and then he said he would say no more without your advice.'

'Thank you,' said Rathbone. 'So perhaps,' he went on speaking directly to Freeman, 'now you have your solicitor's advice you are prepared to explain exactly how it was that you lied to us about being in the grounds talking to Rainbird when you were supposed to be checking your equipment.'

'All right, I did arrange to meet him,' said Freeman, 'but I was a few minutes late because I got chatting to some people who were having coffee so I was a bit pushed for time and we only had a few minutes together. We agreed we'd arrange to meet again to discuss details and I went back indoors. I swear he was alive when I left him.'

'So what was the purpose of your meeting?'

'He offered to give me some advice. He said it was confidential and he didn't want to risk our conversation being overheard.'

'What was the nature of his advice?'

'I told you, it was confidential.'

'Are you saying you were prepared to go to this clandestine meeting without an inkling of what it was about?'

Freeman fidgeted in his chair. 'I think I'd like to have another word with my solicitor in private.'

Rathbone stood up and spoke into the microphone. 'Very well. Interview suspended at three thirty.' To Freeman he said, 'You may have ten minutes.'

When they reassembled Rathbone said, 'Right, sir, you arranged to meet Mr Rainbird. Exactly where was the meeting to take place?'

'In a place we both knew. Whichever of us got there first would be standing near the cypress tree close to the edge of the lake.'

'Which of you suggested that particular place?'

'I did.'

'Any particular reason?'

'It was just a convenient landmark, that's all.'

'Of course, you both knew the grounds reasonably well, having been there on at least one previous occasion. But there hasn't always been a heap of large chunks of cut timber, has there?'

'Not that I remember. What difference does it make?'

'The difference is that in the hands of a strong man – such as yourself, for example – a heavy piece of timber could easily fell a slighter man, who could then be pushed into the water and left to drown.'

'That's an outrageous suggestion!' Freeman shouted.

'Please, Inspector,' Nugent intervened, 'it is obvious that whatever your witness happened to observe he or she did not see my client attack Mr Rainbird or you would have produced them. I must insist that you come to the point without any more beating about the bush.'

'Very well, I would like your client to explain the nature of this advice.'

'He has assured me that it has no bearing whatsoever on the death of Mr Rainbird.'

'I am not prepared to accept his assurance,' said Rathbone, 'and I would remind him that since Mr Rainbird's death one person has been murdered and another has died under circumstances which are not yet fully explained. We do, however, believe that these deaths are connected and that your client is in possession of information which would be of help to us in our enquiries.' He turned to Freeman, 'I must therefore insist that you reveal this advice, otherwise I shall have no alternative but to detain you for further questioning.'

Freeman gave a resigned sigh. 'All right then, I'll tell you.'

FOURTEEN

'Right,' said Rathbone, 'let's have the full story – and make it the truth this time.'

'Lance rang me up a short while before the Dallington Manor party weekend,' Freeman began. 'He'd already booked and paid and I thought at first he was calling to say he couldn't come after all. My events are very popular – especially the parties – and sometimes I have a waiting list so if anyone drops out and they let me know in good time I can offer their place to someone else, but it wasn't anything like that. He said he'd recommended my events to quite a few people in the past – he mentioned regulars like Trixie and Stan Day, the Harlands and some others – but he was sorry to say he didn't feel he could recommend me any more unless I made certain changes to the wording on my prospectus.'

'What changes did he want you to make?'

'Can't you guess?'

'You tell me.' Rathbone's tone made it clear that he was not prepared to accept anything but direct answers.

'All right,' said Freeman with evident reluctance, 'he'd found out – he didn't tell me how – that my degrees were, well, I wasn't entitled to them. He said he'd keep my secret if I had a new prospectus printed without the degrees, but he wanted something else.'

'So he was blackmailing you. How much did he want?'

'It wasn't exactly blackmail . . . I mean, he wasn't asking for money. He isn't . . . wasn't . . . hard up, he had a good job and as you probably know he drove a brand new BMW.'

It was clear that Rathbone was beginning to lose patience. 'Yes, we are aware of the make of his car,' he snapped, 'so please get to the point. If it wasn't money, what the hell did he want?'

'He wanted me to employ him – professionally, that is – to handle my accounts. He said he could help me reduce my tax liability.'

'Mr Freeman,' said Rathbone, 'are you seriously expecting us to believe that the pair of you went through all this subterfuge simply to discuss a straightforward matter of business?'

'It's the truth,' said Freeman stubbornly. 'Lance insisted on it. I've always found him . . . a bit odd in some ways. I think we touched on this aspect of his character the first time we met and the word "autistic" was mentioned. I'm sorry, but there's nothing else I can tell you.'

'There's a great deal more you can tell us. You can start by repeating exactly what passed between you during that conversation down by the lake.'

Freeman glanced at Nugent, who nodded. After a pause, during which he sat with knitted brows, Freeman began speaking, slowly at first but with increasing confidence as memory returned. 'As far as I remember,' he began, 'I started by apologizing for turning up a bit late but he brushed that aside. He said he understood why I felt it necessary to have some qualifications when advertising my courses, but insisted that I remove those fake degrees from my prospectus. I assured him that I'd have new ones printed without them, and then he went on to say he could save me money if I trusted him with my accounts.'

'Did he say in so many words that if you didn't agree he'd tell all the punters at this event that you were a phoney?'

'No, he didn't.'

'You expect us to believe that was all he wanted in return for not divulging something that could ruin your business . . . make you a laughing stock?'

'You can believe what you like. I don't remember every precise word, but that was the gist of what he said.'

'So what did you say in reply?'

'I was in a bit of a hurry so I just said that was fine; I promised to get in touch when I got back home and we'd discuss details. I then went straight back to the Orchard Room . . . as I've already told you more than once,' he added wearily.

'It must have troubled you that he was still in a position to influence you . . . or that he might make some further demands on you,' said Rathbone.

'On the contrary, it crossed my mind that maybe the reason why he was being so secretive was that he didn't want his employers to know what he was proposing – in other words, he was hoping to make something on the side and was relying on me to be equally discreet.'

Rathbone gave a short, staccato laugh. 'You have the effrontery to ask me to accept that gave you some sort of influence over him?' He leaned forward and locked his eyes on to Freeman's. 'I put it to you that you have been telling me a cock and bull story from start to finish, that having unmasked you as a phoney Lance Rainbird was blackmailing you for substantial sums of money and rather than pay up you felled him with one of those lumps of wood and left him unconscious in the water to drown.'

'Really, Inspector . . .' Nugent began, but it was Freeman who responded.

'You're the one who's telling the cock and bull story and you haven't got a shred of evidence to back it up,' he shouted angrily. 'What I've told you is the truth, and I'm not saying another word.'

As if he had not been interrupted, Rathbone continued. 'Having disposed of Rainbird you were then threatened with exposure by John Grayson, the man who called himself Romeo. He happened to be sitting unobserved in the seat under the cypress tree and witnessed what happened, so you had to get rid of him. You found an opportunity to tamper with the brake pipe of his van while he was entertaining members of your party and so caused the accident that killed him.'

'That's not true. I never went near the van from the time he arrived to the time he left,' said Freeman, in response to a glance from Nugent.

'You were later threatened with exposure by one of the waiters, Reg Law, who had also stumbled on the truth,' Rathbone continued, 'so you disposed of him as well.'

'That's absolute rubbish.'

'Inspector,' said Nugent, 'unless you can produce evidence to back any of your allegations I must insist you release my client immediately.'

Rathbone stood up. Sukey could sense his feeling of frustration as he said, 'Wait here. I'll be back in a moment.' He signalled to Vicky and Sukey to remain seated and went out, slamming the door behind him. Five minutes passed, during which no one said a word. Then Rathbone returned and switched off the recording. 'All right, Mr Freeman,' he said, 'on condition that you are willing to let us take your fingerprints and a DNA sample you are free to go for now, but we may want to talk to you again so please keep us informed of your movements.'

'What a load of poppycock!' Rathbone snorted the moment the door closed behind Freeman and Nugent.

'You reckon he pulled that story out of the air, Guv,' said Vicky.

'Of course he did – and you have to hand it to him, it's not bad for something cooked up at short notice and under pressure.

But ask yourselves why, having got Freeman over a barrel, would Rainbird demand nothing in return for his silence but a bit of business for his firm? DCI Leach agrees with me – he's our man all right but he's as slippery as an eel and so far we haven't been able to pin him down.'

Faced with a sudden mental image of Rathbone in hot pursuit of an eel with a giant pin in one hand, Sukey had difficulty in keeping a straight face as she said, 'Maybe it wasn't quite as simple as that, Guv.'

'Meaning?'

'There's been quite a lot in the media lately about firms exploiting loopholes in the tax laws for wealthy clients to save them huge sums of money that should have gone to HM Revenue and Customs.'

'I suppose that's a point,' Rathbone conceded. 'But a small outfit like Freeman's could hardly be expected to generate megabucks. It could,' he went on after a moment's thought, 'enable Rainbird to put in his back pocket fees that should have gone to his firm, which would explain all the hush-hush business. But no, whichever way you look at it, it smells like something Freeman has cobbled together in a desperate attempt to hide the truth. And think for a moment about how Reg Law died – strangled. Did you notice Freeman's hands? They'd have had no trouble choking the life out of a slightly built young man like Law, who might well have overheard something incriminating. Remember what he said to his mate, Gunn? No,' he insisted, 'Freeman's our man – he had means, motive and opportunity; all we need is . . .'

He stopped short, having momentarily run out of breath.

'Evidence, Guv?' said Vicky.

'Exactly. So bloody well get busy and find me some! I'll see you back here first thing in the morning.'

'What do you reckon?' said Sukey when she and Vicky returned to the CID office. 'Do you really think he did it?'

'Of course. Don't you?'

'I'm not sure. I know that story about tax evasion and so on is feasible, but from what we know about Rainbird – which admittedly isn't much – blackmail wouldn't seem to be his line. But of course, you never know what people are capable of. Maybe forensics will come up with something.'

'Which will take forever,' Vicky commented.

'Maybe Mr Leach will manage to pull some strings and get the tests fast-tracked,' said Sukey, 'and in the meantime perhaps we'd better start by having a word with Mr Ashman. He knew Rainbird personally so maybe he can shed some light on his character.'

'I guess that's our best bet to start with it,' Vicky agreed. 'He said he was staying at the hotel until today, so he's probably gone back to London by now. We'll have to call him at his office in the morning.'

'He may have decided to stay another day. Why not check with the hotel?'

'I suppose it's worth a try.' Vicky picked up the phone and punched in the number. 'Good evening, is Mr Ashman still in the hotel, please? He is? May I speak to him? Thank you.' There was a pause before she said, 'This is DS Armstrong speaking, Mr Ashman. I understand you're staying at the hotel until tomorrow and we'd like a word with you before you leave . . . yes . . . that's splendid, thank you so much. Good night.' She ended the call and gave a thumbs-up sign. 'We're seeing him at half past nine tomorrow. At the hotel. Meet me here at eight thirty as usual.'

'Fine,' said Sukey. 'At least we can show Sir that we're being proactive.'

When they arrived, Ashman was waiting in reception with his suitcase beside him.

'Good morning, please sit down,' he said. 'I was glad to get your call; as a matter of fact I've been on the point of calling you, but decided it would probably be a waste of your time.'

'Why should you think that, sir?' asked Vicky.

'I told myself you'd probably already thought of what I was going to say.'

'That's possible, sir, but let's have it anyway.'

Ashman took off his glasses and polished them with a hand-kerchief. It seemed to Sukey that it was more to hide discomfiture than of necessity. He put them back on his nose and cleared his throat. 'I've spent a lot of time walking round the grounds,' he said. 'Lance had been twice before and was looking forward to

coming again. I suppose I was trying to . . . how shall I put it
. . . imagine what it was about the place that appealed to him.
Of course, parts of the grounds are still taped off by your officers
so I could only observe from a distance the actual place where
his body was found, but one thing I did notice and that was a
great heap of timber close by. It occurred to me that a lump of
that in the wrong hands could be used to attack someone. I do
understand, of course, you still don't know the exact cause of
death, but . . .'

'Mr Ashman,' Vicky broke in, 'I can assure you that in addition to various other features of the crime scene we are aware
of that pile of timber. Is there anything else you want to draw
to our attention?'

Ashman fiddled with the handle of his suitcase. 'I've been
talking to a member of the staff. I bore in mind Inspector
Rathbone's reminder that they had all been interviewed by the
police, but as a matter of fact this young man approached me.
He's a waiter but he wants to be a journalist – particularly a
crime reporter.'

'Yes, we know about him and we've taken a full statement
from him,' said Vicky.

'Oh yes, he told me, but he'd become aware that Lance is a
friend of mine and he asked me if I could tell him something
about him, something personal, that might be of interest to a
potential reader. He went on to assure me that what he was
writing wasn't for publication – he had a friend, a professional
journalist, who promised to help him.'

'And what did you tell him?' asked Sukey.

'I made it very clear that I wasn't prepared to answer that kind
of question to a journalist, but I've been giving it some thought
and I wondered if I should tell the police. That's why I was
thinking of calling you and the fact that you've approached me
has made up my mind.' He took a deep breath and said, 'Lance
had many fine qualities and as far as his professional life was
concerned I'd be prepared to vouch for his integrity, but he could
be rather difficult on one particular subject – religion.'

'Are you saying he was a deeply religious man?'

'On the contrary – he was almost fanatically against any form
of religion, especially Catholicism. It's one of the few subjects,

apart from music, on which he expressed any strong opinion . . . or any opinion at all for that matter. Most of the time he kept his head down and got on with his work, but mention religion and it was like waving the proverbial red rag in front of a bull. Unfortunately it was the cause of an unpleasant incident in our firm; one of the staff in his department is a devout Christian and on one occasion he accused Lance of blasphemy. According to reports, it seemed for a moment that they were about to come to blows, but then the accuser backed down and mumbled something about how the persecuted are blessed and the kingdom of heaven is theirs. I seem to remember hearing something like that at Sunday school,' he added, 'but of course that was a long time ago.'

'It comes from a passage in the Bible known as the Sermon on the Mount,' said Sukey in response to an enquiring glance from Vicky. 'Did Lance ever tell you why he felt such antipathy towards religion?' she asked Ashman.

'Not really, except that it had something to do with an experience he had as a child.'

'We know that his father died when he and his brother were quite small,' said Vicky. 'Their mother had to work as a teacher to support them so she sent them to a boarding school run by some religious order.'

Ashman nodded. 'That could account for it; I'm told some of these people are very strict disciplinarians. Maybe he had one caning too many.'

'Or some of the teaching may have had a profound effect on him psychologically,' Sukey suggested.

'Whatever the reason, you've given us another avenue to explore, so thank you for your time, sir,' said Vicky. 'Would you be kind enough to give us the name and address of the person who had the confrontation with Mr Rainbird?'

'I'll have to check his address when I get back to the office. I have a feeling he's on some kind of compassionate leave at present on account of a bereavement in his family. His name is Luke Grayson.'

FIFTEEN

'How about that?' Vicky exclaimed as they returned to the car park after saying goodbye to Ashman. 'Co-incidence or what?'

'It has to be Romeo's brother,' said Sukey. 'There can't be two people with that name who work for the same firm as Rainbird and have recently suffered bereavement.'

'So Rainbird was a devout atheist,' said Vicky, after mulling over this new piece of information for a moment, 'who once said something which infuriated Luke Grayson, who according to Ashman is an equally devout – and somewhat militant – Christian.'

'We know that the Grayson brothers had Christian parents who named them after the evangelists and took them regularly to church and so on,' said Sukey, 'but apart from that Luke never mentioned religion to us, or showed any sign of militancy either. He expressed shock when we told him about Rainbird's death, and it's odd that he didn't mention the fact that they worked for the same firm – or that he'd had a disagreement with him. Maybe that was because he was so upset about the accident to his brother,' she added as an afterthought.

'Perhaps he was being extra clever,' Vicky suggested.

'How do you mean?'

'Let's suppose for a moment that Luke Grayson is a total fruitcake who regarded Rainbird as an instrument of Satan because of his atheism. Rainbird said something that he regarded as particularly outrageous and almost led to a stand-up fight. And suppose he knew Rainbird was coming here and followed him with the intention of killing him.'

Sukey shook her head. 'That doesn't add up. If he managed to contain his anger and show a Christian attitude after the scene in the office over what he regarded as blasphemy, he's hardly likely to pursue the man to Dallington Manor at a later date to exact some kind of atonement. From what Ashman said he's a man of pretty high principles; don't forget he was horrified at the thought of his brother John having contemplated blackmail. That would have been avarice – one of the seven deadly sins.'

'It doesn't sound rational,' Vicky agreed, 'but maybe we're not dealing with a rational person.'

'You mean "some kind of psychopath", as Freeman put it? In which case, what DI Rathbone calls Freeman's cock and bull story would have to be true.'

'He's not going to give up on Freeman without a struggle and neither is DCI Leach,' said Vicky, 'but we'll have to tell them what Ashman said.'

They drove back to headquarters and went straight to Rathbone's office. 'It's sure to be a red herring,' was his immediate reaction, 'but I agree, it's an odd coincidence.'

'Grayson might be able to tell us something more about Rainbird's character, sir,' said Sukey. 'He might have suspected him of having been guilty of another of the seven deadly sins.'

'Besides blasphemy, you mean?'

'Well, yes – although I'm not sure which of the sins that comes under,' she admitted. 'Pride, perhaps.'

'Anyway, you'd better have another talk to Grayson,' said Rathbone. 'We don't want to leave any loose ends.'

'Will do, sir.'

Back in the CID office, Vicky rang the headquarters of Ashman, Lee and Edwards and asked to speak to Luke Grayson. When she put down the phone she said, 'He's quite willing to talk to us but naturally wants to know what it's about. As you heard me say, we want to know why he never mentioned the scene between him and Rainbird. He refused to discuss it over the phone but he's invited us to his office so that we can talk in private. He's given us an appointment for tomorrow afternoon.'

'That's nice; it's a long time since I had a trip to London,' said Sukey. 'By the way, I've just had another idea. Why don't we ask Justin Freeman if Rainbird ever expressed any particular opinion about sacred music during any of his events?'

'That's a thought,' Vicky agreed. 'I believe he lives near Reading. With luck we might be able to call on him tomorrow morning on our way to see Grayson.'

*   *   *

Freeman lived in a flat in a small development on the London side of Reading. 'I've spoken to Nugent,' he said when they arrived, 'and he advised me to find out what you want to talk to me about but not to answer any further questions about my own movements without him being present. I might add,' he went on as he ushered them into a comfortably furnished sitting room with a view over the river, 'that I found DI Rathbone's manner somewhat overaggressive, but having had time to cool down I can understand why I'm still a suspect and as I'm totally innocent I'm as anxious as anyone to establish the truth. Please sit down – ' he indicated two armchairs – 'I've got coffee on the go; would you like some?'

'That would be nice; thank you,' said Vicky. 'We'll come straight to the point,' she said as he brought a jug of coffee and some cups, 'we've been trying to find some more information about Lance Rainbird, and one of the things we've established is that he had a particular antipathy towards any form of religion.'

'It's odd you should say that,' said Freeman. 'I haven't so far put on an entire programme of sacred music, but now and again I include a work with a religious theme in a programme featuring a particular composer. For example, I recently did one on the work of Berlioz and included part of his oratorio *The Childhood of Christ* which as you may know is based on the flight of the Holy Family into Egypt, and I included *Vespers* in a programme on Rachmaninoff. I noticed that Lance didn't stay and listen to either of those particular works, but I never thought to ask him about it and he didn't miss anything else.'

'Were there any occasions when something cropped up in conversation – for example a reference by someone to a sacred work not in the programme but possibly by the composer featured in the programme?' asked Sukey.

Freeman took a few mouthfuls of coffee and thought for a moment before saying, 'I can't think of any particular occasion – although I do remember that now and again a piece would be under discussion about which Lance did not have anything to say, which was unusual. I have no idea what the piece was; I'm sorry but I really don't think I can help you.'

'So you were never aware of any open hostility between him and any other member of the group at Dallington Manor?'

'Not on the subject of religion. As I may have mentioned, some of the people got a bit irritated with him now and then, but open hostility – no, none that I observed.' He glanced from one to the other. 'Have you been able to find out why he was so against religion, or religious belief?'

'We think it may have something to do with his childhood,' said Vicky. 'As a matter of fact we're on our way to talk to someone who may have more information. At least you have gone some way to help us to eliminate the members of your party.'

'From which I gather you are still no nearer to solving the case?'

Vicky stood up. 'Thank you very much for your time, sir – and for the coffee.'

The head office of Ashman, Lee and Edwards was in a modern building in the City of London. A receptionist checked their IDs, issued them with badges and directed them to the department where Luke Grayson was employed. When the lift reached the tenth floor he was waiting for them and without a word of greeting escorted them to a small room a short distance along the corridor.

The minute they were seated he said, a little irritably. 'I can't for the life of me think what my differences with Lance Rainbird have to do with you.'

'As you are no doubt aware, Mr Grayson,' said Vicky, 'we have not yet been able to establish how Lance Rainbird met his death, but we have to consider all possibilities. We think he may have been attacked before his body was found in the lake and we are naturally interested in anyone who might have any kind of grudge against him.'

Grayson shook his head in apparent disbelief. 'You've come all this way to question me about an argument I had with him in the office? I admit I did get very angry with him because he spoke blasphemy against the Lord, but I realized that in losing my temper with him I was guilty of the sin of anger, so I controlled myself and forgave him. Not that he appreciated the sentiment.'

'Your account of the argument has already been confirmed by other witnesses, sir,' said Vicky, 'but what we find surprising is that when you learnt of his death you merely expressed shock.'

'What did you expect me to say? I can't pretend I was heartbroken.'

'Of course not,' said Sukey, 'but why did you not mention at the time that you were colleagues?'

'I had other things on my mind.' It was clear that Grayson was beginning to lose patience. 'Perhaps you have overlooked the fact that I had just lost a brother who was very dear to me.'

'By no means, sir,' Vicky assured him, 'and you have our deepest sympathy in your loss, but the fact remains that, in view of the ill-feeling between you – which it seems to us was not confined to this one particular event – you expressed nothing but shock nor any, how shall I put it, Christian feelings when you learned of his death.'

Grayson shrugged. 'I have long regarded him as one of the lost. I have prayed earnestly that he might come to know the Lord, but . . .' He made a slightly helpless gesture.

'Did you ever ask him what made him so obsessively against religion?' asked Sukey. 'Maybe it was due to some traumatic experience in his past.'

'What do you take me for – some sort of counsellor? If he had problems there are professionals who deal with that sort of thing.'

'And that is all that you have to say about the relationship between you?'

'Absolutely.'

'One more thing, sir,' said Sukey. 'Where were you between eight o'clock and midnight last Friday?'

Grayson stood up. 'This is outrageous!' he exclaimed. 'Are you suggesting I'm some kind of fanatic? I assure you, the idea of physical violence is not in my character. Are you seriously suggesting I might have pursued Rainbird to Dallington with the intention of murdering him?'

'It's a purely routine question, sir,' Sukey assured him. 'We have to put it to everyone connected with the case.'

'All right, if you must know I was at the Ritz hotel, making final arrangements for my mother-in-law's one hundredth birthday party the following day. Do you want the names of the restaurant manager and the maitre d'?'

'That won't be necessary, sir,' said Vicky, 'and thank you for your time.'

'As far as I'm concerned it was time wasted,' said Grayson. 'By the way,' he added, 'I have checked with my father the date when John made that call you were so interested in. It was soon after eight o'clock on the Friday evening – the first day of the Schubert music party at Dallington Manor.'

On the way back to reception, Vicky said, 'You can't seriously regard him as a suspect!'

'No, of course not.' Sukey chuckled.

'Then why . . .?'

'I just wanted to wipe that sanctimonious expression off his face. "There are professionals who deal with that sort of thing",' she mimicked. 'Isn't he capable of any kind of compassion? What sort of a Christian does he think he is?'

Vicky nodded. 'I take your point. And did you notice his self-righteous manner when he told us about the time of Romeo's call? As if he was saying "just because you've offended me is no reason for me to fail in my obligations"?'

'At least he told us something we wanted to know. Suppose we're right in our assumption – that Romeo overheard the exchanges between Freeman and Rainbird. We know from what Ashman told us that he'd found out someone was a phoney – could it have been Freeman he was talking about? He had access to the Internet on his mobile so maybe he already knew about the phoney degrees and had just learned that Rainbird knew about them as well. He had a grudge against Rainbird for being rude about his singing so perhaps he was hoping he'd be able to put a bit of pressure on him . . . maybe get him to say something complimentary.'

'So he went back to his van and rang home to tell his folks what he'd overheard. He obviously didn't see Rainbird being attacked, or lose his balance and fall in the water. If he had, he'd have raised the alarm.'

'Instead of which he must have spent the next couple of nights in the van, done his act on Sunday as arranged and left soon after.'

'And soon after that conversation with Freeman, Rainbird

ended up in the water – but we still don't know how,' Vicky sighed.

As they were about to return to reception to hand in their badges, a young blonde woman wearing a very short skirt and teetering on very high heels hurried after them. 'Excuse me,' she said in a low, breathless voice, 'are you two ladies the police officers who've been talking to Luke Grayson?'

'That's right,' said Vicky.

'I'm glad I caught you. I'm Barbara Baker; I work in the same office as Luke and poor old Lance. Luke was away from his desk for a couple of minutes when you rang so I took the call,' she explained.

'So it was you who picked up the phone when I asked to be put through to him?'

'That's right. As soon as June on reception mentioned police I was naturally dying with curiosity so I hung around, trying to catch what was going on. It was obvious Luke wasn't best pleased at whatever you said. After you arrived and he went off to meet you we chatted among ourselves and wondered if it had anything to do with the way he used to wind up poor old Lance. I know it's wicked to say so, but between you and me several of us wouldn't have minded so much if Luke was the one who popped his clogs.'

'Let's get this straight,' said Vicky. 'Did you and the other people in your office witness what we understand was quite a fierce argument that took place recently between Lance Rainbird and Luke Grayson?'

'That's right.'

'You implied that this was something that had happened before.'

'Oh yes.' She glanced over her shoulder. 'Look, it's a bit public here. I've slipped out for an early tea break to have a private talk to you. Why don't we go down to the staff restaurant and find a quiet corner?'

'All right,' said Vicky. 'We could do with a cup of tea. How long is your tea break?'

'Just twenty minutes. That should be plenty of time for what I want to say.'

They went to the counter for cups of tea – and in Vicky's

case a hefty slice of chocolate cake – and sat down at an empty table.

'Right,' said Vicky, plunging a fork into her cake, 'tell us what Lance and Luke used to argue about.'

'Luke was usually the one who started it. He's a real goody-goody and used to have digs at Lance, who had a thing about church and stuff.'

'What sort of thing?'

'He obviously thought it was all a load of cobblers and wasn't afraid to say so. Luke seemed to go out of his way to get his back up and then start preaching to him about God.'

'Was anyone else in your office involved in these exchanges?'

'No, we just sat and listened. We thought it was all a bit of a laugh.'

'How many people are in your office besides Luke Grayson – and Lance Rainbird, of course?'

'Three – Sue, Helen and me. Luke's the only one who had his knife into Lance; the rest of us thought he was OK – quite nice in fact. Not exactly good-looking,' she added, 'but there was something about him, especially his voice. Not that he ever said much unless it was something about work – except to Luke during one of their spats.'

Sukey had been listening carefully to these exchanges. She took advantage of a momentary pause and said, 'Did Lance ever make a pass at any of you?'

Barbara shook her head. 'Now and again, when we were packing up to go home and chatting about our plans for the evening, he'd look sort of wistful, as if he wished he had plans, but he never asked if any of us was free or anything like that and we didn't expect him to. He seemed to be a bit of a loner.'

'So you don't really know anything about his social life.'

'No. He never talked about himself, but once or twice I've seen him leaving the building at the same time as Mr Ashman and they seemed to know each other quite well.'

'So he wasn't really a ladies' man?'

'Not that we knew of, but we all wondered if perhaps he had a girlfriend – or possibly several – tucked away somewhere. He was quite sexy in an odd sort of way. And there was something about him that made us think he quite enjoyed getting under

Luke's skin.' She looked at her watch and hastily gulped down the rest of her tea. 'Sorry, I've got to go now. I don't know if any of this has helped; we really hope you find out what happened to Lance. We miss him.'

SIXTEEN

'If you ask me, that was a wasted journey for us as well,' Vicky observed as they left the building. 'Ashman had already told us about the row between Grayson and Rainbird, and knowing the strongly opposed feelings the two of them had about religion it's hardly surprising that it was just one of many.'

'That's true,' Sukey agreed, 'but at least we've learned a bit more about the character of both men and I can understand the way Barbara and her pals feel about them. Grayson told us he used to pray that Rainbird would come to faith, yet according to Barbara he constantly went out of his way to wind him up and presumably goad him into uttering one of his "blasphemous" opinions. Maybe he was trying in a roundabout way to give him a chance to redeem himself – although it seems an odd way to go about it,' she added after a moment's reflection.

'So the women all found Rainbird "quite sexy in an odd sort of way", weren't put off by his anti-religious views and found Grayson a pain in the backside,' said Vicky, showing a touch of impatience with this line of reasoning. 'So where does that get us? We'd already learned from people in Freeman's group – and Freeman himself mentioned it – that some women seemed to find Rainbird's voice attractive, but no one's appeared to have noticed any atmosphere or tension between the married couples that might have hinted at a husband consumed by jealousy. I honestly can't see that we've learned anything remotely useful.'

'I'm not suggesting Rainbird was pushed into the lake by a jealous husband,' said Sukey. 'It's just something to add to what up to now has been a pretty thin character sketch of Rainbird the man as opposed to Rainbird the victim.'

'If he is a victim,' Vicky pointed out. 'Surely Doc Handley will do the PM soon.'

'We've already come to the conclusion that he was attacked,' Sukey reminded her. 'All we're waiting for is the precise cause of death. Going back to what we've learned about Rainbird this afternoon, I think Barbara was trying to sell us the idea that Rainbird's private life might be worth investigating.'

'If that's the case, why didn't she say so?'

'Perhaps it's because she's got someone in mind but isn't sure. If it got around that she'd been spreading false rumours she might lose her job.'

'Well, he's a free agent so there's no reason why he shouldn't have a bit of nookie if he wants to,' said Vicky. 'I wonder if it was Luke Grayson's wife?' she added mischievously. 'Probably not – in any case, she was celebrating her Mum's birthday the day after he died so it would have been difficult to look cheerful if her lover had just popped his clogs. Still, that was Saturday and I don't suppose the news had reached the firm by then. Do you think we should check Luke's alibi?'

'Now you're winding me up,' said Sukey with a touch of exasperation.

'Sorry, only kidding.' Vicky grinned. 'Let's get back to the car; I think it'd be a good idea to get out of London before the rush hour.'

'If you say so. I was hoping to do a bit of window shopping, but . . .'

'No time for that,' said Vicky firmly.

'OK, Sarge.'

The traffic on the motorway was moving freely and they were back at headquarters shortly after seven. Rathbone had left a message informing the team that the post-mortem on Lance Rainbird had revealed no alcohol or toxic substance in his body and no evidence of a condition that might have caused loss of balance or a dizzy spell. Death was due to drowning, but before entering the water he had suffered one or possibly two blows to the back of the head. There were traces of sawdust in the wound, which appeared to have been inflicted by some kind of blunt instrument.

'I guess for "blunt instrument" we can read "chunk of timber",' said Sukey.

'Well, we'd already figured that out as a possible cause of the injuries,' said Vicky, 'but we still can't be sure they were the result of a deliberate attack. He could have slipped, fallen heavily backwards on to a lump of wood, did it again in his struggles to get up and then went slithering down the bank in a semi-conscious state and into the water.'

'And we've already thought of that scenario,' Sukey sighed.

'So just suppose,' Vicky went on, 'that Sir and Mr Leach decide to charge Justin Freeman with murder, the motive being fear of exposure at having made false claims about his qualifications. I don't know what you think, but I doubt if the CPS would allow the case to get to court. And even if it did, any barrister worth their salt could have shown – as we've done – that it was possible for Rainbird to have sustained his injuries by accident.'

'So without further evidence, there's no case against Freeman,' said Sukey. 'Not that I ever really thought he did it anyway, and after meeting him it's more than just a hunch.'

'Do you still think Rainbird's death could have been an accident, then?'

Sukey shook her head. 'On the contrary, I'm convinced he was attacked and left unconscious in the water to drown. Someone had a grudge against him. The trouble is we know so little about him.'

'So what do you suggest we do about it?' Vicky persisted. 'I can't see Sir granting us another day's leave to go to London to probe into Rainbird's social life. Mr Ashman didn't seem to know anything about what he did in his spare time; on the contrary he described him as a very private individual. That goes some way to confirming what Barbara said – although he didn't work in the same office so he wouldn't have picked up anything the women said about Lance's sexy voice and so on.'

'I guess we'd better do our reports on today's interviews and then go home,' said Sukey. 'It will be interesting to see what Sir's reaction is when he reads them. If you're right and he insists we keep digging for evidence against Freeman perhaps we should poke around in *his* private life.' Privately, she was working on another idea that had just come to her – an idea she was not prepared to share with Vicky for the moment, and certainly not with DI Rathbone.

When Sukey reached home she found a message from Harry. 'Where have you been? I'm pining for a sight of you,' he said. 'Please call.'

She picked up the phone and punched in his number. 'It's only been a couple of days since we saw each other,' she said.

'So what? I want to see you every day. What about now? Have you eaten yet? Dad and Freddie have suddenly decided to fly up to Scotland to meet some friends for a few days' golf so I'm languishing here alone. Shall we go out, or how about a take away?'

'I'd rather eat in if you don't mind. I've got plenty of stuff in the freezer; I'll take something out and we can have a drink while it's defrosting. It so happens I was going to call you anyway. There's something I want to talk to you about.'

'With you in no time.'

He arrived within five minutes. His first words, when he was free to speak, were 'Are you *very* hungry?' He nuzzled her ear. 'How about defrosting whatever it is on the lowest, slowest setting?'

'Not all that hungry,' she whispered. 'The defrosting can wait.'

An hour or so later, when they were in the kitchen with a glass of wine while a casserole defrosted in the microwave, he said, 'You said you wanted to talk to me about something.'

'I want to run an idea past you.'

He was instantly alert. 'Something tells me you need my help on the Dallington Manor murders. Ah, I see I'm right,' he added, noticing her raised eyebrows. 'It's been obvious for days that your enquiries have run into the sand. DI Rathbone's pet suspect hasn't been charged yet and the body count is rising. What do you want me to do? My investigative skills are at your disposal.'

'Harry, you're absolutely right, we're getting nowhere. The PM result has only confirmed what we already knew and potential witnesses are dying off like flies. All DI Rathbone can think of is looking for more evidence against Freeman, but the more Vicky and I ferret around, the more I'm convinced that he didn't kill

Lance Rainbird or either of the others. Harry, you will swear to treat what I'm going to ask you to do – and anything you manage to dig up – as completely off the record until I give you the go ahead to tell your editor.'

'You know you can trust me,' he said, putting a hand over hers. 'What do you have in mind?'

'You mentioned a few days ago that you'd be covering the trial of the six people who've been accused of running a cannabis farm in a Gloucestershire village.'

'That's right – the case against them opens tomorrow. It'll probably last for days and my boss has decided it'll be cheaper for me to stay in a B and B during the week rather than drive to town and back each day and charge mileage. But I don't understand your interest – surely you don't think Rainbird's killer is somehow mixed up in the cannabis farm case?'

'No, of course I don't. It's just that I was wondering if while you're in town you could find time to do a spot of research for me.'

'What kind of research?'

'We know very little about Rainbird's background. He wasn't exactly a social animal; something of a loner in fact, and it's been suspected that he had some kind of personality disorder although another suggestion is that he had some traumatic experience as a child. We do know that he was what someone described as "a devout atheist" who'd been accused of blasphemy by one of his colleagues, who's a committed Christian. What we – Vicky and I – found particularly interesting is that one of his female colleagues describes him as "sexy in an odd sort of way", and one or two witnesses mentioned that he had what one of them described as a "mellifluous" speaking voice.'

'You're wondering if he had a love life and you want me to do a little poking around for you. I take it he lived in London?'

'Yes, in Richmond. He owned quite a large house there; it was pretty run down and he managed to get a bank loan and have it renovated and divided into flats. He lived in one of them and the rest are let.'

'That suggests he was quite well off,' said Harry. 'You mentioned colleagues, so I presume he had a full-time job as well?'

'He worked for a very well known firm of accountants. He'd been with them for five years and one of the partners, it seems, took him under his wing and acted as his financial adviser.'

'What's the name of the firm?'

'I don't think you need to know that,' said Sukey. 'We've visited their head office and spoken to the people who knew him. As far as DI Rathbone is concerned there's nothing further to be gained from any further enquiries there and I don't think for a moment that he'd authorize another trip to London to probe into Rainbird's social life. All he's interested in is getting evidence to support his case against Justin Freeman.'

'Who, I take it, you don't think is the killer?'

'No I don't, but it seems obvious I'm the only one who believes his version of events.'

'Which is?'

'Sorry, you don't need to know that either.'

'You're not giving me much to go on,' Harry grumbled. 'I take it I can claim expenses if I undertake your commission?' he added.

She punched his arm and then gave him a kiss on the cheek. 'I'll pay you in kind,' she whispered. 'Will you do it? It might lead to the biggest scoop of your career.'

'With such an inducement, how could I refuse?'

'You're a star.'

'I'm a very hungry star,' he complained. Surely that casserole must be ready by now.'

She jumped to her feet. 'Of course – I was forgetting. Give me a few minutes to cook the vegetables.'

There was very little conversation over the meal. When they had finished, Harry said, 'Are you working next weekend?'

'No, it's my weekend off. Why?'

'Come to London and spend it with me. We can do some sleuthing together – when we're not otherwise engaged.'

SEVENTEEN

On Thursday morning Rathbone, together with DS Vicky Armstrong and DCs Sukey Reynolds, Mike Haskins and Tim Pringle, were summoned to DCI Leach's office. 'No prizes for guessing what this is about,' Leach began when they were all assembled. 'Dallington Manor; we seem to be getting nowhere with this case so treat this as a brainstorming session. I've received all your reports; I know they've been circulated round the team and I hope you've got all the details at your fingertips, but just to bring everyone up to speed I'll run over the story so far. Come in and sit down everyone,' he added with a touch of impatience as the group stood in a cluster just inside the door.

When they were all settled, Leach resumed. 'I spent most of yesterday reading and rereading your reports,' he began. 'Nothing jumped out at me, but it's obvious we're missing something. Of the three deaths that occurred over the weekend, only one – that of the young waiter Reg Law – was unmistakably murder. We suspect that Lance Rainbird's death was not an accident, but the PM didn't throw up anything to either confirm or kill off our suspicions and our enquiries seem to have run into the sand. As to the fatal accident to John Grayson's van; it's been established that it was caused by the brakes failing on a particularly dangerous stretch of road because the pipe carrying the brake fluid had become detached, but we don't know if it came adrift by accident or was due to sabotage. Is everyone with me so far?'

There was a general nodding of heads and replies of 'Yes, sir.'

'We have established that Justin Freeman does not in fact possess the qualifications – namely degrees from certain American universities – that he claims on his prospectus. He eventually admitted under questioning that Lance Rainbird, who we know had an Open University degree in music in addition to his Oxford degree in maths, had discovered this fact and tackled him about it. It was put to him that Rainbird threatened to expose him as a fraud unless he paid substantial sums of money to keep quiet and that he killed him rather than submit to blackmail. He strongly denied the accusation but admitted that Rainbird had demanded, at a pre-arranged meeting in the hotel grounds, that he remove the bogus degrees from his prospectus and he'd agreed to do that. He also admitted that Rainbird wanted something else in return but he refused at first to say what it was. Eventually, under further pressure from DI Rathbone, he offered what was obviously a hastily thought-up story to account for the fact that Rainbird had requested a clandestine meeting.

'We later learned that Rainbird had very strong views about religion which caused conflict between him and a colleague. Vicky and Sukey followed up this aspect of his character and uncovered the fact that he and John Grayson's brother Luke were colleagues and that it was with Luke Grayson that Rainbird had some very heated arguments. It became evident that Grayson had been less than frank during earlier interviews so Vicky and Sukey made an appointment to see him at his office. Acting on one of Sukey's famous hunches –' a brief smile flitted over Leach's features and he gave a sidelong glance in Sukey's direction – 'she and Vicky called in to see Freeman on their way to interview Luke Grayson. What Freeman said in response to their questions added very little to what we already knew about Rainbird, but since that visit Sukey has experienced further doubts about Freeman's guilt. Would you like to add anything to that, Sukey?'

'Not really sir, except to say that I was probably the only person to give some credence to Freeman's story when he first told it, although I didn't mention my doubts about his guilt to DI Rathbone at the time. My son did a degree in Business Studies; from time to time we discussed various topics covered by his course and one of them was taxation. I'm not claiming to be an expert, but it did seem to me that Freeman's account was at least feasible. And when we visited him at his home his manner was very frank and open; he didn't exactly apologize for his outbursts during his interviews but he did say he understood why he was a suspect while insisting that he had nothing to do with Rainbird's death.'

'So,' Leach resumed, 'the question is: where do we look that we haven't looked before?' He got up, indicated a flip chart

standing beside his desk and picked up a marker. 'Right, everyone
– let me have some ideas. Yes, Mike?' he said as DC Haskins
raised a hand.

'Well, sir, we interviewed all the staff at Dallington Manor
after Rainbird's death and questioned them about their movements
at the crucial time. We also asked if any of them witnessed
anything suspicious or that could in any way help to establish
how he came to be in the water. As you know from our reports,
sir, we didn't turn up anything helpful there. However, speaking
for myself, I didn't ask any of them specifically if they had
observed anything of particular interest about Rainbird's relationship with any of the guests and none of them mentioned anything
of that nature worth pursuing. Once they'd given satisfactory
accounts of their movements we eliminated them from our
enquiries. We know that at least one of the waiters – Mal Carter
– has worked at the hotel long enough to be there during several
of Freeman's previous events. There may be others; do you think
it's worth having another talk to them?'

Leach turned to Rathbone. 'What do you think, Greg?'

'I think it's a good point, sir. In fact, Vicky and Sukey have
already put further questions to Carter.'

'Yes, I have their reports, but it appears they were focusing
on relationships between the attendees at Freeman's party.'

'That's correct, sir.'

'I agree; the point Mike makes is an interesting one,' said
Leach. 'I think it might be worth pursuing. Right, any more
ideas?' He glanced round and DC Pringle raised a hand. 'Yes,
Tim?'

'Well, sir, I see that Vicky – DS Armstrong – mentions in her
report a comment by one of Rainbird's female colleagues that
he was "quite sexy in an odd sort of way" and suggested he
might enjoy "a bit of nookie". I was wondering whether it might
be worth enquiring among his neighbours to try and find out
whether any of them have noticed any regular female visitors,
especially one wearing a wedding ring.'

Leach raised an eyebrow. 'Are you suggesting that he might
have had some sort of liaison with a married woman and that
her husband found out about it and pursued Rainbird to Dallington
Manor with the intention of murdering him?'

'I know it does sound a bit far-fetched, sir,' Pringle admitted. 'I just thought a bit of house-to-house near his home might throw up some detail of his private life that could possibly give us a lead.'

'It's true we know virtually nothing about his private life,' said Leach, 'and whereas I'm not sure there's much mileage in Tim's initial suggestion, we haven't paid a visit to his home which, as you know, is in London. We asked the local police to ask if anyone had noticed any suspicious characters hanging around the house but nothing of any interest emerged. I think perhaps we should have a look in his flat to see if there's anything that might, as Tim suggests, give us a lead. Yes, Sukey?' he added as she raised a hand.

'It had occurred to me that Rainbird's private life might bear investigation, sir. It so happens that I'm not on duty this weekend and a friend has invited me to London. I'd be willing to give up some time during my visit to call at Rainbird's address if you think it worth while.'

'That sounds a handy arrangement,' said Leach. 'You'll have to clear it with the local police, of course. I presume there were keys among Rainbird's possessions, Greg?'

'Oh yes, sir – house keys and car keys. The hotel manager wants to know when his car can be removed and I've told him we're waiting to make arrangements with his solicitor, a Mr Horace Nielson, who will come and collect it, together with his personal effects. Rainbird's friend Mr Ashman kindly put us in touch with him; as you all know, it was through him that we learned of the connection with Luke Grayson.'

'Excuse me, sir,' said Haskins. 'Do we know who stood to benefit from Lance Rainbird's death?'

'I understand from Mr Nielson that he's left his entire estate to be divided between several well-known charities, so even if he was murdered – and don't let us lose sight of the fact that we're still not a hundred per cent sure – it wasn't for his money. Right, we've turned up a couple of new avenues to explore. Any other ideas?'

'Going back to the possibility that women found Rainbird attractive, sir,' said Vicky, 'one or two of the people in Freeman's party hinted at the same thing. We already have all their names and addresses, but no phone numbers. We could easily get them from directory enquiries, of course, but as Freeman has expressed his willingness to cooperate we could ask him for them, explaining that we want to ask the same sort of questions Mike has suggested putting to the hotel staff. I'm thinking particularly of the lady in the wheelchair, Charlotte. She gave the impression of being very observant; she was positive that Rainbird had something on his mind because he was unusually quiet over dinner. She was equally certain that he was murdered, but she wasn't able to add to anything we already knew about people's movements.'

'Yes, that's worth pursuing as well,' said Leach. 'It'll be interesting to hear how Freeman reacts to the request; if he makes excuses about confidentiality it might indicate he's not anxious for us to question them further.' Throughout the discussion he had been making notes on a pad and he pressed the intercom. His PA came in and he tore off some sheets and handed them to her. 'Run me off half a dozen copies of those right away, please.'

'Certainly, sir.'

'Right, I think that session has been worthwhile,' he said as she went out of the room. 'So, take your team back to the office, Greg, go through those notes, come back to me if anyone has anything further to add, otherwise allocate the tasks and tell them to get on with them. You can issue a statement to the press telling them we're now treating the death of Lance Rainbird as murder; I'll attend tomorrow's briefing and take questions. Meanwhile, I'll report to the Superintendent.'

As they left DCI Leach's office Rathbone said, 'If anyone wants coffee they can get it from the machine and bring it to my office in fifteen minutes.'

'It's OK for him; he makes filtered coffee in his own fancy machine,' Vicky muttered in Sukey's ear as Rathbone headed for his office. 'No instant stuff in a plastic cup for Sir.'

As the team clustered round the drinks machine in the CID office, Mike Haskins said, 'Any idea how he's going to play this, Sarge?'

'My guess is he'll allocate the new lines of enquiry to those of us who suggested them,' said Vicky. 'With the exception of Tim's idea, which Sukey seems to have bagged. You never mentioned you were off on a jolly to London this weekend,' she added. Her tone invited further information and Sukey was aware of curious glances from the others, but she ignored them.

'I only got the invitation yesterday evening,' said Sukey, 'and in any case there was always the chance that something might break and all leave cancelled.'

'Instead of which the most interesting job has landed in your lap,' said Tim. 'Even though it was my idea,' he added with a touch of resentment.

'Most interesting in more ways than one,' said Vicky, giving Sukey a sidelong glance which she pretended not to notice. She finished her coffee and threw the plastic cup into the bin. 'Let's go and get our orders.'

'Right,' said Rathbone when they assembled in his office. 'We came away from Mr Leach's office with basically three lines of enquiry to follow up: Rainbird's private life, his possible relationship with a particular member of staff and ditto with one of the members of Freeman's party. Sukey, you will take care of the first; Mr Leach has made it clear to me that as you're going to be in London on a social visit the only expenses you'll be entitled to claim are those directly connected with the time actually spent in your investigations in and around Rainbird's home. And in the meantime you can help Vicky go through the list when she gets it from Freeman. Understood?'

'Yes, Guv,' said Sukey.

'Mike, you will interview the staff at Dallington Manor and I'm going to draft in DC Penny Osborne to help you,' Rathbone continued. 'I think she should be the one to talk to Gunn about Reg Law, but give her a thorough briefing first. This will involve more than one visit, and bearing in mind the hotel staff work shifts arrange as much over the telephone as possible in advance to keep mileage claims to a minimum. Is that clear?'

'Perfectly, Guv,' said Mike. 'Do you think I should speak to the hotel manager first, out of courtesy?'

Rathbone nodded. 'Yes, he won't like it so be diplomatic. Vicky, you will get on to Freeman and sweet talk him into coughing up the list of phone numbers. As soon as you get it, you and Tim can settle down to some telephoning, OK? Is everyone clear what they have to do? And before anyone asks what I'll be doing,' he added before anyone had a chance to speak, 'it occurs to me that Justin Freeman's private life might be worth looking into as well. I might look up one or two of his former colleagues. Any questions? No? On your way then.'

Back in the CID office Vicky said, 'I guess we'd better take a little time to decide how we're going to approach people. They'll all have had their fill of questions and a bit of what Sir calls "sweet talk" might be necessary. That should take us up to lunchtime; meet me back here at two.'

EIGHTEEN

'So, now that we're on our own, are you going to come clean about your trip to London?' asked Vicky as she and Sukey settled with their lunch trays at a table in a corner of the canteen. 'Is lover boy there on some special assignment for which he needs your expert assistance?'

'He's there to cover the trial of the cannabis farmers at the Old Bailey,' Sukey explained. 'I don't think he wants me around for my expertise – just my company over the weekend.'

'Lucky old you,' said Vicky. 'Whenever I have a free weekend Chris seems to be extra busy with the hotel full of people taking special offers. Your Harry manages to land some interesting jobs,' she went on. 'I'm expecting to hear any day that he's decided to start writing detective novels based on his experiences as a crime reporter.'

'I'm not sure I want to encourage that idea,' said Sukey. 'He'd be forever running his ideas past me for feasibility. Anyway, in answer to your question, his editor has decided it's cheaper for him to stay in a B and B in town while the trial lasts than to commute every day. I'm not all that keen on the idea as it means I don't see him during the week while the trial lasts and it could go on for ages. But when I mentioned I was free this weekend he suggested I join him, and needless to say I jumped at it.'

'Well, I hope you'll be staying in something more exotic than a B and B,' said Vicky before taking another bite from her tuna baguette and washing it down with a mouthful of apple juice.

Sukey hesitated; she ate a forkful of chicken salad to give herself time to decide how far she was going to confide in Vicky. 'I'm going to suggest he finds a quiet hotel somewhere in the Richmond area, within striking distance of where Lance Rainbird lived,' she said.

Vicky gave her a shrewd glance. 'Just between ourselves, how much are you going to tell him about what you're planning to do? He's a journalist first and foremost and he's sure to put two and two together. He's probably done his own ferreting around; for all you know he may have located Rainbird's address and done a few house-to-house enquiries of his own.'

'I wouldn't put it past him, but if he'd come up with anything useful I'm sure he'd have told us,' said Sukey. 'Look Sarge, can you forget rank for a moment?'

Vicky glanced round to make sure no one was within earshot, but lowered her voice just the same. 'You're going to tell me something you don't want to get back to our newly promoted Sir?' Sukey nodded. 'You have my word. Do tell,' she went on eagerly.

'Like DCI Leach, I had this feeling we were missing something significant, something that would give us a definite answer to the question as to whether Rainbird was murdered or not – and if so throw up some sort of lead. We've pulled out all the stops to find evidence and a motive; the nearest we've got is that stuff about Rainbird tackling Freeman about his phoney degrees and wanting to do his accounts, but it's all circumstantial and it seems that even Sir is beginning to have his doubts. Knowing Harry was going to be in London I asked him if he'd be willing to do a spot of sleuthing around Rainbird's house in his spare time and let me know if he came up with anything.'

'I hope you didn't confide in him too much,' said Vicky dubiously. 'You've told me more than once how persuasive he can be.'

'I promise you I didn't tell him anything he didn't need to know,' said Sukey. 'I didn't say anything about Rainbird's connection with Luke Grayson or the rows about religion, or even tell him the name of the firm where the two of them worked.'

'And then you just happened to mention that it was your weekend off and he suggested you join forces in the sleuthing?'

'Well, yes. I've made him swear not to breathe a word to his editor – or anyone else – until I give him clearance.'

'In that case all I can do is wish you the best of luck!' said Vicky.

Sukey swallowed the last mouthful of chicken salad and raised her glass of mineral water in salute. 'Thanks, Sarge!'

When the team foregathered in the CID office at two o'clock DC Penny Osborne joined them. 'I've been working with the Gloucestershire mob on the cannabis farm case, Sarge,' she said to Vicky. 'They've got connections in our area, but DI Rathbone said . . .'

'Yes, I know,' Vicky said briskly. 'As the case has gone to court he thinks they can manage without you from now on, and you're needed here to help us on the Dallington Manor case.'

'Oh, great!' Penny's eyes sparkled. 'I've picked up bits of info about it from James and it seems it's quite a puzzler.'

'James who?' asked Vicky.

'PC James Bond,' Penny explained.

'So you've been chatted up by Double Oh Seven?' said Sukey. 'I thought you and PC Dandridge were an item.'

'Oh, we are, but I asked James about the Dallington Manor case out of interest. Anyway, Inspector Rathbone told me to forget the cannabis farmers and meet you here, Sarge,' she said to Vicky.

'That's right,' said Vicky. 'The situation so far is that we've been concentrating on asking questions about people's movements, has anyone seen anything suspicious, the usual stuff, but we haven't gone into relationships among the people who were present at the time of the deaths. We're pretty sure that Lance Rainbird was murdered and you may have heard that we've questioned one suspect, but we haven't found enough evidence to charge him and DCI Leach wants us to spread the net a bit wider. One area about which we know little or nothing is Lance Rainbird's private life. We know quite a lot of his history but so far no one has checked on his flat or talked to his neighbours. He lived in Richmond and it so happens that Sukey will be in London at the weekend so she's been assigned to that job.'

'Not exactly the short straw,' Tim muttered in Mike Haskins' ear.

'Yes, we know it was you who put forward that suggestion,' said Vicky, 'and you know why the job has landed in Sukey's lap instead of going to you. You have to accept that you can't win 'em all.' She turned to Penny. 'Mike and Tim will fill you in on everything we've dredged up so far and then we have to start making some telephone calls. Sukey, Sir wants us – you and me that is – to spend the next couple of days trawling through the people in Justin Freeman's party. That could take time – he'll probably want to contact them all before we do, just to warn them to expect to hear from us. Will you give him a call? I'll join the others in case they need any guidance.'

'Right, Sarge,' said Sukey. 'I just hope he hasn't gone off somewhere to take a break.' She went to her desk and called Freeman's number. To her relief, he answered after the first couple of rings.

'Is there any news?' he asked. 'I've been turning things over in my mind since your visit in case I'd forgotten something, but nothing came to mind.'

'We think it's possible that Lance Rainbird had some kind of relationship or dealings with someone who was at Dallington Manor over the weekend, either a member of the staff or one of the people in your party,' Sukey explained. 'You've known him for some time because he's been on other events, and presumably a few others among your regulars have known him for a while. Apart from his arguments with Eric Bowen, and the fact that he had a certain appeal to some of the ladies, have you noticed anyone else he spent time with or seemed to have something in common with?'

There was a short silence before Freeman said, 'After you let me go back to the hotel to collect my stuff I was buttonholed by a chap called Ashman. He said he was a colleague of Rainbird's and he asked me more or less the same question. From what he said it's obvious that different people had different impressions of the man.'

'What did you tell him?'

'What I'm about to tell you, that is I hadn't noticed him being particularly intimate with anyone. Like I said before, he'd talk to anyone about music, but in some ways he seemed to be a bit of a loner. I can't speak for everyone in my party, of course.'

'I was coming to that,' said Sukey. 'Would you let us have their phone numbers, so that we can contact them and ask them the same question?'

Freeman gave an audible sigh. 'They aren't going to like it,' he said. 'As it is, a few of them have cancelled their bookings for my next event, saying they found it too upsetting. I can't afford to lose any more.'

'I quite understand,' said Sukey, 'but we have instructions to contact them and it's only out of courtesy that I'm speaking to you first. They will of course have given the hotel all the necessary details when they checked in, but we thought we'd put you in the picture before we start ringing around.'

'That's very considerate; thank you. I'm as keen as you are to get to the bottom of this so I'll do everything I can to help. Supposing I call, say, the first few names on the list, tell them to expect to hear from you and then email you with their details. While you're speaking to them I'll ring another batch and then do the same. How will that be?'

'That's absolutely fine,' said Sukey. A thought struck her and she said, 'Would you put Miss Charlotte Lang and her companion in the first batch, please?'

'No problem.'

Sukey went over to the corner in the office where Mike, Tim and Penny were planning their strategy under Vicky's supervision. 'Freeman's more than willing to play ball,' said Sukey. She outlined the procedure he had suggested.

Vicky nodded approvingly. 'At least he's a well organized sort of chap,' she said.

'I guess he has to be,' said Sukey. 'There must be more to running events like his than choosing the music. By the way, I asked for Charlotte Lang's details to be in the first batch.'

'Any particular reason?'

'Only that she mentioned how one or two of the women seemed to warm to Rainbird in much the same way as the ones in his

office. She might on reflection think of a particular one he spent
some time with.'

'It's possible, I suppose,' said Vicky. 'To be honest, I'm not
sure this is going anywhere. I'm pinning my hopes on your visit
to his flat.'

When Sukey called Charlotte Lang's number Millie answered.
She sounded flustered and said in a low voice, 'Who is it, please?'

'This is Detective Constable Reynolds,' said Sukey. 'We had
a chat at Dallington Manor – you remember?'

'Yes, yes, of course I remember; it was about poor Mr Rainbird,
wasn't it? But I don't understand why . . .'

'We still don't know what happened to him and we are making
further enquiries. May I have a word with Miss Lang, please?'

'Oh dear.' Millie sounded uneasy and Sukey could picture her
casting an anxious glance over her shoulder. 'The fact is, she's
watching her favourite programme on the television and I can't,
that is, she won't like being interrupted.'

'That's no problem,' said Sukey. 'I need to talk to you as well
so we could have our chat first and then I'll wait until Miss
Lang's programme is over.'

'All right, although I can't think what you want to ask me
about. I'll just go in the next room and pick up another phone.'
There was a click and a few moments passed before she came
back on the line and said, 'Here I am. How can I help you?'

'You've told us where you were and what you were doing the
night Mr Rainbird's body was found and I remember you saying
"Mr Rainbird never talks to me – not that I particularly want
him to". Why did you say that? Didn't you like him?'

'Well, it's a bit hard to explain,' said Millie. 'I didn't exactly
dislike him; it was just, well something about him . . . and the
way some people . . . that is, some women . . .'

'Can you be a bit more specific?' asked Sukey, as Millie
seemed at a loss how to continue.

'Oh dear; I'm not sure how to put it.' Sukey sensed that she
was embarrassed. 'I heard one of the women, Mrs Pearson I
think it was, say what a nice voice he had and she said it was
– now, what was the word she used to describe it?'

'Mellifluous?'

'No, it wasn't that, although I did hear someone else use that word. I think what Mrs Pearson said began with s.'

'Sexy?' suggested Sukey.

'Yes, I think that's what it was.' Sukey could almost see her blushing. 'And then,' Millie went on, 'she said, "He is quite sexy; I wonder if he's got a lady friend tucked away somewhere".'

'If you don't mind my saying so, you sound a little shocked at the suggestion.'

'I just don't like that kind of talk, that's all. Maybe that's what put me off Mr Rainbird. Oh, excuse me; Miss Lang has just rung her bell – that means she wants her tea. I'll ask her to speak to you while I'm making it.'

'For goodness' sake, I told you all I know,' said Charlotte when she came on the line.

'I'm really very sorry to bother you, Miss Lang,' said Sukey. 'As you'll have gathered, we are no nearer to finding Mr Rainbird's killer, and—'

'Oh, you've at last accepted that he was murdered,' Charlotte broke in. 'I told you so, didn't I? All that waffle about an "unexplained death" was just to cover up the fact that you weren't doing your job properly, and while your lot were messing about another two people died. I wonder you can sleep at night.'

'There are times when it can be a problem,' Sukey admitted. 'What we are trying to find out now is whether people have noticed Mr Rainbird appearing to have, how can I put it, an especially close relationship with anyone in particular, someone he spent more time talking to than anyone else?'

'Close relationship – Rainbird?' Charlotte gave a staccato laugh. 'None that I've ever noticed. As I've already told you, some women seemed to find him attractive on account of his voice. I've even noticed the women in the office or on reception looking at him in a gooey-eyed sort of way.'

'Well, that's something we hadn't thought of,' said Sukey. She resisted the temptation to add 'I take it *you* weren't susceptible to his charm' before thanking Charlotte for her time and ending the call.

'That's something to pass on to Tim and Mike,' said Vicky

when Sukey relayed the gist of her conversations with Millie and Charlotte. 'I suspect "gooey-eyed" was an exaggeration – she really is a spiteful old cow; I wonder how Millie puts up with her.'

'Maybe she doesn't have a choice,' said Sukey. 'As for Charlotte – well, I might turn crabby if I was suddenly faced with the prospect of spending the rest of my life in a wheelchair. How about you – any luck with the names on your list?'

'So far I've only spoken to Julie Pearson. She wasn't at Dallington Manor last weekend of course, but she and her husband knew Rainbird from previous events. It's obvious they never understood why we've been treating his death as unexplained; she said they suspected all along that he'd been murdered. She confirmed what we learned from the Days; they quite liked Rainbird but agreed that he didn't say anything much about himself. She did confirm what Charlotte told you about the female staff; she said even Mrs Chapman, who always appeared very brisk and businesslike, seemed to warm to him, but she never noticed him show a particular interest in, or be attentive to, anyone in particular.'

By the end of the day all the members of the team had ticked off a few names on their respective lists without any positive results. 'Let's hope for better luck tomorrow,' said Vicky as they cleared their work stations and went home.

At the press briefing the following morning DCI Leach made a statement to the effect that the death of Lance Rainbird was now being treated as murder and a new line of enquiry was being pursued. He appealed to anyone who had a personal acquaintance with Rainbird or knew anything about his private life to come forward. Despite requests from many of the journalists present he refused to answer any questions.

NINETEEN

A t five o'clock on Friday, Rathbone summoned his team for a debriefing.

'You first, Vicky,' he said. 'Did you and Sukey learn anything useful from any of Freeman's mob?'

'Nothing specific, Guv,' said Vicky, 'but so far we've only managed to make a dozen calls each so there are still a few people to track down. Some of them were out so we'll try them again; in the meantime the consensus seems to be that Rainbird was pleasant and polite to everyone but not much of a conversationalist and tended to shy away if anyone asked him anything like a personal question. As we already know, he was always ready to contribute to a discussion about music – it was in that sort of situation that the spats with Bowen arose – and he was quite friendly with the Pearsons, but not really intimate with them or anyone else.'

'Not a lot of help, but keep at it,' said Rathbone. 'Have you anything to add to that, Sukey?'

'I'm afraid not, Guv.'

'How about you, Mike? Have you learned anything interesting from any of the staff?'

'Well, sir, it soon became evident that the female staff often exchange titbits about things they've noticed about the guests and there seems to have been quite a lot of gossip about one or two members of Mr Freeman's group. One member of the house-keeping staff noticed a condom that didn't get flushed away in the toilet of a room occupied by a single gentleman and it so happened that the guest in the room next door was a single lady who one of the waitresses had noticed seemed to be on very friendly terms with the gentleman in question.'

'I don't suppose the gentleman in question was Lance Rainbird?'

'No such luck, I'm afraid, Guv.'

'Why doesn't that surprise me? Did you have any luck with Gunn, Penny?'

'As it happens, Guv, he did say something that might be significant.' Penny consulted her notes. 'I began by reminding him of something he said to Mr Chapman when he rushed in to tell him he'd found Reg's body, something suggesting that he knew his friend was worried because he'd said he "might have done something stupid". DS Armstrong and Sukey saw Gunn the next day and asked him to be a bit more specific; it seemed that it arose out of a phone call he'd had from Law on Sunday afternoon. He said, "I can't remember the exact words but the gist of it was that he should have gone to the police instead of trying to be clever" and then he said "Sorry, I've got to go" and ended the call; Gunn thought it was probably because the guests had started to come back for their tea.'

'Thank you, that's refreshed all our memories,' said Rathbone. 'I take it you've got something to add to that?'

'Yes, Guv. After I'd reminded him of all that he said, "That sounds about right; as you can imagine, I was still in a hell of a state. It had all been such a terrible shock. I'd calmed down a little but I was still really distressed." He then went on to say, "Ever since it happened I've been going over and over in my head, trying to think of something . . . anything . . . that might give a clue." At that point he got a bit weepy so I gave him a moment to pull himself together.'

'All right, get on with it,' Rathbone interrupted, as Penny broke off to scroll hastily through several pages of the reports.

'Sorry, Guv, just finding the right spot,' said Penny. 'Ah, here we are!' She appeared nervous – probably, Sukey thought, because she found Rathbone's manner intimidating. She cleared her throat and said, 'Law *had* remembered something else; he said "I've been thinking perhaps I should tell the police about Reg's call so I'm glad to have this chance." He said he'd remembered asking Law what he meant about trying to be clever instead of going to the police; again, he couldn't recall the exact words but it was something like "you'll never believe who I heard having a . . ." and then he said "got to go, tell you later" and ended the call. I asked Gunn if Reg had sounded normal when he made the call and he said, "I had the impression that he was really anxious to tell me something, but for some reason had to break off – probably because someone else was trying to attract his attention. He was on duty at the time".'

'And that was it?'

'Yes, Guv. He kept repeating how much he missed his friend and would do anything to help nail his killer, but he really couldn't think of anything else. I asked him if Law had said anything on a previous occasion to suggest he'd noticed anyone saying or doing anything out of the ordinary, but he was quite certain that he hadn't.'

'Well, it's not much to go on, but we have to look into it,' said Rathbone. He flipped through the pages of the open file on his desk. 'Law made that call to Gunn at three fifteen on Sunday afternoon. Let's assume for the moment, first that whatever he was talking about had a direct bearing on Rainbird's murder, and second that the killer heard him making that call and decided he had to be silenced. Any comments?'

'Sunday afternoon – that would be the time when the waiters were setting up the afternoon teas,' said Vicky. 'If your assumption is right, Guv, that would narrow down the number of people who might have overheard the call. The music lovers would have been in the Orchard Room.'

'Good point, Vicky. Make a note to ask everyone on your list from now on if they happened to have noticed any absentees from the Orchard Room at the crucial time, and double check with any of the others you've been in contact with, including Freeman. Mike and Tim, you've been talking to the staff; go over your list and narrow it down to those who were on duty when Law made that call.'

'Right, Guv.'

'Chapman will know, or one of the office staff,' said Rathbone. 'Next question: has anyone any idea what Law meant by "doing something stupid" and "trying to be clever"?'

'Whatever it was, he said he should have gone to the police, so he obviously thought it had some bearing on at least one of the deaths,' said Tim.

Sukey raised a hand. 'I think I can answer that one, Guv.'

'Right. Let's have it.'

'I was having dinner with Major Matthews on Sunday evening, his son Harry was there and he received a call on his mobile during the evening. He didn't say what the call was about, but I could see that it disturbed him. He told me later that it was from Keith Gunn, telling him that Reg Law had been murdered.'

'How the hell did Matthews know Gunn?' demanded Rathbone. 'Has he been poking his nose into our case again?'

'He admitted to me that he's been taking a particular interest in the Dallington Manor case, Guv. As you all know, he's the senior crime correspondent on the *Echo* and like all reporters he's always on the lookout for a scoop. Anyway, after he got the call from Gunn he told me that Law had called the *Echo* on Saturday – the day before Rainbird's body was found – asking to speak to a crime reporter. The call was passed to Harry; Law said he'd seen a man he didn't recognize talking to someone he thought might be Rainbird the evening Rainbird's body was found. Harry naturally wanted to hear more; after questioning Law he wasn't convinced he'd actually seen anyone, but he advised him to tell the police. Then Law tried another tack; he said he knew something that would make a nice titbit for the *Echo*. Again, he wouldn't give any details and this time he wanted a promise of payment in advance. Harry said it didn't work like that; he'd have to be satisfied there was something in this "titbit" and if so to decide what it was worth. Law said he'd think about it; he never called again and Harry decided it was probably a try-on and thought no more about it.'

'Unfortunately for him, he didn't take Matthews' advice,' Rathbone commented. 'Law's call to Matthews was made the day before he was murdered,' he went on thoughtfully. 'Well, if Law really did see anything significant before calling Matthews on Saturday he obviously didn't mention it to Gunn at the time. I strongly suspect that he'd seen or heard something more just before making the call to Gunn and someone overheard what he said. I want to know who that person is.

'I suppose it's possible more than one person heard the call or possibly even noticed whatever Law was so exercised about without realizing its significance or making the connection.'

'That could mean someone else could be in danger, Guv,' said Sukey. 'Both Bowen and Gunn and one or two other people talked about a serial killer. Vicky and I did our best to reassure them.'

'Serial killers do it for the pleasure of killing,' said Tim. 'It seems to me that our man is just trying to cover his tracks.'

'Which he's done quite successfully so far,' said Rathbone. 'Is everyone clear about what they have to do? Right, now I'll tell you what I've found out about our friend Justin Freeman. Apart from the phoney degrees, there are some other inaccuracies on his prospectus. He claims to have been a lecturer at Branwell College in Taunton until his retirement, after which he set up his business running these music events. I made an appointment with the Principal, a Doctor Lloyd, and he confirmed that Freeman had lectured there for some years but retired early on the grounds of ill health. I expressed surprise, saying he appeared pretty fit, and after a bit of hesitation Lloyd admitted that was a cover-up; he'd been caught having an affair with one of his students. The girl wasn't under age and had been quite willing, so there was no question of police involvement, but Doctor Lloyd feared damage to the college's reputation so Freeman had agreed to the early retirement story.'

'Freeman told Stan and Trixie Day a bit about himself,' said Vicky. 'He said he was a widower with one son who lives in South Africa with his wife and children, and he visits them for a few weeks every winter. It looks as if being on his own with his family so far away made him look around for some female company and he found it in the wrong place.'

'It happens,' Tim commented. 'Perhaps the girl took the initiative; teenagers are sometimes attracted to older men.'

'Oh, I haven't come to the end of the tale yet,' said Rathbone with a hint of relish. 'He wasn't a widower, his wife divorced him. The fling with the student wasn't the first of his shenanigans but she'd stuck it out for the sake of their son, because up to then he'd been more discreet about his affairs. Anyway, when the dust had settled after the divorce the ex-wife went off to join the son, who by this time was married with a couple of kids and living in South Africa. At least that part of the story is true; he does visit the grandchildren for a couple of weeks in the winter.'

'And when did he get the idea for starting his music conventions?' asked Mike.

'He'd probably been planning it for some time as something to do when he retired, but it all went pear-shaped. After the divorce he was financially pretty stretched and his only asset was the house, which he'd been allowed to keep as part of the settlement. Everything else had either gone to his wife or been swallowed up in expenses. To raise some capital he put the house on the market and then his fairy godmother came to his rescue in the shape of the purchaser. She's a wealthy lady who took a shine to him; the feeling was mutual and they're now an item. She's having the house made over and the plan is for them to move in together as soon as it's ready for them.'

'Sounds a nice cosy arrangement,' commented Mike. 'I wonder if the fairy godmother keeps him on a tight rein or whether he still has the occasional fling.'

'If he does, it can't be with anyone in the Dallington Manor party or it would have been commented on,' said Penny.

'Perhaps he was the single gentleman who was careless with the condom,' Tim suggested. 'We'd better check the room numbers.'

'Do you think Rainbird might have dredged all this up from somewhere, Guv?' asked Mike. 'The threat to publicize that bit of scandal, plus the phoney degrees, would have put him in an even stronger position to demand hush money.'

'Exactly,' said Rathbone. 'As you may have noticed, I still have my doubts about Freeman's story that all Rainbird wanted to talk to him about was a reduction in his tax liability. As far as I'm concerned he's back in the frame.'

'Why not pull him in for further questioning, Guv?' said Mike. 'He is still on police bail.'

'Not without at least one hard bit of evidence,' said Rathbone. 'If we pull him in purely on the basis of his having told a few porkies to the Days we'll have Nugent threatening to bring a case against us for harassment.' He closed his file, put it into a drawer in his desk, stood up and reached for his jacket. 'Right, that's all for today. Usual time tomorrow everyone – except you, Sukey, of course. It would be great if by some miracle you could find something in Rainbird's flat, or learn anything from the neighbours, anything that would help us find his – and young Law's – killer.'

'I'll do my best, Guv,' said Sukey.

*   *   *

It was a little after half past nine when Sukey's train reached Waterloo. Harry was waiting for her and in a short time they were in the car and heading out of central London. 'I hope you like Greenings,' he said. 'It's a small privately owned hotel and the rooms are really comfortable. Mrs Greening is a splendid cook and she's happy to do evening meals to order.'

'And a full English breakfast?' asked Sukey.

'Of course.'

'I was afraid of that,' she sighed. 'I love it, but it's so bad for the figure.'

'There's nothing wrong with your figure,' he assured her. He patted her thigh and she felt her flesh tingle in response. 'Now, the court isn't sitting tomorrow so I thought the two of us could try our luck with some house-to-house enquiries. Another advantage of Greenings is that it's within easy reach of the house where Lance Rainbird used to live.'

'We can do better than that,' said Sukey. 'I've got the key to his flat.'

'No kidding? How did you manage that?'

'I reminded DI Rathbone that it was my weekend off, told him I'd been invited to spend it with a friend in London and offered to give up a little of my valuable time doing a bit of house to house. He referred the suggestion to DCI Leach who gave it his blessing.'

'Great. I take it you didn't mention our arrangement?' They had stopped at a traffic light and he turned to look at her. 'Something tells me you have; am I right?'

'Not exactly, but it does make a difference because Rathbone knows about the call you had from Gunn.'

The traffic has started moving again. 'Go on,' said Harry.

'It emerged during our enquiries that Reg Law had told Keith Gunn about how he'd called you on Saturday with that story about having seen someone talking to Rainbird and then trying to sell you a titbit about something else, but nothing came of it. Rathbone wanted to know why Gunn had called you immediately after finding Law's body so I had to tell him.'

'Are you saying I can't go with you to Rainbird's flat, then?'

'No, but I've arranged to meet an officer from the local police at Rainbird's address. I have to show my ID and get the OK to go in, and I don't want you around while that's going on. I suggest you drop me off near the house and then go and wait somewhere nearby but out of sight until I've done the necessary with whoever comes round to check me out. I'll call you on my mobile as soon as the coast is clear. How does that sound?'

'It sounds fine to me,' said Harry. 'Here we are at Greenings hotel.' He took her suitcase out of the boot and locked the car. 'Are you hungry, by the way? It's gone ten but I dare say Mrs Greening could rustle up a sandwich.'

'I'm fine, thanks. I had a burger and a coffee on the train.'

'Good.' He took her hand and squeezed it. 'I promise you'll find our bed *very* comfortable,' he whispered as he pushed the front door open.

'I'm sure I shall,' she whispered back.

TWENTY

S ukey awoke the following morning in a blissful state of relaxation after a wonderful night. She glanced at her travelling clock; it was a little after eight. Sunlight was filtering through the rose-printed curtains, promising a fine morning. She gave Harry, still fast asleep at her side, a gentle shake. After a moment he stirred, rolled over, put an arm round her and gently kissed her cheek.

'Sleep well, love?' he whispered.

'Like a baby. And you?'

'Likewise. Isn't it great being in a full-size double bed? Not that I'm complaining about yours, it isn't that small but . . .'

She snuggled against him. 'I know what you mean.'

'As a matter of fact, I've been thinking just lately . . .' he began.

'What?' she asked after he left the sentence unfinished.

'Never mind; perhaps we can talk about it some other time. We've got plans to make for today and I'm hungry. Who's first in the bathroom?'

*   *   *

'That was a super breakfast; thank you so much,' she said as Mrs Greening, a pretty brunette in her late thirties, whisked away her empty plate.

'I'm glad you enjoyed it. Would you like some more toast?'

'No thank you, but I'd love some more coffee. I don't think I'll want to eat another thing until dinner,' she said to Harry when Mrs Greening had refilled their cups and moved on to the next table.

'I'm hoping you'll find room for some lunch,' he replied, stirring milk into his coffee, 'because I've got a special treat lined up for you.'

'What's that?'

'It's a surprise. Let's plan our strategy for this morning.' He glanced round the dining room; there were still a few people there and none of them appeared to be taking any notice of anyone else, but he was careful to give nothing away as he said, 'What time have you arranged to meet your, er, opposite number?'

'Half past ten. Is that OK with you?'

'Whatever you say; by the way, are you happy to have dinner here?'

'If the dinners are as good as that breakfast, I'm more than happy.'

'Good. I'll book it with Mrs Greening and then we'll have a look at the map to check the best route to your friend's house. I suggest we get there a few minutes early in case there's a problem with parking.'

'Good thinking.'

Lance Rainbird's flat was in an imposing Victorian house on the corner of a quiet street not far from Kew Gardens. Harry had already made a note of a convenient turning where he could wait for Sukey to call him, so they drove straight to the house and drew up outside just as a police car appeared from the opposite direction.

'How's that for timing?' he said as she got out of the car.

'Perfect. See you later.'

One of two uniformed constables got out of the car and approached her. 'I'm PC Connor,' he said. 'Can I take it you're DC Reynolds from the Avon and Somerset force?'

'That's right.' She showed him her ID.

'The first we knew about Mr Rainbird's death was when a woman from the news desk of the local paper rang us hoping for a story,' he told her. 'She picked it up from a brief report in one of the national dailies but we couldn't tell her anything. We know absolutely nothing about the gentleman and no one claiming to know or be related to him has approached us, so we've had no occasion to call here. I understand he was found drowned in a lake in the grounds of a hotel in Somerset.'

'That's right,' said Sukey. 'We began by treating it as an unexplained death.'

'We assumed it was an accident, but as it didn't concern us we didn't pay much attention to it until we got your call. Are you now treating it as suspicious?'

'Death was definitely due to drowning, but we weren't sure at first how he came to be in the water,' said Sukey. 'We're pretty sure now that it was murder and our enquiries have led us to believe that there may be something in his residence to give us a lead.'

'Believe or hope?' said Connor.

She gave a rueful smile. 'Good question. I can guess what you're thinking. I have to admit that clues have been pretty thin on the ground so far, which is why I'm here. Anyway, my DI instructed me to let your people know as a matter of courtesy.'

'We appreciate that. He probably knows that all the neighbours will have read about it and it's more than likely at least one of them will be calling us to say that a strange woman has been seen at the flat. You might be challenged by one of the residents.'

'I'm hoping to speak to some of them while I'm here,' said Sukey, remembering in the nick of time not to say 'we're hoping'. She took the keys to Rainbird's flat from her pocket. 'Are you happy to let me go in?'

'Of course; we're just here to make sure you're who you say you are. Perhaps you'd like one of us to come in with you, in case there's a problem?'

'You think the killer might have murdered him for the flat and taken up residence there?' said Sukey, and he gave a slightly self-conscious grin. She had a feeling that he might have been hoping to stand around and watch while she carried out her search, which was the last thing she wanted. Not that Harry's – strictly unauthorized – presence was an essential part of the exercise, but an extra pair of eyes was always useful. 'I'm sure he's more likely to keep well out of the way,' she said. 'If he moved in here, someone would be sure to see him and ask questions.'

Before he could respond there was a shout of 'Here, Jim!' and the sound of an engine revving.

'It looks as if you're needed elsewhere,' said Sukey, greatly relieved at the diversion.

'Good hunting,' said Connor as he hurried back to the car, which raced away with its siren sounding and blue light flashing.

As soon as it was out of sight Sukey called Harry and said, 'Come and join me; the coast is clear.'

A few minutes later he appeared and slid into the place vacated by the police car. 'This looks a pretty affluent neighbourhood,' he commented. 'Lots of big houses and all well maintained. Did you say Rainbird owned this one?'

'That's right. Let's go in.'

There were stone steps leading up to the front door, to the right of which were four bell pushes numbered one to four. Each had a name beside it, the first being labelled Rainbird. A downward slanting arrow indicated a flight of steps to the right and was marked simply 'Basement Flat'.

'Which floor did he live on?' asked Harry.

'I've no idea, but I think it might be the first floor right,' she said. 'I'm pretty sure I saw a twitch of the lace curtains of the one on the left, so there's someone at home. The name according to the label to Flat Two is Fellows and my guess is it's a woman. That means there's at least one potential witness for us to question and the nosier the better. Right, let's go in.'

The front door gave on to a spacious entrance hall. A light brown carpet covered the floor; on the far wall was a table bearing a large vase of orange tulips, which on inspection proved to be imitation although, as Sukey commented, deceptively lifelike. Above the table was a heavy unframed mirror and to the right was a flight of stairs, carpeted to match the hall. 'No expense spared here,' commented Harry.

On either side of the hall was a door, each bearing a shiny

metal number. The door of number two opened a fraction and a wrinkled face crowned with luxuriant white hair peered out. 'Can I help you?' said the woman in a voice that reminded Sukey of the rustle of tissue paper.

'We hope we haven't disturbed you,' said Sukey. 'We've come to have a look round Mr Rainbird's flat.'

'Oh.' The woman sounded surprised. 'I didn't know it was up for sale already. We heard the poor gentleman had an accident and died, of course, but no one has told us when or where his funeral will be.'

'I'm afraid we don't know anything about the funeral,' said Sukey. 'I wonder if we could come and see you after we've had a look round the flat.'

'Of course.' The wrinkles deepened into a smile of delight. 'I hope you like it. It would be nice to have a young couple living here.'

'That's interesting,' said Sukey as she opened the door to Flat One. 'She obviously didn't see the police outside the house, but she saw us.'

'Maybe she was dozing and the sound of the siren woke her up,' Harry suggested. 'We can find out later. This is nice,' he went on as they stepped inside. They were in a spacious hall with doors on all sides; on the wall opposite the front door was a long case clock that showed the time at a quarter past two. He walked over to inspect it. 'Either it's shown that time for ages or it simply needs winding. Freddie would love it; she's nutty about clocks.'

'Never mind the clock; we're here to look for clues, remember?' She opened the first door on the left, which turned out to be a storage area containing a vacuum cleaner and an assortment of cleaning materials. A few jackets hung from hooks along one wall and Sukey checked every pocket, but found nothing of interest. The next door led into a dining room, with a light oak suite of table, six chairs and a matching sideboard. On the table was a single place setting, with a neatly folded napkin on one side and an upturned crystal tumbler on the other.

'Ready for his next meal,' commented Harry. 'It would suggest that he was a very well organized chap. I wonder why he needed a place this size, though. You said he was a loner.'

Sukey shook her head. 'As he owns the house he probably

found it convenient to live here so he could keep an eye on his tenants. That's something we might find out by talking to the neighbours.' She walked round the room and pulled out the drawers in the sideboard, which contained the usual assortment of cutlery and table linen. In the cupboards were crockery and glasses, all of good quality. 'No bottles of booze,' she said. 'He wasn't a drinker himself and it doesn't look as if he kept anything to offer visitors – which he probably never had anyway.'

'So he didn't fall in the lake by accident after having a few too many,' said Harry. 'That must have come out at the PM, so why did it take you so long to decide it was murder?'

'Various reasons,' said Sukey.

'Which I don't need to know, I suppose.'

'Correct. Come on, we've finished in here. I'd like to try the kitchen next.'

'Any particular reason?'

'Maybe.'

The first door on the right of the hall led into the kitchen. It was well equipped, with a cooker, fridge-freezer, washing machine and dishwasher, the walls lined with a range of storage cupboards and drawers. After a perfunctory inspection of the contents, Sukey bent down and opened the cupboard under the sink. A bin for rubbish disposal swung out, the lid rising automatically. She lifted out the plastic liner, shook it and inspected the contents. 'Nothing there,' she muttered in evident disappointment. 'Ah, what have we here?' She reached into the back of the cupboard and pulled out a second plastic bag, which she lifted up and shook. There was the unmistakable sound of glass clinking against glass. She reached inside and pulled out two empty wine bottles. 'Voila!'

'So he was a tippler after all,' said Harry. 'It must be significant to make you so excited.'

'I don't think he drank the wine himself,' said Sukey, 'but he had a visitor who obviously did.'

'A woman?'

'We do have reason to believe that he may have had a woman friend. If she was a regular visitor here someone would have spotted her. I have great hopes of Mrs Fellows.' She put the bag containing the bottles back in the cupboard.

'Don't you want them as evidence?'

'Whatever prints are on them they certainly aren't the killer's. Let's try the bathroom.'

The bathroom, like the kitchen, was well equipped with modern appliances. Everything was spotlessly clean; a cabinet over the handbasin contained a small assortment of men's toiletries. 'No shaving gear or toothbrush,' commented Harry.

'He was going away for the weekend,' Sukey reminded him. She sniffed and said, 'I can smell some sort of fragrance, but I don't think it's aftershave. Can you smell it?'

'I noticed it too – and I've just recognized it,' he said. 'It's the one Freddie uses. So Rainbird's mystery visitor is a woman, one who uses a very distinctive perfume.'

'So it would seem. I wonder . . .' Sukey took a pair of tweezers from her shoulder bag and opened the door to the shower. She bent down and began probing in the drain. After a few moments she drew out several hairs and placed them in an evidence bag. She then examined the drain in the hand basin, with similar results. Having labelled the bags she stowed them away. 'That was worth doing,' she said.

'I take it you're hoping to find hairs of different colours – his and hers?' said Harry.

'And different DNA readings as well. Next stop, the bedroom.'

Sukey went straight to the bed and turned back the cover. She bent down and sniffed. 'The perfume's even stronger in here.' She slipped a hand under the pillow and pulled out a woman's handkerchief. 'Eureka!' She took out another evidence bag, labelled and sealed it and stowed it away with the others. 'There's another door at the end of the passage. Let's have a look in there.'

The room was sparsely furnished and had obviously been used by Rainbird as his home office as it contained nothing but a desk, a filing cabinet and one chair. On the desk were a lamp, a telephone and a laptop. 'He probably did his research on that,' said Harry.

'I guess so. Let's see if we can take a look at some of his files.' She switched on the laptop, waited till the desktop appeared and clicked on the Internet browser. A window appeared demanding a password. 'I was afraid of that.' She shut it down. 'Never mind; if DI Rathbone thinks it's important he'll get the techies on to it. I think it's time to pay Mrs Fellows a call. Perhaps she'll give us a cup of coffee.'

Mrs Fellows had not been idle. She led the way into her sitting room where a woman, slightly younger than herself, was sitting on a sofa. 'I told Mrs Palmer some people had come to view the flat and she was naturally very interested. I said you were going to pop in to see me so I invited her to join us. I hope you don't mind.'

'Not at all,' said Sukey, 'but there's something I have to tell you first. I'm Detective Constable Reynolds from the Avon and Somerset Police.' She held up her ID.

'The police!'

The eyes of both women widened and they exchanged excited glances which quickly turned to consternation. 'Does that mean Mr Rainbird's death wasn't an accident?' said Mrs Palmer.

'I'm afraid it does,' said Sukey. 'We weren't sure at first exactly what happened to him and at first it seemed it could have been an accident, but now we're fairly certain he was murdered.'

'How dreadful,' said Mrs Fellows, her papery voice reduced to a whisper.

'I wonder if his lady friend knows about it,' said Mrs Palmer.

'We gather he had a lady friend, but we don't know anything about her,' said Sukey. 'Have you seen her?'

'Oh yes,' they both said eagerly. 'She doesn't come very often – at least, we only see her occasionally but of course she may come when we don't see her.'

'Could you describe her?'

'Oh dear.' Apart from recalling that 'she's quite nice looking, about the same age as Mr Rainbird and always very nicely dressed,' neither woman was able to give anything approaching an accurate description.

Sukey was beginning to feel discouraged when Harry suddenly said, 'If you saw a picture of her, perhaps you'd recognize her?'

'Oh yes!' they both said eagerly. 'Have you got one?'

Sukey shook her head. 'If we knew who she was we wouldn't be asking you these questions,' she pointed out gently. 'Well, thank you anyway. We mustn't take up any more of your time.'

Both women apologized profusely for their failure to say anything useful and Sukey and Harry made their escape. The minute they were back in the car Sukey said, 'We haven't got any picture to show them, so what on earth was the point of that?'

'You don't need to know – not for the time being anyway.'

'So what do we do now?'

'It's getting on for lunchtime. Didn't I say I had a surprise for you?'

TWENTY-ONE

'You said something about a special treat,' said Sukey, as Harry turned into the drive at Greenings and pulled up in a parking space, 'so what are we doing back here?'

'I thought we should change into something a bit less casual,' said Harry. 'Jeans and a sweat shirt aren't quite suitable for where we're going.'

'Which is where?'

'You'll see.'

Realizing there was no point in asking further questions, Sukey followed him up to their room, where she changed into the simple dress she had brought to wear for dinner, brushed her hair and checked her make-up. She slipped on a jacket and did a brief twirl in front of him. 'Will this do?' she asked.

He pretended to study her with a critical eye before giving her a hug and saying 'Perfect – as always! I hope those are comfortable,' he added, indicating her low-heeled pumps. 'There'll be nowhere to park where we're going so you'll have to do a bit of walking.'

'Where to?'

'You'll see.' Meanwhile he had changed into a grey suit with a plain blue shirt and striped tie. He glanced in the mirror, brushed his hair and said, 'Right, let's go.'

'Hang on a moment while I put these evidence bags in the safe. Just in case we get mugged,' she explained. 'Unlikely, I know, but I'd hate to have our morning's work wasted.'

At Richmond station they took a train, emerging into the

daylight of Piccadilly at Green Park Underground station. The sun was warm and there was a hint of spring in the air. Harry took her arm. 'It's not far now,' he said. A few steps further on he stopped at the entrance to the Ritz. 'Here we are.'

Sukey's eyes widened. 'Are we having lunch here?'

'I told you it was a special treat. I've made a reservation in the Rivoli Bar. Come along.' When they were seated at their table he said, 'How about a champagne cocktail to celebrate?'

'I'd love a champagne cocktail, but what are we celebrating?'

He ordered the drinks from the waiter standing at his elbow before lowering his voice and saying, 'In case you hadn't noticed, it's exactly a year since our adventure in that tattoo parlour – remember?'

'How could I ever forget?' She glanced round the bar; it was already busy, the few unoccupied tables bearing cards reading 'Reserved'. 'This is lovely,' she said. 'Whatever made you think of it?'

'Dad told me he and Freddie stayed here one weekend a couple of years ago. They were feeling a bit flush as they'd just won a prestigious golfing tournament and decided to put a bit more to the prize money and treat themselves to a weekend of luxury. I'm afraid I couldn't run to a weekend – and in any case it wouldn't have been as convenient for our researches as Greenings.' The waiter returned with their drinks and he raised his glass. 'Let's drink to the memory of a very special day!'

'The day you nearly got the two of us killed,' she reminded him. 'Being here has just reminded me of something,' she added as they sipped their drinks and studied the menu. 'When Vicky and I interviewed Luke Grayson . . .'

'Who's Luke Grayson?'

'The brother of John Grayson, the one who calls himself Romeo. He works for the same firm of accountants as Rainbird.'

'Which you said I didn't need to know,' he reminded her.

'You still don't. Luke Grayson came to identify his brother's body; he told us quite a lot about his family but during a conversation Rainbird's name came up. He expressed surprise and shock, but he didn't mention he was a colleague. When we found out he'd withheld that information DI Rathbone told us to see him again.'

'And what reason did he give?'

'That isn't important. What is interesting is that he stated that on the Friday evening Rainbird was killed he was here, making sure everything was in order for his mother-in-law's one hundredth birthday party the next day.'

'I see what you're getting at,' said Harry. 'You obviously think it's significant for some reason, but before we go any further let's decide what we're going to eat. Do you fancy one of these dishes to share? They look interesting.'

'Good idea. Which one shall we have?'

Harry beckoned the waiter. 'What do you recommend?' he asked.

'The savoury hors d'oeuvres are very popular with our regular guests, sir.'

'That sounds a good recommendation,' said Sukey. 'Let's have those. Vicky and I found Grayson's attitude a bit arrogant,' she said as the waiter left to place their order. 'It was only to give him a bit of aggro that I asked him where he was the night Rainbird died. He expressed outrage, said he was here and suggested very scornfully that if I didn't believe him I could check with the maitre d'.'

'And as you happen to be here you think you might as well do just that?' said Harry.

'It seems too good a chance to miss. I've no idea how big the party was but I doubt if it would have been held in here. When the waiter brings our food he'll tell us the right person to ask.'

'Mr Luke Grayson?' The events manager consulted his computer. 'Ah yes, he gave a luncheon party for fifty guests. It was exactly a week ago today.'

'That's right,' said Sukey. 'It was his mother-in-law's one hundredth birthday and I understand he was particularly anxious that everything should go without a hitch. He even said he spent the previous evening here, going over all the details. Presumably that would have been with you?'

The man smiled as if the recollection struck a chord. 'Oh yes, I remember. He was *most* particular and spent at least an hour going over everything – although,' he stopped for a moment and referred back to the computer, 'actually it wasn't the evening, it was the morning. He insisted on going over every detail to make sure we were quite clear about his instructions: the menu, the wines, guests seated in the correct order and so on.'

'Yes, he is a stickler for detail,' said Sukey, 'but I understand everything went well on the day.'

'I can personally vouch for that. Are you planning a similar function? Did Mr Grayson recommend us?'

'Not exactly; it just cropped up in conversation. Thank you for your help.'

'My pleasure, madam.'

'What do you think we should do next?' said Harry as he and Sukey left the hotel. 'I don't suppose you have Grayson's home address?'

'As it happens I don't, but even if I did there's no way I'd use it without DI Rathbone's say-so. My remit while I'm in town is to check Rainbird's flat and chat to some neighbours, and that's what I've done; end of story.'

'But Grayson's come up with yet another lie,' Harry protested. 'Surely you can't let him get away with that. If he checked his party arrangements at the Ritz on Friday morning he would have had plenty of time to be at Dallington Manor in time to kill Rainbird and be back well before midnight.'

'That's true, but what's the motive?'

'You said he works in the same office as Rainbird and we know Rainbird had some stuff on Freeman that he wouldn't want spread round. Suppose he had some dirt on Grayson as well.'

'It's possible, but a previous DCI who was asked for a character reference when I transferred from the Gloucestershire force mentioned that I was inclined to be what he called a loose canon, and DCI Leach said the same after the tattoo parlour adventure, as you call it. I'm not going to risk yet another rap on the knuckles for the same thing. The best I can do is report this to Rathbone when I get back.'

'Is he on duty today?'

'As far as I know.'

'Then why not give him a call now and tell him what you've found out?'

'It's tempting, but how do I explain why I started questioning the events manager while I was having lunch with you? He has no idea you're the reason I'm doing this weekend in town.'

'You don't have to let him know about me. Tell him you've got a rich uncle; I'm sure you can think of something.'

'Vicky knows I'm meeting you because I'd already told her I'd asked you to do a bit of ferreting around near Rainbird's place for me. She promised to keep it quiet for the time being, but if I told Rathbone about this and he shared it with the others she might feel duty bound to say you're the one who invited me to London and took me to lunch at the Ritz. I've got to think this through.'

'All right,' he said resignedly. 'It's still quite warm so let's go for a stroll in Green Park.'

The mild weather had attracted a number of people to the park. There were families with children; some had spread blankets on the grass and were enjoying picnics while others were strolling along the paths, stopping every few yards to admire the flowers. 'Let's hire a couple of deckchairs,' Harry suggested. 'Maybe you'll think better sitting down and relaxing. Or you might have a little nap while you digest your lunch.'

'Which was delicious,' said Sukey. 'Thank you so much, Harry.'

They sat for a while without speaking. Around them, pigeons were pecking in the grass, occasionally taking off with a noisy flapping of wings when chased by a shrieking child. Sukey closed her eyes, reflected on everything they had learned that day and tried to decide how she should handle it. She found herself praying. *Please Lord, tell me what I should do!*

Harry was the first to break the silence. 'About this chap Grayson,' he said. 'You've got the rest of today and most of tomorrow to get in touch with him. If you leave it till you get back to work to tell Rathbone what you've just learned, my guess is you'll get a rocket for not reporting it right away. He's sure to want it followed up and it would make more sense to do it while you're here rather than have to make another trip to London. In that case you might even have to pay for your own ticket as a penalty for neglect of duty,' he added with a sly grin.

'You know something,' said Sukey, 'I think you're right. I'll call him now.' Rathbone's response was as Harry had predicted. 'We have to follow this up, if possible while you're still in town. I remember asking Ashman for his home address. I've got it here somewhere. Yes, here we are.' He dictated an address and telephone number. 'Got that?'

'Yes, Guv.'

'Go and tackle the bugger right away and keep me posted.'

'Will do, Guv. You were right,' she said as she put her phone away. 'He lives in Isleworth; have you any idea where that is?'

'It's not that far from Richmond,' said Harry. 'Let's go back to the hotel and look up the address.'

A little over an hour later they were parked outside an impressive house in what was evidently a prosperous area. Every property had a large front garden and a wide drive with parking for two and in some cases three cars. The drive at number twenty-five, however, was empty. 'There's obviously no one at home,' said Sukey.

'Why don't you ring the bell?' Harry suggested. 'There might be someone in who could tell you when he'll be back.'

Sukey shook her head. 'I want to catch him unawares,' she said.

'Give him a call later on,' he suggested.

'I don't think so; it might be awkward if his wife answered the phone. I've got to go carefully. If only I could think of a way to catch him face to face – wait a minute!' she exclaimed. 'Tomorrow's Sunday and being so religious he's sure to go to church. But which church, I wonder? If we knew, we could check the times of the services.'

'Maybe he goes to one near here,' said Harry. 'Let's drive round a little.'

They had not gone far when Sukey noticed a spire rising above some trees a short distance ahead. 'That looks like a church,' she said. 'Let's try and find it.'

The church was in a quiet street a short distance further on. It was set back from the road and there was a forecourt with half a dozen spaces, one of which was reserved for the vicar and the other for the church secretary. A single car was parked in one of the unreserved spaces and Sukey gave a squeak of excitement. 'That's his car!' she exclaimed.

'Are you sure?'

'Of course I'm sure. He was driving it when he came to identify his brother's body. He must be doing something in the church.'

'Shall we go in?' said Harry.

'Not you; he'll assume you're a copper and ask for an ID. You go somewhere out of sight and wait for me to call you.' She got out of the car and watched him drive away before crossing the road to the church and opening the door. A heavy curtain shielded the interior; she pushed it aside and went in. It was a typical Victorian church, with oak pews on either side of the nave and a stained glass window above the altar. On the right of the chancel steps was a pedestal on which a woman was arranging foliage and flowers. A man was seated in the front row of pews, watching her. It was clear that neither of them had heard her come in. She walked quietly up the carpeted aisle and sat down beside him.

'Good afternoon, Mr Grayson,' she said.

His head jerked as if pulled on a string. 'What the he—' He managed to bite back the expletive. 'How did you know I was here?'

'I'm a detective, remember? It's what we do.'

He glared at her. 'Haven't I answered enough of your stupid questions?' he hissed. 'This is sheer harassment.'

'Luke, what's this about? Why should a detective want to talk to you?' The flower arranger had evidently overheard and stood staring at Grayson with a half-open daffodil in one hand.

Sukey stood up. 'Mrs Grayson?'

The woman's face turned scarlet. 'No . . . I'm . . . that is, I do the flowers and Mr Grayson is kind enough to give me a lift to the florist and then to the church.'

'How kind of him,' said Sukey, 'but perhaps you can do without him for a few minutes while he and I have a quiet chat about one or two things.' She turned to Grayson. 'Shall we find somewhere a little more private?'

'But . . .' the woman began.

'It'll be all right, Cynthia,' said Grayson. He turned a look of sheer malice on Sukey and said, 'Come on, let's get this over.' He led the way to a corner at the back of the church where a small circle of chairs was arranged round a table on which copies of the parish magazine and a brochure advertising open learning courses were laid out. 'Will this do?'

'Fine,' said Sukey. 'It shouldn't take long.'

'This is exceedingly embarrassing, to say the least,' he said in a low voice. 'If you have to ask more of your perpetual nit-picking questions, why did you have to come here instead of to my office?'

'It so happens I'm in London for the weekend and a friend took me to lunch at the Ritz,' Sukey began. 'Does that ring a bell?'

'Should it?'

'You gave a party there for your mother-in-law's one hundredth birthday last Saturday.'

'So what if I did? Don't tell me you're thinking of holding a similar function there?' The idea seemed to amuse him, the subtext of the remark being, *I doubt if you could afford it.*

'Not exactly,' said Sukey. 'If you would cast your mind back to my recent visit with my colleague, DS Armstrong, to your office, you may recall that when you told us you were at the Ritz on the Friday evening you suggested – rather sarcastically as I remember – that I could check your alibi with the maitre d'.'

'So?' he said. His tone became less confident as if he sensed what was coming next.

'I did just that – or rather, I spoke to the events manager. He agreed that you were there on Friday to check the arrangements, but was quite positive that you were there in the morning, not the evening. So I'm asking you once again, where were you on that Friday evening between eight o'clock and midnight? At home with your wife?' If so, I'm sure she'll be happy to confirm it.'

'My wife had gone to collect her mother, who lives in Manchester. She was bringing her back in the morning.'

'So you were at home on your own?'

'Yes.'

'Can you prove it?'

'Why should I have to?'

'This is a murder enquiry, Mr Grayson. Anyone who might have a motive to commit the murder and who has no alibi is naturally under grave suspicion.'

'What possible motive could I have for killing Rainbird? The idea is preposterous.'

'But you don't have an alibi either.'

'Yes, he has!' Sukey and Grayson swung round. The flower arranger, evidently overcome with curiosity, had approached unobserved and stood behind them with an expression of sheer horror on her face. She moved across and put a hand on Grayson's shoulder. 'I can tell you who was with him. I was.'

He pushed her hand away and said, 'Stay out of this, Cynthia.'

'And have you suspected of murder? You think I'd stand by and let that happen? He was with me on the Friday before the party, Detective whatever your name is. All evening . . . and all night.'

TWENTY-TWO

Luke Grayson broke down and wept, racking sobs that seemed to tear the heart out of him and leave him gasping for breath. The woman sat down beside him, took his hand and tried to soothe him, murmuring words in his ear that Sukey, who had withdrawn a short distance to give them some privacy, could not hear. She recalled the time she had sat at his side as he shed quiet tears for his dead brother. Then, she felt nothing but compassion for him in his grief. She felt no compassion for him now; instead the words 'How are the mighty fallen' came into her mind. She waited until he had become calmer before saying, 'I'm Detective Constable Sukey Reynolds of the Avon and Somerset Police. May I know your name, please?'

'I'm Cynthia Franks.'

'Well, Mrs Franks, as you will have gathered, I have already interviewed Mr Grayson in connection with the death of one of his colleagues, Lance Rainbird, who was found drowned a week ago yesterday in the grounds of a hotel near Clevedon. Perhaps he told you about that?'

Mrs Franks shook her head, 'No, he didn't. He never talks about anything to do with his work.'

'That's a little surprising, don't you think? The death of a colleague by drowning isn't exactly "anything to do with work", is it?' Mrs Franks made no reply. 'We weren't sure at first how he came to meet his death,' Sukey continued, 'but our enquiries have now established that his death wasn't an accident; he was murdered.'

'That's awful, of course,' said Mrs Franks, 'but as I've just told you, Luke was with me on the day you mentioned so he couldn't possibly have had anything to do with it.'

'We have learned from witnesses that there was considerable friction between Mr Grayson and Lance Rainbird, chiefly because Rainbird held very strong atheistic opinions and often offended Mr Grayson with his blasphemous remarks. That's correct, isn't it?' she said to Grayson.

He nodded. 'I believe he made some of his most outrageous statements with the deliberate intention of offending me,' he said.

'I remember you telling me something about the arguments you had with him from time to time, Luke, but you didn't tell me he was dead,' Mrs Franks said reproachfully. 'Why not?'

He made a helpless gesture. 'It didn't concern us . . . and we have so little time together.'

'But you couldn't possibly have had anything to do with his death, so why did you lie to the police?' she persisted.

'It was because of *her*.' He jerked his head in Sukey's direction. 'She had the cheek to ask me where I was at the time Rainbird was killed and I told her I was at the Ritz and suggested she check with the manager and the maître d' if she didn't believe me. The detective sergeant who was with her assured me that wasn't necessary; she probably agreed with me that her *subordinate* –' he managed to inject a hint of condescension into his tone – 'had overstepped the mark and I naturally assumed she believed me. It wasn't an outright lie . . . I mean I was there, it was just the time . . . it never entered my head that *she* would actually go and check up on me.'

'You were right, we had no reason not to believe you,' said Sukey, 'but it so happened that the opportunity arose and it seemed to make sense to take advantage of it.'

'And now my sin has found me out,' said Grayson. He looked up at Cynthia Franks. 'I'm sorry I got you into this; will you forgive me?'

'There's nothing to forgive,' she assured him. 'We have both sinned; we must both pray for forgiveness.'

'Mrs Franks,' said Sukey, 'are you prepared to swear that you were with Luke Grayson between the hours of eight p.m. and midnight the day of Lance Rainbird's murder?'

She drew herself erect and said, 'Yes, Constable Reynolds, I am.'

Sukey sank into the passenger seat of Harry's car and closed her eyes. 'That,' she said, 'was the most distressing interview I've carried out in a long time.'

'I was getting worried,' said Harry. 'In fact I was about to walk back to the church and put my head round the door when I got your call. Do you want to tell me about it?'

'Luke Grayson,' she said, 'is a broken man. A devout Christian, a pillar of the church and highly respected in the local community, he's been caught out having an extramarital affair with Mrs Cynthia Franks, a fellow member of his church, for the past three years.'

Harry whistled. 'Don't tell me they were having it off in the vestry!' he exclaimed.

'Oh no, it wasn't quite as bad as that. She does the flower arrangements; she doesn't drive so he takes her there, waits while she does her stuff and then brings her home. Apart from the convenience it gives them a bit of time together, but I can't believe anything improper goes on in the church.'

'It must have scared the pants off him when you walked in.'

Sukey managed a chuckle. 'It gave him the shock of his life; the look on his face had to be seen to be believed. I said I wanted a word with him in private so we went to a quiet spot at the back of the church, leaving Mrs F to get on with her flower arranging. But curiosity got the better of her and she managed to overhear me challenging him about his whereabouts on the Friday evening Rainbird was killed.'

'I think I can guess what's coming next,' said Harry. 'She realized he needed an alibi so she said he was with her.'

'Exactly.'

'Do you think she was telling the truth?'

'It's hard to say. I asked her if she'd be willing to swear to it and she said she would. He begged her not to and assured her he had nothing to do with Rainbird's death, but she wouldn't budge. I took her details and said I'd be reporting to my superiors and they'd both be hearing from us again.'

'From what you've told me about Grayson he's a pretty self-righteous bloke,' said Harry. 'I've never met him, but I'm inclined to think he deserves to get his comeuppance.'

'He was all but wailing and gnashing his teeth,' said Sukey. 'It was quite pitiful; he was alternately apologizing to her and then saying "I'm ruined" and "Whatever's to become of me?" Oh, and at one point he said "God be merciful to me, a sinner". I should have felt compassion for him, but I couldn't help feeling it was a bit of rough justice. I felt sorry for her, though. She obviously adores him and seemed as concerned for his reputation as he was. She asked me for assurance that it wouldn't get into the papers, but of course I couldn't give it.'

'Do you know how the affair started?'

'Grayson and her late husband used to play golf together and when her husband died he used to visit her from time to time to take her out shopping, bring her to church to the services and every so often to arrange the flowers and so on. He confided in her that his own marriage was on the rocks so they used to console each other. One day they somehow ended up in bed, and it went on from there.'

'I take it you'll be feeding all this back to Rathbone?'

'Of course, but what I need now is a nice strong cup of tea. I'll call him when I've had that.'

Harry switched on the ignition. 'Right, let's go back to Greenings.'

Rathbone's reaction to Sukey's report was the most positive since the day he was forced to admit there was insufficient evidence to charge Justin Freeman with Rainbird's murder.

'Well done, that was a smart piece of work,' he told her. 'I'm not too optimistic about the hair and the handkerchief; lots of women use perfume and it seems unlikely that there'll be a match between any of the hair in Rainbird's flat and that of anyone known to be at Dallington Manor when he was killed. We might have more luck with his laptop. Go back to his flat and pick it up. I'll get the techies on to it first thing on Monday. Enjoy the rest of your weekend.'

'Thanks, Guv. He sounded almost pleased,' she told Harry as she ended the call and told him what Rathbone had said.

'Do you want to go and pick up the laptop right away or shall we leave it till the morning?'

'Let's do it now so we have tomorrow free.'

As they reached Rainbird's flat Mrs Fellows opened her door. 'I saw your car outside,' she said. 'Have you any news?'

'We've been getting on with our enquiries,' said Sukey, 'and my Inspector has instructed me to collect something from Mr Rainbird's flat.'

'Oh!' She sounded surprised. 'Mr Rainbird's lady friend was here a little while after you left. I heard her go into the flat.'

'Did she say why she was there?'

'I didn't actually speak to her. I had a telephone call from my daughter; it went on for quite a long time and I think she must have left by the time I finished because I never heard her go.'

'Well thank you for telling us, Mrs Fellows. We apologize for disturbing you.'

'Now what would the mysterious lady friend be so anxious to retrieve?' said Sukey as they entered Rainbird's flat. 'At least it wasn't the laptop, it's still here,' she added, opening the door to the small room he used as an office. 'Perhaps it was something she didn't want anyone else to see, like a diary or some letters.'

'But why leave it for a week after her lover died to come and look for whatever it was?' said Harry.

'Maybe she hadn't realized she'd lost it. Or maybe it was the first opportunity she had to come here without her husband knowing.'

'You think she's married?'

'The fact that the visits seem to have been quite infrequent makes me think that's more than likely,' said Sukey. 'Anyway, we don't know what she was looking for or whether she found it, but as we're here it might be worth ferreting around a bit more.'

After several minutes of fruitless search they were about to give up when Harry said, 'I've just had a thought. I mislaid my wallet a couple of months ago and I was going bananas trying to find it. Guess where it was?'

'You tell me.'

'It was under my bed. It had fallen on the floor and I must have kicked it out of sight and I suddenly remembered . . .' He was already on his knees by the bed, groping with the fingers of one hand. 'Got it!' he said as he got to his feet and brandished a small notebook that he was holding between his thumb and one finger.

'Well done!' said Sukey. 'It looks like a diary; with luck it will give us a serious lead. Be careful how you handle it; just drop it on the bed.'

'You're thinking of fingerprints?'

'And DNA. If they prove this belonged to the owner of the scented hanky and the hair, and we can somehow find her, she might possibly mention the name of someone who might have a motive for killing her lover. It's a pity those two old dears couldn't give a decent description between them.'

'There may be other residents in the house who've noticed this woman's comings and goings,' said Harry. 'Maybe one of them could remember enough for an E-FIT.'

'You're right.' Sukey glanced at her watch. 'What time does Mrs Greening serve dinner?'

'Eight o'clock. We've plenty of time to ring a few more bells if that's what you're thinking.'

'I'll just put that in an evidence bag,' said Sukey, indicating the little book. 'Luckily I still have one left.' Having dealt with that she put the laptop into its carrying case and handed it to him saying, 'I think it'd be better if you wait in the car. This shouldn't take long.'

There was no one in at number four, but a woman of about fifty answered their knock at number three. 'Mr Rainbird?' she said in reply to Sukey's question. 'Yes, Mrs Fellows told us he'd been murdered and how the police had been asking her questions. She's a bit cross with herself for not being able to help.'

'How well did you know Mr Rainbird?'

'Hardly at all, really. We used to meet in passing of course and exchange greetings, but we didn't stop to chat or anything. He was always very pleasant and polite, but he did keep himself to himself.'

'Do you remember anything special about him?'

'He had a very nice voice,' she said. 'I saw him come in once or twice with a lady,' she went on after a few moments' further thought.

'Could you describe this lady?'

The woman closed her eyes. 'Let me think. She had light brown hair, quite short but beautifully cut, a slim figure, good features, not a lot of make-up. Oh, and she wore a rather nice perfume; but I'm afraid I don't know what it's called.'

'Did you ever hear Mr Rainbird calling her by name?'

'I'm afraid not.'

'But you'd recognize her if you saw her again?'

'Oh certainly. Poor thing, she must be very upset.'

'I'm sure she is,' Sukey agreed. 'Thank you, you've been very helpful.'

'Any luck?' asked Harry as she got into the car.

'A bit, I think. The woman at number three gave quite a promising description and could possibly give enough detail for an E-FIT if DI Rathbone thinks it's worth doing. And I'm sure she'd recognize the perfume on the hanky. Anyway, I think we've done more than enough for today. Let's go back to Greenings and freshen up for dinner.'

Sunday was warm and sunny. Harry and Sukey enjoyed a trip on the London Eye followed by a river cruise before crossing the Millennium Bridge and visiting Tate Modern, where they browsed for a while before having lunch in the restaurant. All too soon it was time to go back to Greenings and collect Sukey's case. Harry took her to Waterloo to catch her train.

'Thanks for a wonderful weekend,' she said.

'It was wonderful for me too. We must do it more often.' He put his arms round her and held her close. 'I'll keep in touch; let me know if you want me to do any more sleuthing.'

When Sukey arrived at work on Monday morning she was eagerly greeted by Vicky.

'How did it go?'

'It was really interesting. I found out Luke Grayson has been telling porkies again. You'll never guess what that holier-than-thou humbug has been getting up to.'

'I'll wait to read your report. Tell me where you went with Harry.'

'All right, we stayed in a nice private hotel near Richmond and we had a great time in between sleuthing. Look, I haven't time to talk about it now; Sir will want a full report.' She switched on her computer. 'See you later.'

'Not unless Sir sends you down to Dallington Manor,' said Vicky. 'We're all off there to go over the grounds with a tooth-comb. If what you've found out about Grayson were to open up a new lead it would give us something to get our teeth into. We haven't dug up anything new here.'

TWENTY-THREE

Sukey was about to sit down at her work station when Rathbone summoned her to his office. She handed over Rainbird's laptop and the four evidence bags.

'You only mentioned three items,' he commented.

'I found the diary – at least, that's what it looks like – when I went back to Rainbird's flat to pick up the laptop,' she explained. 'The woman in the opposite flat heard my key in the lock and popped out to tell me that his lady friend had also been to the flat that afternoon, after my morning visit. That struck me as odd and my first thought was that she'd come to pick up his laptop, but fortunately it was still there. Then I got to wondering whether she'd been looking for something else – something compromising, perhaps, something she was afraid might betray her identity if it fell into the wrong hands.'

'Her husband's, for example?' suggested Rathbone.

'Yes, Guv. Thinking it might have been something like letters, I had another search in the bedroom and this time I found the diary. Maybe that was what she was after, but it was out of sight and she obviously didn't think of looking more closely.'

'And you did. Good work; where was it?'

'I happened to remember something a friend once told me; he'd mislaid a wallet and couldn't find it anywhere. Then he remembered he was by his bed last time he had it and wondered if he'd dropped it and kicked it under the bed, which is what happened. So I groped around under Rainbird's bed, and there it was.'

'Have you read it?'

'No, Guv. I thought it might be worth checking for prints and DNA before a close examination. I'm not even sure it's a diary,' she added, peering at the little book in its evidence bag, 'it might be just an address book.'

'You were right not to handle it; we can't be too careful. I'll get forensics to check it over. Anything else?'

'While I was there I took the opportunity to speak to another of the residents, on the off-chance of getting a better description of Rainbird's visitor. I struck lucky – or at least I got a more promising description than Mrs Fellows and her friend could rustle up between them. It might be worth sending an artist to do an E-FIT.'

'I'll think about that when I've read your full report, but first I'd like to know if you've had any further thoughts about this woman who swears Grayson was with her on Friday night. You seemed fairly sure at the time that she was telling the truth, but you say she's a devout Christian, so would she really be prepared to take the oath if she was just covering up for him?'

'She said she would, but maybe she was taking a chance that I'd accept her word and it wouldn't actually come to that. She did ask me if I could keep the affair out of my report, but of course I had to say that wasn't possible. She seems absolutely besotted with Grayson, but I can't think why.'

'I take it you haven't a very high opinion of him then?'

'It's occurred to me before that his so-called devout Christianity didn't altogether ring true. Now it seems nothing but sheer hypocrisy; all he seems to be concerned with is the damage to his own precious reputation. He did offer her some sort of apology for having got her into a mess, but I could tell he was thinking mainly of himself.'

'Hmm, you've given me quite a bit to think about,' said Rathbone. 'As soon as I've seen your full report I'll have a word with DCI Leach and we'll decide if there's any mileage in taking it further. The big question of course is motive. Maybe the laptop will yield something useful so I'll get the techies on to it right away. Go now and get on with your full report. When you've done it,' he added as she got up to leave, 'you can drive down to the hotel and give Vicky and the lads a hand. She's organizing a fingertip search of the grounds; the cigarette stub wasn't any use by the way as there was no DNA match to anyone who was there at the crucial time, but I'm convinced there's some hard evidence around somewhere if only we look in the right place.'

'Let's hope you're right, Guv.'

Sukey entered her report in her computer, saved it and sent it to DCI Leach and DI Rathbone with copies to the rest of the team. She then went to her car and drove to Dallington Manor, where she found Vicky, Mike and Tim taking a coffee break.

'I've been told to report to you for orders,' she said. 'I gather we all have to go round on our hands and knees looking for evidence.'

'It's a question of leaving no stone unturned and no bit of exposed earth left unexplored,' said Vicky with a grimace.

'At this rate we'll all end up with back problems,' grumbled Tim, 'and every time we start poking around in a flower bed the gardener nearly has a nervous breakdown.'

'Get your girlfriend to give you a nice soothing massage,' said Vicky. She finished her coffee and stood up. 'Right, back to work.'

'So where would you like me to start searching, Sarge?' asked Sukey.

'It's time someone checked the rubbish skips; they're all hidden away round the back of the hotel, close to the kitchen door. You can give me hand with that.'

'Surely they'll have been emptied since the murders?'

'That's where we're in luck. They should have been emptied last Wednesday, but the rubbish disposal people were on strike all last week so the stuff has been piling up. Chapman's been on to the Council whingeing about a health hazard and the possibility of a plague of rats. The strike has been settled but the stuff hasn't been collected from here yet and I'm making sure it isn't until we've given the entire area a thorough going over.'

'Including going through all the smelly stuff?' said Sukey.

'I'm afraid so. Just think for a moment; if you had some small item you wanted to get rid of without the risk of it being found, where would you hide it?'

'Somewhere you hoped no one would think of looking,' said Sukey. 'I see what you're getting at.' She pointed to the food bins.

'Right, so let's put on some gloves and masks and make a start.' Vicky spread a large plastic sheet on the ground and they began their unsavoury task. They worked well together and the time passed surprisingly quickly; needless to say Vicky took the opportunity as they carefully inspected every scrap of the rotting waste to quiz Sukey about her weekend with Harry.

'It was brilliant,' Sukey said. 'He was a great help; in fact he found one piece of evidence that I'd have missed – only I had to be careful not to tell Sir that he was there with me. I wonder . . .'

'Thought of something else?' said Vicky as Sukey left the sentence unfinished.

'Yes, but I don't think it had anything to do with the case. It was on the Saturday morning; we'd just woken up and Harry said how nice it was to be in a double bed. And then he said, "As I matter of fact I've been thinking lately," and then he broke off. I asked him what he'd been thinking, but he just said, "Never mind, we can talk about it some other time", but he's never referred to it again.'

'You know what?' said Vicky. 'I think he's going to ask you to marry him – or at least to shack up with him.'

'Oh dear,' said Sukey. 'I'm not sure I'm ready to think about that just yet. Let's try and get this job over before lunch.'

After two hours of back-breaking work they completed their task without finding anything significant. Vicky said, 'Thank goodness that's done. Let's bag it all up and get some lunch.'

'I'm not sure I fancy food after wading through that lot,' said Sukey.

'You'll feel better after a clean up and a drink,' Vicky, assured her.

When they reached the bar Tim and Mike were already there. 'Where's Penny, by the way?' asked Sukey.

'Sir has sent her off to talk to a woman who claims someone

tried to snatch her baby,' said Mike. 'I think she was glad of the chance to get away from here.'

'I can't say I blame her,' said Tim. 'I reckon our DI is on to a loser with all this grubbing around for evidence. I don't think he has a clue what he expects us to find.'

'We won't know ourselves until we find it,' Mike pointed out between swigs from his beer mug. 'I'm surprised DCI Leach doesn't decide to downgrade the case. He probably would if anything big cropped up, but things have been surprisingly quiet lately.'

The conversation turned to other topics until they had finished their lunch. 'OK Sarge,' said Mike, 'I take it you want us to carry on with crawling round?'

'No, I thought you'd like a change so I want you to help Sukey and me sort through the rubbish. We've already done the messy stuff, but there's loads of recyclables; bottles, plastics, cans and so on and black bags full of other dry waste.'

They set about their respective tasks without a great deal of optimism, but half an hour later Sukey made a discovery. While delving into the contents of a container full of newspapers, catalogues and junk mail, she found a pair of white cotton gloves. 'I think I've got something here,' she said as she held them up. 'These aren't women's gloves, like the sort you buy in a shop to wear with a summer outfit. In any case, if a guest had left them in her room they'd have been handed in as lost property.'

'So what do you reckon?' asked Vicky. 'They look to me like the ones waiters wear when they're serving.'

'I don't remember seeing any of the waiters here wearing gloves,' said Mike.

'That's true,' said Sukey, 'they're more the sort of thing they wear at formal dinners with a tux and a black tie. We could find out whether there's been an event like that here recently.'

'So what if there has?' said Tim. 'What possible connection could there be with our case?'

'You're forgetting something; Reg Law was manually strangled and Doc Handley was pretty sure his killer was wearing gloves. If he wore these he's probably smart enough to know about DNA and so forth so he'd want to get rid of them as quickly as possible. The obvious thing to do was drop them in one of the rubbish bins and tip in some stuff on top of them. In the normal course of events the bin would have been emptied the week after the murder, but thanks to the strike that didn't happen.'

'You may well be right,' said Vicky. 'We'll definitely get forensics on to these, but first I'm going to find out if anyone recognizes them and can suggest who might have worn them and when.'

'Does that mean we can give up sorting through the rest of this stuff?' asked Tim hopefully.

'Sorry guys, I'm afraid not. You carry on searching while I go and check on the gloves.' She went to reception and showed them to Maxine. 'Do you recognize these?' she asked.

'They're just an ordinary pair of waiter's serving gloves,' said the receptionist after a quick glance. 'Where did you find them?'

'They were in one of the rubbish bins. I don't remember seeing any of your waiters wearing white gloves, though.'

'They don't normally, but a couple of weeks ago we laid on a dinner for a consortium of business people; it was a formal occasion so all our waiters were formally dressed. We hired the outfits, but as far as I know everything went back. I suppose that pair must have got overlooked.'

'When was this formal dinner?'

'I think it was the week before last; I'll just check.' Maxine consulted the register. 'Yes, here we are; it was on the Wednesday, a couple of days before Mr Freeman and his party arrived. Is it important?'

'It might be. Do you know which waiters were on duty that evening?'

'I can find out for you. Mrs Chapman will know.'

'Thank you.' Vicky went outside and called Rathbone.

'That's certainly an odd place to find those sort of gloves,' he said, 'but the most likely explanation is that one of the waiters didn't remember to hand them in, nobody noticed a pair was missing before the rest of the stuff went back, so he just ditched them.'

'Do you think it's worth checking them for DNA, Guv?'

'I suppose we'd better.' Rathbone's tone was dismissive. 'But I think we might be on to something a lot more promising. I called the techies; one of their boys was already here checking a mobile so I asked him if he could have a quick look at Rainbird's laptop. He got into it in no time, and there's some very interesting stuff in it. Tell Sukey to come back here right away; she might as well bring the gloves with her and I'll hand them over to forensics for the usual checks.'

'What do you want the rest of us to do, Guv?'

'Just keep on with the search.'

When Sukey entered Rathbone's office she found him with a pen in one hand and a diary at his elbow while apparently studying the open laptop.

'Come and look at this lot,' he said, his voice and expression positively gleeful. She sat beside him and looked at the screen. The file was named Freeman and listed every detail of the man's personal history, including his date of birth, his parentage, his marriage and divorce, education and qualifications. The latter consisted of nothing more significant than the results of his secondary school and sixth form college examinations and a degree course in music that he didn't finish. 'There's a list of various jobs, none particularly significant, and he carried on with his music studies in his spare time. There's no doubt he gained a very extensive musical knowledge, which eventually led to his appointment at Branwell College.'

'Rainbird didn't do things by halves, did he?' said Sukey. 'I wonder what made him make this check in the first place. Maybe something Freeman let slip roused his curiosity. Or maybe he just has an abnormally curious nature. We've already agreed that there was something odd about him – a personality problem perhaps.'

'He certainly seems to have taken a more than usual interest in a lot of the people he associates with. There's a lot of stuff about various people; even his cleaning lady gets a mention. "A pretty Polish lady who pretends not to understand if I point out something she's missed". He makes a comment about his neighbour, the old busybody you spoke to. He's written, "If I enjoyed a chat it wouldn't be with her". Then there are titbits about the girls in his office that he picked up while listening to their gossip.'

'This is fascinating stuff, Guv, but I don't see how it helps us in our search for the Dallington Manor killer.'

'Aha, I've saved the best till last.' With a gesture that made Sukey think of a conjuror producing a pack of cards from the air, he called up a file named Luke Grayson. 'Have a look at that while I get a refill, but don't spend much time on the early stuff; the last couple of pages are where it gets interesting. Do you fancy a coffee?' he added, somewhat to her surprise.

'Thanks, Guv, that'd be great.' She scrolled down the screen and felt her pulses tingle with excitement as intimate details of Grayson's private life emerged. She soon learned that Mrs Franks was not his first lover. Before she came on the scene he was having an affair with a lady member of the golf club which came to an end when she suffered a stroke and died two years after the relationship started. 'There's something odd here, Guv,' she said when Rathbone returned to his seat. 'Yvette Daniels, the woman he'd been having an affair with for a couple of years, died just over five years ago, but Mrs Franks told me her affair with Grayson started about three years ago, soon after her husband died.'

'I thought you'd pick up on that,' said Rathbone. 'There's no mention here of another affair before the one with Franks, and as he seems to be something of a Casanova I doubt if he'd wait a couple of years before finding another floozie. Geoffrey Franks died about the same time as Mrs Daniels. The question is, was it just a slip of the tongue on Cynthia Franks' part when she was in a state of considerable distress, or was it a deliberate lie? If it was a lie, we need to know the reason; in any case it not only throws doubt on Grayson's alibi but also, if he's aware of the existence of this dossier, gives him a powerful motive for murder.'

'For murdering Rainbird perhaps, Guv, but we've been working on the assumption that Rainbird and Law were killed by the same person. Law was killed on the Sunday – but of course, that was the day Grayson was here to identify his brother's body.'

'So he knew somehow that Law was about to sell his story and had to kill him as well. Maybe you're right about the gloves, Sukey; if they have Grayson's DNA in them the case is as good as in the bag. By the way, when did Rainbird start his present job?'

'According to Mr Ashman, Guv, Rainbird started working for his firm about five years ago; it's obvious from these entries that it didn't take him long to twig that Grayson was up to no good. In addition to his extreme curiosity, he must also have exceptional powers of observation.'

'Plus a very keen ear, which would enable him to listen into private conversations in the office – and possibly account for his interest in music. It's time we had a further word with Grayson and his lady love.'

'There's one thing that puzzles me,' said Sukey. 'Barbara Baker, one of the girls in Grayson's office who had a private word with us after we'd interviewed him, didn't mention anything suggesting that Grayson had been leaving the straight and narrow, but they seemed to think it more than likely that Rainbird had some sort of love life. We know now that they were right, but there's no hint of anything personal in this.'

'He obviously doesn't feel the need to keep a record of his own love life,' said Rathbone.

'Let's hope the diary I found in his flat – if it is a diary – will give us a lead, Guv.'

'I suppose it might be useful if we could identify this mystery woman, but first things first. I'll report this to DCI Leach right away; my guess is he'll tell us to pick up Grayson and the Franks woman and bring them here for interview.'

TWENTY-FOUR

'The missing baby was found safe and well so I've brought DC Osborne back into the Dallington Manor case,' Rathbone told Sukey on his return from Leach's office. 'My instructions are to leave Vicky and Tim to carry on with the search; Tim and Penny will interview Cynthia Franks while you and I tackle Grayson. I take it you have Franks' address.'

'Yes, Guv. She lives in Isleworth, not far from Grayson but in a slightly less prestigious part.'

'Within easy reach of London then; good, we can all travel most of the way together. I don't imagine you're keen to drive into the city centre and in any case I'd prefer to go by train.

Once we get there we'll bé going in separate directions. Work out some details and times and get back to me.'

'Will do, Guv.' She logged on to the Internet, retrieved the information she needed and called him back. 'It's quite straightforward; we get a train from Bristol Parkway to Waterloo; from there you and I get the tube to St Paul's and Penny and Tim go by British Rail to Isleworth. I've no idea how far her house is from the station but if it's a long way they can probably get a taxi.'

'I'm not authorizing any taxi fares,' said Rathbone. 'They can go by bus, and if there isn't a bus they can walk from the station; the exercise will do them good. And there'll be no advance phone calls to make appointments. We'll get there at a time that suits us and catch the blighters with their pants down.' After making a few calculations, he decided that they should time their arrival so as to reach their respective destinations in the middle of the afternoon. 'If my reckoning is correct,' he continued, 'Grayson will have had lunch but will probably plan to leave early; on the other hand, if he was too shaken to face the office after having his cover blown he'll have called in sick and be skulking at home, or he'll have flown to the arms of his lady love for solace.'

'In which case he'll be there when Tim and Penny ring her doorbell,' said Sukey.

'I've thought of that; I'll tell them to be sure their phones are charged up and to call me immediately if he is.'

By three o'clock they were at Waterloo Station. 'Good hunting,' said Rathbone before Tim and Penny went to buy their tickets. 'Feel free to call me if there's anything significant to report or you need further instructions. Sukey, I hope you managed to find your way round the underground during your weekend here.'

'I did use it a couple of times, Guv, so I've a good idea how it works. I've been checking the map and I think I can manage to get us to St Paul's station.'

'Then lead on. By the way, I'll leave it to you to take over the questions when we come to the subject of his religious beliefs; you're more up in that sort of thing than I am.'

He sounds like a kid going to a football match, thought Sukey as she led the way down the escalator leading to the platforms.

He's pinning a lot on this; I hope he's right, but I still think
those gloves have something to do with the case and I don't see
how Grayson could have got hold of them. In any case, if he
really did go to Dallington Manor with the express intention of
throttling Rainbird with his bare hands, surely he'd have had the
nous to take his own gloves.*

The question was still hovering at the back of her mind as
they went up to the desk, where the receptionist, whose name
Sukey recalled was June, was speaking on the phone. The recog-
nition was evidently mutual; her face registered a slight unease
at their approach; she said something in a low voice and put the
phone down before saying in a tone that was intended to sound
normal and relaxed but was in fact neither. 'Good afternoon, Ms
Reynolds! What brings you here again?'

'We want to see Mr Luke Grayson.' Rathbone held up his ID
and June's eyes widened as she studied it.

'I'll tell him you're here, Inspector,' she said hastily. She
pressed buttons and said, 'Mr Grayson, Detective Inspector
Rathbone and Detective Constable Reynolds are here to see you.'
She held the receiver a short distance from her ear as a series of
indignant squawks came from it. She listened for a few moments
before saying, 'Very well, Mr Grayson,' and cradled the instrument. 'He says it's extremely inconvenient but he can spare you
a few minutes. If you take the lift to the tenth floor he'll meet
you there. Oh, just a moment, please.' She held out two visitor
badges. 'Please take one of these and sign in.'

'We won't be staying long, and this –' Rathbone held up his
ID for a second time – 'will do just as well as one of those.'

As before, Grayson was waiting by the lift; without a word
he conducted them to a convenient room, flung open the door
changed the notice outside from 'Free' to 'Occupied' before
entering behind them and sitting down without inviting them to
join him. His face was a dull red. 'I don't know what the hell
this is about, but at least you might have had the courtesy to let
me know you wanted to speak to me again. This is extremely
embarrassing, to say the least.'

Rathbone pulled up a couple of chairs and made sure Sukey
was comfortably seated with her notebook at the ready before
sitting down himself. 'You'd have preferred advance warning, no

doubt, and a more convenient time and venue,' he began, 'so that you could avoid giving your colleagues any more reason to gossip – and probably take the opportunity to call Cynthia Franks and make sure the two of you got your story straight in case we were planning to talk to her as well.'

'How dare you bring her into it?' Grayson spluttered. He looked appealingly at Sukey. 'You know our story, Constable Reynolds and you know the reason I lied about the time I was at the Ritz hotel. Cynthia is prepared to risk her reputation by swearing that she was with me that night.'

Sukey could not resist saying quietly, 'When it comes to reputations, I seem to remember you were more concerned with your own than hers.' He compressed his lips and avoided meeting her eye.

'May I remind you, Mr Grayson, that we are conducting a murder enquiry,' said Rathbone. 'I admit that at first we could see no possible reason to suspect you of killing Rainbird. As you yourself pointed out, what possible motive could you have?'

'Exactly,' said Grayson, 'so why waste my time and yours with further pointless questions?'

'Because,' Rathbone said, 'we have discovered that you have a very strong motive. Lance Rainbird knew all about your guilty secret.'

Grayson's mouth fell open. 'How on earth . . .?' he began.

'It's amazing what one can find out using the various social networking services on the Internet. It was not difficult for one of our technical experts to read the files on Mr Rainbird's laptop and discover not only your affair with Mrs Franks but also details of a previous liaison. I put it to you, Mr Grayson,' Rathbone went on, 'that he wanted something from you which you were reluctant to give him and that, armed with this information which no doubt you wished to remain secret, he put some kind of pressure on you, threatened you with exposure, if you refused his demands. What did he want as a payment for his secrecy – money, promotion?'

'I . . . I simply have no idea what you're talking about,' said Grayson. 'He never made any demands on me; I had very little to do with him that wasn't directly concerned with work.'

'Except during your rather vitriolic exchanges over religious matters,' said Sukey, as Rathbone invited her with a glance to put the next question.

'Well, yes.'

'We understand that you are – or claim to be – a committed Christian.'

'That's true. I wouldn't be surprised to learn that in common with a lot of young people nowadays, you are either a pagan or have no beliefs at all.'

'On the contrary, I too am a Christian. We are told not to judge others, but I'm afraid I tend to feel rather judgemental about hypocrisy. Did Lance Rainbird by any chance accuse you of hypocrisy?'

By this time it was evident that Grayson was feeling very uncomfortable. He clasped and unclasped his hands and hesitated before saying, 'He may have done. He said a lot of very offensive things.'

'Did it not occur to you that to call you a hypocrite would imply that he knew something about you that would suggest that you did not always practise what you preach?' He did not answer. 'So in your heart of hearts you knew that particular accusation was justified.'

'I can assure you I never paid any attention to anything Lance Rainbird said. At first I tried to reason with him, bring him to faith, I even prayed for him.' He made a slightly despairing gesture. 'But I've told you all this before.'

'Indeed you have, but now we want to know more about things you didn't tell us,' said Rathbone. 'Your affair with Mrs Franks, for example; she stated that she was with you on the night that Lance Rainbird was murdered and you did not contradict that statement. Why not?' Grayson remained silent. 'Now, what about the second murder at Dallington Manor on Sunday, two days after the first?'

'A second murder?' Grayson appeared stunned. 'Who else was murdered?'

'One of the waiters. You didn't know?'

'Of course I didn't. How could I have known?'

'But you were in the neighbourhood on Sunday because you were in Bristol to identify your brother's body – just a short drive from Dallington Manor. We have reason to believe that Reg Law witnessed the attack on Rainbird, that his attacker became aware of this and decided that he too had to be silenced.' Before Grayson had time to reply Rathbone's phone rang; he made an excuse and left the room. When he returned his face was grim. 'Mr Grayson,' he said, 'that call was from one of the detectives who are at this moment interviewing Mrs Franks.' He sat down and leaned forward so that his face was just a few inches from Grayson's. 'After some intensive questioning, Mrs Franks has retracted the statement I have just referred to. It appears that you have no alibi after all.' As Grayson appeared to have lost the power of speech, Rathbone said, 'Luke Grayson, I am arresting you on suspicion of the murders of Lance Rainbird and Reginald Law.' He briefly recited Grayson's rights before standing up and opening the door. 'Shall we go?'

'Can't I at least call my wife and tell her not to expect me home? Oh God, I've just remembered; we've got some people coming for dinner this evening. What shall I tell her?'

'You may tell her what you like.'

There was a telephone on the table; Grayson picked it up with a trembling hand, called reception and asked for an outside line. There was a short pause before he said in a voice thick with embarrassment, 'Marjorie, something's come up and I have to be away this evening . . . possibly overnight . . . well, I'm afraid you'll have to put them off . . . I'm very sorry dear, I haven't time to explain at the moment . . . I'll call you again as soon as possible.' He put down the receiver and stood up. 'At least let me pick up my coat and briefcase.'

'Constable Reynolds will collect them for you.'

It was nearly half past seven when they reached the headquarters of the Avon and Somerset Police. While the duty sergeant was admitting Grayson and arranging for him to be escorted to an interview room to await questioning, Rathbone took the opportunity of asking Tim and Penny for a brief report on their interview with Cynthia Franks.

'She was at home on her own when we arrived,' Tim began, 'and as you can imagine she was pretty shocked to see us. She said it wasn't very convenient and could we come back later? We said we couldn't agree to that as we naturally assumed she was hoping to call Grayson, so after a bit of havering she let us in. We then asked her if she would like to have a woman friend with her while we were questioning her, but it was obvious that was the last thing she wanted.'

'In the forlorn hope of keeping her affair with Grayson under wraps, of course,' said Rathbone. 'Anyway, all we know at the moment is that she's retracted her statement about spending the night with lover-boy. What made her do that?'

'Without giving details we told her that we had evidence that Grayson had a very strong motive for killing Lance Rainbird and asked her whether she was still prepared to swear that he was with her the night he died.'

'She didn't answer immediately,' said Penny, 'which could only have meant one thing; she had lied to us to give him an alibi in the total belief in his innocence, but was now having her doubts. It was as if she was wrestling with her conscience.'

'That was the moment Penny said something about bearing false witness, and the poor thing just fell apart,' said Tim. 'We found a half bottle of whisky and gave her a drop of that and waited until she had control of herself. She said she didn't know where Grayson was the night Rainbird died and she'd only said it to help him.'

'She loves him very much,' said Penny. 'It was bad enough to have learned how deceitful he was, but the thought of him being capable of murder was just too much to stomach. I felt really sorry for her.'

'Then she started worrying about whether she was going to be in trouble for wasting our time,' said Tim. 'I said we couldn't be sure but thought it unlikely.'

'That'll be up to DCI Leach, but probably not,' said Rathbone. 'Well done Penny for appealing to her conscience; that was a master-stroke.'

Penny's face lit up at the compliment. 'Thank you, sir.'

'You two might as well go home,' said Rathbone. 'Sukey and I will have a preliminary chat with Grayson; he may want to call his solicitor before saying anything.'

'What about tomorrow, Guv?' asked Tim.

'You can sit in while Vicky, Sukey and I give Grayson a more thorough grilling.'

'And the search at Dallington Manor?'

'Forget that. I really think we've got our man this time.'

Grayson, his face expressionless, sat at the table while a uniformed officer stood impassively behind him. Rathbone switched on the video recorder; he and Sukey sat down facing him. 'This will be only a short interview, Mr Grayson, as it is already after eight o'clock. Before we go any further, would you like to have a word with your solicitor? You are entitled to call him, or if you prefer we can ask a duty solicitor to attend.'

'My solicitor lives in London and I can hardly expect him to travel to Bristol at this ungodly hour,' said Grayson. 'In any case, I believe he is on holiday at the moment.'

'Are you prepared to answer my questions without legal advice, then?'

Grayson passed a hand over his eyes. 'I haven't anything new to tell you that I haven't already told you,' he said wearily. 'All right, Cynthia lied to give me an alibi and I didn't contradict her so it was natural that you should wish to check with her a second time. I admit it's come as a shock that she has withdrawn that statement, but I was never happy about her telling untruths on my behalf. All I can do is repeat what I originally told DC Reynolds and her sergeant, that I spent the night at home alone but I can't prove it.'

'Do you still maintain that you had no idea that Rainbird knew about your love affairs, especially the current one with Mrs Franks?'

'It never entered my head. As I've said before, I never got to know him and I always thought of him as a loner.'

'So it would surprise you to know that in addition to his researches into your love life he had certain information about a number of other people?'

'I'm beginning to think nothing would surprise me. Perhaps one of them killed him; I certainly didn't.'

'Most of them are mere acquaintances and above suspicion – his cleaning lady for example – but it so happens that Rainbird approached one of them and pressured him into taking certain actions.'

'So who is this person? Why isn't he sitting here instead of me?'

'He has been eliminated from our enquiries.'

Grayson's shoulders sagged and he seemed to sink deeper into his chair. He made an effort to pull himself together, but Rathbone said, 'You appear to be very tired, so I think we'll leave it until you've had some rest. This officer will make you comfortable for the night and bring you some food.' He switched off the recorder. 'Sleep well.'

TWENTY-FIVE

The uniformed officer led Grayson away and Sukey and Rathbone went back to the CID office.

'Good night, Guv,' said Sukey as she put on her jacket and slung her bag over her shoulder. 'See you in the morning.'

'Can you spare a couple of minutes?'

'Yes, of course.'

She followed him into his office. He closed the door, waved her to a chair and went to the coffee machine. 'Fancy a cup?' he said.

'Not now, thank you.'

She watched him while he prepared his drink. He seemed to move more slowly and deliberately than usual, taking his time about filling the cup with coffee and stirring in milk and sugar, as if he needed time to think about what he was going to say. She knew him well enough to recognize the signs and guessed that he had something on his mind; his next words confirmed it.

'You and I have worked together for several years now, haven't we?' he said as he sat down.

'That's right, Guv.'

'Forget the Guv for a moment. This is between friends, OK?'

Sukey nodded and smiled. 'That's fine by me.'

'We've had a few chats about things other than the job,' he continued. 'I recall sharing some of my family problems with you and you always lent a sympathetic ear. And you seemed genuinely pleased when I told you how well things had settled down.'

'It's always good to hear of a real-life happy ending,' she replied. Just in time she checked the impulse to say 'Guv'. 'Forgive me if I'm wrong, but I have a feeling something else is troubling you; I hope all is well with your boy. He must be in his senior school by now.'

'In his second year and doing very well thank you. No, this isn't a private matter; it's this wretched Dallington Manor case. I was so sure Freeman was our man, but we couldn't find enough evidence to hold him, let alone charge him. And then, when we looked more closely at his story it did seem feasible. We've got you and Vicky to thank for that.' He broke off to take a mouthful of coffee. 'When you found out about Grayson's love life, plus the information the techies found in Rainbird's laptop, everything seemed to point to him and I felt just as confident as I had over Freeman. And now I'm beginning to have my doubts about him as well.' He rapped the desk with his knuckles in frustration. 'My first case as a DI and I'm really struggling. I have a feeling DCI Leach is beginning to have second thoughts about recommending me for promotion.'

'I'm sure that's not true,' she assured him. 'It is one hell of a case and we've all been feeling pretty frustrated, but I'm sure Mr Leach knows that you're doing everything you possibly can to get a result. I have to admit I share your doubts about Grayson; there's no doubt he had a motive but the only evidence we have against him is circumstantial and not enough to detain him. But if neither he nor Freeman is our man, the question is where else to look? From a quick scroll down Rainbird's laptop there doesn't appear to be anyone else there with means, motive and opportunity.'

'You're right,' he agreed despondently. 'In fact Freeman is the only one actually known to have been at Dallington Manor when both Rainbird and Law were killed, with Grayson another possibility on the grounds that he had an even stronger motive and has no alibi, plus he was actually in the neighbourhood the day of Law's murder. We'll have a thorough go at him tomorrow and see how long it will be before he breaks. And if he doesn't break, I can't for the life of me think where to look next.' He took refuge once again in his coffee, swallowed and then waved the empty cup to and fro as he continued, 'I'm pretty sure of one thing; Rainbird and Law were killed by the same person. Rainbird's murder was premeditated, Law was killed out of necessity – he simply became a threat and had to be eliminated. But who carried out those murders? Where else do we start looking? You know what, Sukey? What we need is another of your famous hunches.'

'I'll see what I can do,' she promised, and he held out a hand.

'You're a mate,' he said, and for the first time that day he appeared to relax. 'Thanks for listening. See you in the morning.'

When Sukey reached home she found a message from Harry. 'Another day in court and none of the accused is cracking so far. How has your day gone?'

'It's getting interesting. Rainbird's laptop has some very interesting stuff in it that we have to follow up.'

'A new lead?'

'Maybe, but I'm not saying any more for now.'

'Not even the tiniest hint?' he wheedled.

'I'm sorry. Like I said, I promise you'll be the first to know once any info is released.'

'OK, I understand.' He yawned. 'It's been a long day and I'm turning in when I've watched the news. Talk tomorrow, love you.'

The next morning Rathbone greeted the team with the news that Grayson had managed to contact his own solicitor who, as he suspected, was on holiday in Austria. His advice was to use the services of a duty solicitor, so it was not until half past nine that Rathbone, Vicky and Sukey, with Mike and Tim as observers, assembled in the interview room, where Grayson and Fiona Girling, the duty solicitor and a woman of about his own age awaited them.

'Right, Mr Grayson,' said Rathbone after completion of the formalities, 'I hope you had a comfortable night.'

'I've known better,' Grayson responded with a shrug.

'And a good breakfast?'

'It could have been worse.'

'Right then. Let's go over the facts of the case. We know that Lance Rainbird was murdered and we know from the evidence in his personal files that he had enough information about your private life to cause you acute embarrassment, to say the least, and possibly financial ruin.'

'One moment, Inspector,' said Fiona Girling, 'my client has told me that he has not personally seen this file and has only your word that the information you refer to was contained in it.'

'It is true that he has not actually seen the file, but when confronted with the information it contains he made no attempt to deny it. In addition, even before this came to light he had lied about his own movements at the crucial time.'

'He maintains he had no intention of lying; it was a natural mistake.'

'One which would have gone unnoticed but for the fact that last Saturday my colleague, DC Reynolds, happened to be in the place he claimed to have been and took the opportunity of checking your client's statement.'

'I should like to hear from Constable Reynolds herself why she is so sure my client was lying about his whereabouts.'

Rathbone nodded at Sukey and she scrolled back in her notebook. 'When my colleague DS Armstrong and I interviewed your client in his office last Tuesday afternoon I asked him as a matter of routine where he was between the hours of eight p.m. and midnight on the previous Friday and he said he was at the Ritz hotel, checking the arrangements for his mother-in-law's birthday party the following day.'

'Do you accept that as a true record?' asked Rathbone. Grayson nodded.

'It so happened,' Sukey continued, 'that last Saturday I was lunching with a friend at the Rivoli Bar in the Ritz hotel and while there I took the opportunity of speaking to the events manager. He confirmed that your client was there on the day in question, but was quite positive that it was in the morning, not the evening.'

'Thank you,' said Rathbone. 'Have you any further questions, Ms Girling?'

'Not for the moment.'

Rathbone turned back to Grayson. 'The fact remains that without the evidence of your lover, Cynthia Franks, who was prepared at first to swear that you were with her but has now formally withdrawn that statement, you have no alibi for the night

Rainbird was murdered in the grounds of Dallington Manor hotel. I put it to you, Mr Grayson,' Rathbone struck the desk with his forefinger to emphasize each point, 'that Rainbird had told you he was in possession of information that would ruin you if it were made public, that he made certain demands as the price of his silence and that, having agreed to meet him, ostensibly to discuss those demands, you knocked him unconscious and pushed him into the lake, where he was later found drowned by a member of the hotel staff.'

'No!' Grayson sat erect in his chair and met Rathbone's gaze without flinching. 'I categorically deny the accusation.'

'And I further put it to you,' Rathbone continued as if Grayson had not spoken, 'that your attack on Rainbird was witnessed by one of the waiters at the hotel, that he too threatened you with exposure, and that two days later you found an opportunity to waylay him and throttle him.'

'That is completely untrue.'

'As untrue as Mrs Franks' original statement that she spent Friday evening and all night with you?'

Grayson had the grace to appear shamefaced. 'I admit I did not contradict her statement when she made it in DC Reynolds' presence. I was not comfortable with it, but . . .'

Rathbone pounced. 'You hoped – and no doubt believed – that Constable Reynolds would accept her statement without question so that you would not be exposed as a liar for the second time. Did you really suppose that an experienced detective would be that naive?'

'I don't deny that to allow her to lie on my behalf was a cowardly act of which I am deeply ashamed.' Grayson's attitude changed from defiance to contrition, but he still met Rathbone's eye without flinching. 'I can only repeat that I was at home alone from midday on Friday until my wife returned with her mother on Saturday morning.'

'I believe the party was on Saturday evening. When did your mother take her mother home?'

'On Sunday afternoon.'

'Did she return the same day?'

'No, she came home first thing Monday morning. By then of course she had learned of my brother John's death in the road accident. My wife is not a churchgoer but she did accompany me to church and sat with me holding my hand while I prayed for him.'

'You are fortunate to have such a devoted and supportive wife,' said Rathbone. 'Perhaps if she was aware that you have consistently been unfaithful to her she would be less sympathetic?'

'That's a cruel thing to say, Inspector,' Grayson protested. 'She was very fond of my brother and shared my grief. And before you put any more offensive questions, it so happens that for reasons which are highly personal my wife has accepted the fact that I have found the need to seek . . . what I might describe as certain solace . . . elsewhere.'

'And she knew the identity of your current mistress?'

'I doubt it; as I said before, she isn't a churchgoer.'

'But she will no doubt be prepared to confirm that she was familiar with your special needs?'

'I'm certain she will, but do you really have to drag her into this? She knows about Lance Rainbird's death, but she has no idea that I'm a suspect for his murder. I shall of course have to explain my sudden absence when I return home.'

'Inspector Rathbone,' said Fiona Girling, 'my client has admitted that his marital arrangements are unconventional but it is obvious that they are totally irrelevant to this case.'

'May I remind you, Ms Girling,' he replied without shifting his gaze from Grayson, 'that this is a murder enquiry and it is our duty to explore every possible avenue in our efforts to find the culprit, no matter how distasteful some people may find it. Mr Grayson, I put it to you again that, fearing Lance Rainbird would divulge the details of your sordid behaviour and so ruin your reputation, and unwilling to accede to whatever conditions he offered in exchange for his silence, you killed him, and subsequently killed Reginald Law because he had witnessed the attack and threatened you with exposure.'

'I can only repeat what I have told you all along – I am totally innocent of these murders.'

Recalling how with one simple question Penny had caused Cynthia Franks to admit that she had given her lover a false alibi, Sukey gave Rathbone a discreet glance. He responded with a brief nod. 'Mr Grayson,' she said, 'as a committed Christian, are you prepared to swear on the Bible that what you have just told us is the truth?'

He solemnly raised his right hand. 'As God is my witness, it is the absolute truth.'

'Does that satisfy you, Inspector?' Fiona Girling gathered her papers together as if the interview was as good as over. 'Apart from a few shreds of circumstantial evidence you have found no valid excuse for detaining my client, or indeed for having arrested him in the first place. I shall be giving him some further advice on that, but I now insist that you either charge him or release him immediately and unconditionally.'

Rathbone got up and left the room. He was absent for a short time; when he returned he said stiffly, 'Thank you, Mr Grayson, you are free to go.' To the group of waiting detectives he said, 'Right, we're finished in here.'

They followed him in silence. The moment they were outside and the door shut behind them he said, 'Right, Mr Leach's office in fifteen minutes. Grab yourselves a coffee and meet me there.'

'Sit down everyone,' said Leach when they assembled in his office. 'At least yesterday wasn't a total write-off; we've finally eliminated a very strong suspect.'

'Fiona Girling was dropping hints about bringing a case against us for harassment and wrongful arrest, sir,' said Rathbone. 'You know what she's like; she may persuade him he has a case.'

Leach shook his head. 'She has an eye to a fee, no doubt, but she must be well aware that we'd contest it and the last thing Grayson would want is to have his dirty linen washed in court.' He chuckled. 'The paparazzi would have a field day. Now, we have to think seriously about where we go from here. By the way, I haven't written Freeman out of the frame, even though Sukey gave him a good character. Greg, I believe you've sent the gloves Sukey found in the waste bin at Dallington Manor and various samples she found in Rainbird's flat for DNA testing.'

'That's right, sir.'

'Did you ask for them to be fast-tracked?'

'Well, no sir. Do you want me . . .?'

'Leave it with me.' Leach made a note on his pad. 'What about the lady's handkerchief Sukey found under Rainbird's pillow?'

'I've kept that, sir. I assumed it belonged to Rainbird's lady friend and even if she had reason to murder him it was unlikely she'd travel to Dallington Manor and strangle him.'

'A reasonable assumption,' Leach agreed, 'but it may yet prove useful so be sure and hang on to it. Now, about the diary that was hidden under Rainbird's bed, you told me you'd sent that to forensics for possible finger prints. Any joy there?'

'I'm afraid not, sir. There are traces of prints on the cover but all badly smudged. They think she probably kept it in her handbag where it would have rubbed up against the usual odds and ends women carry around with them. It's not a diary, by the way; it's an address book.'

'In that case it might yield some useful information. Go through it and see if you can identify any addresses within a reasonable radius of Rainbird's flat. Yes, Vicky?' he said as she put up a hand.'

'We learned from our enquiries among the people in Freeman's group, sir, that some of the women found Rainbird attractive. Do you think it might be worth finding out which of them attend his events regularly, if they live fairly near him, if they're married and whether their husbands normally accompany them?'

'You're thinking of one of them being the owner of the handkerchief and the diary, with her jealous husband being our man, I take it?'

'It seems like a possibility, sir.'

'Good thinking. OK Greg, get your people busy. That's all for now.'

TWENTY-SIX

When the team reported to Rathbone the following morning he summoned them to his office and said, 'I see no point in spending further time ferreting around at Dallington Manor, so Mike, Tim and Penny can go and start work on the cases that have come in the past couple of days. I'll be with you in a moment to allocate the jobs.'

'Right, Guv,' said Mike. Sukey noticed that all three appeared relieved at the decision.

'Vicky,' Rathbone continued, 'you will get hold of Freeman and get him to check his records and let you know which of the married couples or women on their own would have been to the same events as Rainbird. If any of them live within, say, a five- or ten-mile radius of Rainbird's pad, make sure you have their address and phone number and come back to me for further instruction.'

'Right, Guv.'

He handed the address book to Sukey. 'You will make a similar check in this. From a quick glance through I notice that not every entry has an address but they all have phone numbers, so one way or the other you should be able to find what you need. Both of you are to report to me as soon as you turn up anything significant.'

'This could either turn out to be a doddle or a monumental task,' said Vicky when she and Sukey returned to the CID office. 'By the way,' she added in a lower voice, 'I had the impression yesterday that Sir wasn't exactly a happy bunny, but he seems to have bucked up today even though we're no nearer a result. Was something bugging him?'

'Why do you ask me?'

'He's been different since his promotion, and I've been wondering if he's asking himself if he's really up to the job. From what you've told me he hasn't got anyone close, so . . .'

'So you thought he might have dropped a hint in my ear? If you must know, as we were leaving yesterday after having eliminated Grayson, he did mention that he was feeling frustrated at the lack of progress on his first case as a DI, but I pointed out that it was one hell of a case and that DCI Leach probably shared his frustration. He seemed to cheer up when I said that.'

'Understandable, I suppose, but Mr Leach didn't say anything to suggest he felt our DI, or any of us come to that, had missed out on anything in particular. Right, I guess we'd better get on with our researches.'

They had been working for a while on their respective tasks. Sukey was checking a telephone number on her computer when Vicky came and tapped her on the shoulder. 'I think I may have found something,' she said.

'I'm glad to hear it,' said Sukey. 'I haven't had any luck so far. What is it?'

'You remember Hugh Pearson?'

'Yes, of course. He was the rather grumpy man in the Aran sweater whose wife couldn't be with him because her sister had flu? What about him?'

'I remember he seemed a bit ill at ease when we spoke to him. And guess what, they live in Richmond. And I'm sure you also remember that the Days mentioned Julie Pearson as one of Rainbird's admirers who always sided with him in his spats with Eric Bowen?'

'You're thinking maybe her husband suspected, or even knew, that she was having an affair with Rainbird and took the opportunity of killing him when she was unable to be with him?'

'And was spotted by Reg Law, who very foolishly didn't go straight to the police but tried to sell his story to the press?'

'It's feasible. He was there on Sunday as well. He could have overheard Law's call to Harry.'

'But Freeman hadn't noticed anyone absent from the afternoon session.'

'That's true, but he was probably feeling a bit stressed at the time, there were over forty people in the group and he might not have noticed. Anyway, I'm going to report this to Sir and see what he has to say.'

'I'm going to take a coffee break,' said Sukey. When she returned to her work station Vicky was on the telephone and Sukey heard her say, 'Three o'clock tomorrow afternoon. That's fine. Thank you very much, Mrs Pearson.'

'Don't tell me you've struck oil?' said Sukey.

'I've had a chat with Mrs P. She sounded very wary at first, couldn't think how she could possibly help with the enquiry, wasn't even there and so forth, but I managed to persuade her that it was just to tie up a loose end. She said she had to have a word with her husband first and she'd call me back, which she's just done. So I have another trip to London.'

'Lucky you. I'm still trawling through the address book. I've got as far as H. without finding anything remotely feasible. Let's hope the rest of the alphabet will yield something useful.'

'With luck you could join me tomorrow,' said Vicky. 'I suppose

I'd better check on the rest of the people on Freeman's list, in case there's another possibility.'

They resumed their respective tasks. It was just before midday that Sukey gave a little squeak of excitement. 'Bingo!' she exclaimed. 'I've found a woman called Pansy with a local number . . . that is, it has the same area code as Rainbird's.'

'That sounds promising,' said Vicky. 'Have you got the address?'

'There's only the number in the book, but I can get the address from directory enquiry if she proves difficult. I'll check through the rest of the book before reporting to the boss.' She quickly flipped through the remaining pages but found nothing else significant.

'Is that the only one?' said Rathbone when she reported her findings. 'There's no address here so I presume it must be someone who lives near whoever our mystery woman is. Give her a call and see what you can get out of her.'

'Will do, Guv.' Sukey went back to her desk and dialled the number. A woman's voice said, 'Hullo, Pansy here. Who's calling?'

'This is Detective Constable Reynolds of the Avon and Somerset CID,' said Sukey. 'I apologize for bothering you, but we've found an address book with your name and phone number in it and we'd like to ask you one or two questions.'

There was a short silence before the woman said, 'I don't understand. Where did you find this book? And why do the police want to talk to me?'

'If you don't mind, I would prefer to explain in person. If we could agree on a convenient time for me to call?'

'Just a minute, how do I know you're the police? You could be a criminal trying to get me to open my door so you could rob me.'

'You are quite right to be suspicious,' said Sukey. 'May I suggest that you get on to directory enquiries and ask for the number of the Avon and Somerset Constabulary. Ring that number and ask to be put through to DC Reynolds of the CID. I'll be here waiting for your call.'

'All right.' Pansy put the phone down. Sukey turned to Vicky. 'Either she knows something and wants to check with whoever owns the book before talking to me, or genuinely suspects me of being a crook. If she doesn't call back I'll check with the DI; my guess is he'll tell me to get the address and turn up anyway.'

It was another five minutes before her phone rang. When she answered, Pansy said, 'You obviously are who you say you are, but I really don't understand why you want to talk to me.'

'As I said, I'd prefer to speak to you in person. Would some time tomorrow afternoon, say half past three, be convenient?'

A resigned sigh drifted over the line. 'Oh, all right. Here's where I live.' She dictated an address in Turnham Green. 'I hope you won't turn up in a police car; I don't want to give my neighbours something to gossip about.'

'I assure you that won't be the case. May I know your full name please?'

'I'm Mrs Pansy Denny.'

'Thank you for your cooperation, Mrs Denny. I'll see you tomorrow.' Sukey put the phone down to avoid further questions. 'Good,' she said to Vicky. 'That fits in nicely with your visit to Mrs Pearson. I'll go and check with Sir.'

'Ask him what we do about transport,' Vicky reminded her.

The following day, after an early lunch, the two detectives headed for Richmond in Vicky's car. When they reached the road where Pansy lived, Vicky drove slowly past the house, an impressive detached property not unlike the house where Luke Grayson lived. 'It's a pretty up market area,' Vicky commented as she pulled into the kerb and waited for Sukey to get out. 'Our mystery woman obviously has rich friends.'

'She may be in the same league herself,' said Sukey. 'I'm not surprised Pansy wanted to check my credentials, though. OK, I'll leave you to your visit to Mrs Pearson. I'll give you a call when I finish here. Good luck.' She waited until Vicky's car was out of sight before walking up to the front door. It opened before she touched the bell.

Mrs Denny was a slim woman in her fifties, immaculately dressed, with beautifully styled hair and discreet but flawless make up. Without a word she ushered Sukey into the house, taking a quick glance over her shoulder as if fearing her arrival might have been observed before closing the door. She led the way across a wide entrance hall and gestured with a manicured hand at a door in the corner. 'I hope this won't take long,' she said as she followed Sukey into the room, 'I have friends coming for cocktails later on.'

'I see no reason why it should take more than half an hour or so,' said Sukey as she sat down in the chair Mrs Denny indicated. The room was small, the only furniture being two chairs and a table on which stood a telephone, a directory and an address book.

Mrs Denny said, 'As I told you over the telephone, I can see no earthly reason why you should be so interested in me that a personal visit is necessary. If, having been satisfied as to your bona fides, I had given you my address, you could have put the book in the post to me and I could have given it to its owner.'

'That's an interesting point,' said Sukey, 'but what if I had asked you the address of the owner so that we could return it to her ourselves. It is a woman, isn't it?' she added as a faint flicker of unease dawned in Mrs Denny's carefully made-up eyes.

'Does that make a difference?' she asked.

'Does the name Lance Rainbird mean anything to you?'

Mrs Denny sucked in her lower lip. 'The name does sound familiar,' she said warily. 'Haven't I seen something in the paper recently about somebody called Rainbird having been drowned . . . in Clevedon wasn't it – oh, I understand now why you're interested.' Her attempt at a laugh had a brittle quality. 'Clevedon's in Somerset, isn't it? But I still don't understand . . .'

'It's true Mr Rainbird was found drowned in the lake in the grounds of Dallington Manor, which is a short distance from Clevedon,' said Sukey, 'but he lived in Kew – as I am sure you are aware,' she added, using Rathbone's technique of looking her subject directly in the eye. 'And it is in his flat that we found this address book.'

Mrs Denny covered her face with her hands. 'Oh my God, Pet, how could you have been so careless?'

'So you do know her? Will you give me her name and tell me where I can contact her?'

'She's my kid sister. I've promised from the beginning that I wouldn't breathe a word to a soul. How can I break my word? I couldn't live with myself if . . .'

'If her husband should find out she's been having an affair with Lance Rainbird?'

'She was heartbroken when he . . . when she heard of his death, and of course she had to hide it, as while it was obviously very shocking everyone had to believe it meant nothing to her personally. Why does it have to come out now?'

'Because,' said Sukey, 'Lance Rainbird's death was no accident. He was murdered. And we believe the owner of this address book can give us important information in our search for the killer.'

'Yes, I understand, but,' she broke off as if she had remembered something, 'did you say you found the book in Lance's flat?'

'That's right. It was under the bed.'

'Under the bed? Oh how stupid of me – I never thought of looking there.'

'So it was you who called at Mr Rainbird's flat on Saturday afternoon? His neighbour heard someone go in and assumed it was his "lady friend" as she referred to your sister.'

'That would have been the old busybody in the flat opposite, I suppose. My sister rang me on Saturday morning; she was very upset because she couldn't find her address book and she was terrified she'd left it in Lance's flat, so she asked me to go round and check, which I did. As I couldn't find it she assumed she'd either lost it somewhere else or simply mislaid it.'

'So both of you have a key to his flat?'

'No, he gave her just the one. She daren't take it home in case her husband notices a strange key on her bunch and asks questions, so she leaves it with me.'

'How long has the affair been going on?'

'It started about three – no, I think it was four years ago. She told me the first things she noticed about him were his smile and his voice and she was attracted right away. She said he was a strange character, didn't talk much; in fact, she told me the only other person he felt really at ease with was a man in his office. Have you spoken to him? I think his name is Ashman; perhaps he could help you. I really don't want Petunia involved.'

'We have spoken to Mr Ashman, but I'm afraid we really need to speak to your sister.'

'And if I refuse to tell you where she lives?'

'I'm sure you are aware that withholding vital information from the police is a serious offence and can result in prosecution.'

Mrs Denny got up and went to the door. 'I need a drink,' she said. 'Can I get you anything?'

'A glass of fruit juice would be nice, thank you.'

'Right, I'll be back in a moment.' She returned shortly after with a glass of orange juice for Sukey and what looked like a gin or vodka and tonic for herself. She sat down, took a mouthful of the drink and sat for a moment turning the glass in her hands. 'Pet's isn't a bad marriage,' she began, 'but it isn't ideal either. She was just twenty-one; I was a couple of years older, we were both pretty hard up and on our own.'

'Your parents were both dead?' asked Sukey.

'Yes. Our mother died of cancer when we were still in our early teens. Dad struggled on for a couple of years – he used to call us his little flowers. That's why he named us after some of his favourites; I'm Pansy Rose and my sister is Petunia L . . .' She broke off and took another mouthful of her drink. 'Anyway, Dad seemed to fade away after Mum died. There wasn't much money left after all the expenses were paid, just enough with what we earned from not very well paid jobs to keep the house. And then this man turned up at the recruitment agency where Pet worked, looking for a job and he obviously fancied her from the word go. He invited her out a few times; then he was interviewed for a job, got it, asked her to marry him and she accepted.'

'Was she in love with him?'

'Not madly; she liked him a lot, but she wasn't happy about leaving me on my own. I told her not to let that stand in her way so she went ahead. It was never an ideal relationship; he really loves her in his own way, which doesn't include much in the way of, well, the thing is my sister has a pretty healthy libido and Morry hardly ever . . .' Evidently embarrassed, she took refuge once again in her drink.

'I get the picture,' said Sukey. 'The chemistry between her and Lance was pretty lively from the time they met. It happens,' she added as thoughts of Harry flitted through her mind. She sternly dismissed them and said, 'I do understand why you're so anxious to protect not only your sister but her husband, but I'm afraid we have to speak to her. So will you please give me her name and address?'

'I suppose I'll have to, but I can't believe Morry would hurt anyone.'

'You'd be surprised at the number of times I've heard that about someone who's turned out to have a violent streak,' said Sukey.

'I think you'll be surprised at what I'm about to tell you,' said Mrs Denny.

As Sukey told Vicky when they spoke a short time later, 'surprised' was an understatement.

TWENTY-SEVEN

Sukey called Vicky as soon as she was out of sight of Mrs Denny's house. Vicky answered immediately.

'I was about to call you,' she said. 'I've just left the Pearsons. Hugh Pearson was there with his wife and to start with he gave me a bit of a hard time, said it was an intrusion and there was no need for a personal call, he'd had to leave his assistant in charge of the shop – he's a pharmacist with his own business – because he wasn't going to let his wife be bullied and so on. I managed to calm him down by explaining that it was a rather delicate matter and we felt a face-to-face interview would be more appropriate, so in the end he agreed, but he insisted on staying with her throughout the interview. Anyway, I think I'm on to something. The handkerchief doesn't belong to Julie Pearson but she recognized the perfume and she's pretty sure one of the office staff at Dallington Manor uses it as well. How did you get on anyway?'

'The address book belongs to a lady called Petunia, and Pansy, whose name is Mrs Denny, is her elder sister. Pansy was equally reluctant to talk because Petunia had sworn her to secrecy. Incidentally it was Pansy who checked Rainbird's flat after Harry and I went there because she was the one with the key. She explained that her sister was afraid to take it home in case her husband spotted it and started asking questions. In the end, I had to dangle the threat of being charged with refusing to divulge vital evidence in a murder enquiry before she agreed to talk.'

'So Petunia is our mystery lady?'

'She's no longer a mystery. You aren't going to believe this.'

'You're kidding!' Vicky exclaimed on hearing the name.

'I have to admit it knocked me sideways,' said Sukey. 'You said you'd left the Pearsons so I take it there's nothing more we can do in Richmond.'

'I can't think of anything else. I'll come and pick you up and we'll head for home. Will you give the DI a call and tell him what you've discovered? I've already told him about the handkerchief but he didn't seem to think it was much to go on. Perhaps he'll be more impressed with your stick of dynamite.'

'Let's hope so.'

To Sukey's surprise, Rathbone received her news with some reservation. 'I admit it does look pretty conclusive on the face of it,' he said, 'but I've had my fingers burned twice through jumping to conclusions without hard and fast evidence. All right, there's a pretty strong motive and opportunity for Rainbird's murder, but we'll need more than that to pin Reg Law's murder on him – unless of course we get a confession out of him. In fact I'm almost beginning to ask myself whether the two killings are related after all.'

'I understand why you feel you have to treat carefully, Guv. I guess you want time to think.'

'I want more than time – I want the results of the DNA test on those gloves you found in the rubbish bin. I'll have a word with DCI Leach and see if he can get top priority for them. Anyway, well done both of you.'

'Thanks, Guv. Vicky is on her way to pick me up and she'll bring me back to HQ to pick up my car. We should be there around seven thirty or eight o'clock, depending on the traffic.'

'I'll be leaving at eight, so if you're not back by then I'll see you in the morning. Goodbye.'

The motorway traffic was heavy and it was nearly half-past eight when Vicky dropped Sukey in the car park and they both headed for home. Having had nothing to eat since the canteen lunch and a bag of crisps picked up at the Membury service area,

Sukey went straight to the freezer and took out a ready meal before responding to the message Harry had left with her answering service.

'I've just got back from a trip to Richmond,' she told him when he answered.

'Richmond? What on earth were you doing there?'

'Interviewing two witnesses. At least, I went to see one and Vicky saw the other. They both lived quite close together, which was handy. Mine was one of the people whose names were listed in the address book we found in Rainbird's flat.'

'I presume they were able to tell you who the book belonged to?'

'It was a woman, and she was.'

'I detect a note of excitement in your voice. Have you struck oil?'

'I think we have, although Rathbone is playing it cool. He was convinced twice that we'd found our man, but we couldn't make it stick so he's scared stiff of making another mistake and he's made up his mind not to get too carried away without more evidence. He's right; there's still more to be collected but personally I'm pretty sure we're on the right track this time.'

'I don't suppose there's any chance of lifting the corner of the curtain so I can have a quick peek inside?'

'Not for the moment, but you could make sure your pencil's sharpened in the hope that there'll be a statement before the end of the week. Is there any news your end, by the way?'

'Yes, great stuff. The evidence against the cannabis farmers was so overwhelming that they threw in the towel and pleaded guilty, so they've been remanded to await trial. I'll be home tomorrow.'

'That's wonderful, Harry. See you then. Good night, love you.'

As a result of pressure from Superintendent Bradley, the results of the DNA on the gloves were waiting for DCI Leach the following morning. He immediately called DI Rathbone and said, 'That's all the evidence we need. Go and pick him up.'

Half an hour later, Rathbone, Vicky and Sukey were on their way to Dallington Manor. When they arrived, Maxine was at the reception desk and Rathbone sent Sukey to speak to her.

'Good morning,' she said, 'could I have a word with Mrs Chapman, please?'

'Certainly; she's in the office. Would you like to go through?'

'Thank you.'

Lily Chapman was seated in front of her computer. She looked up in surprise as Sukey entered, carefully closing the door behind her. 'Is there something you want?' she said, a little uneasily.

'That's a nice perfume you're wearing,' said Sukey. There was no reply. She took out of her pocket the transparent evidence bag containing the handkerchief. 'It's the same as the perfume on this. Do you recognize it?'

Lily Chapman gasped and put a hand to her mouth. After a moment she said in a barely audible whisper, 'Where did you find it?'

'It was under the pillow in Lance Rainbird's bed.'

Lily Chapman wept for several minutes, mopping her tears with the handkerchief. It was as if the pent-up grief at her lover's death had been released. Sukey waited patiently until she was calmer before saying. 'So you admit this belongs to you?'

'Yes.'

'Does your husband know about the affair?'

Lily nodded. 'He'd been watching us and he'd noticed the number of times he made excuses to ask for me at reception over something about his room or whatever. Then he started wondering why I had to visit my sister so often and he just put two and two together and one day he tackled me about it. We had a terrible row – the first since we were married – and then he broke down and started to cry and say it was his fault because he couldn't . . . that is . . . oh, it was dreadful, I felt sad for him too. Then he calmed down and begged me to forgive him, and of course I did.' Her look of distress changed to one of apprehension. 'Is that the only reason you're here, just to return my handkerchief?'

'I'm afraid not,' said Sukey gently. 'This is going to . . .'

Before she could finish, Maxine burst into the room. 'Lily, I can't believe this. Maurice has been arrested!'

'Arrested!' Lily appeared stunned. 'What is he accused of?' she asked Sukey. 'He didn't mean . . . I mean . . . that is, he hasn't done anything.'

'We need to ask him some questions,' said Sukey.

'What about? If it's about Lance . . . he didn't kill him . . . all he did was . . . it must be a dreadful mistake.'

'I'm afraid I can't tell you any more for the moment,' said Sukey. Every vestige of colour had drained from Lily's face and she collapsed into her chair. 'Will you take care of her, Maxine? I have to leave now, but if necessary I'll arrange for one of our people to look after her while her husband's in custody.'

Maurice Chapman sat in the interview room staring fixedly at Rathbone. Sukey, seated on Rathbone's right with Vicky on his left, noticed that his normally florid features seemed to have lost much of their colour. For the first time she looked closely at his hands, which he kept spread out on the table; like Freeman's, they had long, powerful-looking fingers. He was solidly built and she estimated that he was tall and strong enough to raise a baulk of timber and bring it down on Rainbird's head with sufficient force, if not to kill him, at least to render him unconscious. Her imagination moved on to imagine those hands gripping Law's throat.

Rathbone switched on the video recorder and warned Chapman that he was being interviewed under caution. Apart from confirming his name, he said nothing but waited for the first question.

'Were you aware that your wife was having an affair with Lance Rainbird?' asked Rathbone.

Chapman nodded. 'Yes.'

'How did you find out?'

'I'd suspected it for some time. He'd been coming regularly to Justin Freeman's music events and at other times as well. After a while I noticed something about the way they looked at each other when he checked in or came to the desk for any reason. I don't think any of the staff noticed it – certainly I never caught the slightest hint of gossip – but I sensed there was some sort of chemistry between them. And I got suspicious when she kept finding excuses to go and spend a couple of days with her sister, so one day I tackled her about it. She denied it at first, but I knew she was lying; in the end she broke down and admitted it and I forgave her. I love her very much.' For a moment he was overcome with emotion and Rathbone waited for him to control himself. 'But I couldn't forgive *him*.' He spat out the word as if it tasted rancid. 'I made up my mind that the next time he came I'd have it out with him.'

'By "having it out with him" you mean you hit him on the head with a baulk of timber that happened to be handy and then stood by and watched him fall in the lake and drown.'

'No!' Chapman half rose in his seat and PC Bond, who was standing behind him, laid a hand on his shoulder. He sank back into his chair and said in a firm voice, 'I wouldn't do that to Lily. I admit I attacked him but he was still alive when I left him.'

'So tell us exactly what happened.'

'I saw him go out into the grounds immediately after dinner and I followed him. He was down by the lake talking to Justin Freeman for five, maybe ten minutes and I sat down under the cypress tree and waited. When Freeman went back into the hotel I tackled Rainbird. I told him I knew about his affair with Lily and said it had to end. He looked at me as if . . . as if I was nothing . . . he sneered at me and said something . . . very insulting.' He broke off and stared at the table for several moments and Sukey guessed that pride prevented him from putting the insult into words. 'Anyway,' he said, 'I lost my rag and gave him a punch in the stomach. I was quite a handy middleweight boxer when I was young,' he added with an unexpected touch of pride.

'Did he fight back?' asked Rathbone.

'No, he staggered backwards and fell over, banging his head on one of the big lumps of timber lying by the edge of the lake. He didn't move for a minute and I was terrified I'd seriously injured him, but after a minute or two he managed to stand up. He was a bit unsteady on his feet but otherwise all right, so I just said something like "stay away from Lily unless you want more of the same" and came back into the hotel.'

'You came back to the hotel,' Rathbone repeated as if he wanted to make sure he had heard correctly, 'and presumably went about your normal business.'

'That's right.'

'And what happened next?'

'I was in my office when I heard a woman screaming and

came out just as Rosie came rushing in. She was hysterical and kept saying there was a man in the lake. I and a member of my staff, who has had some first-aid training, hurried to the scene and pulled the man out of the water; Ben tried artificial respiration but that didn't work so we called an ambulance. When it arrived the paramedics said he was dead and called a doctor.'

'Did you recognize the man?'

'Of course I did. It was Lance Rainbird.'

'And what were your feelings at that moment?'

'How do you think I felt? Shock, horror . . . disbelief, you name it. It seemed obvious at the time that it was just a dreadful accident, but you're now saying it was murder; well, all I can say is that he was conscious and on his feet the last time I saw him so someone else must have killed him after I left him. My chief concern after we learned that he was dead was for Lily. It was natural for her to appear upset, but she made heroic efforts to conceal the fact that she was affected personally. I'm really proud of her for that.'

'I'm sure you are. How did you feel when the police began interviewing everyone in an attempt to find out exactly how Rainbird came to be in the water?'

'It was disturbing for everyone, of course, but we all did our best to cooperate with the investigating officers.'

'It didn't occur to you to tell us at the time exactly what had happened?'

'I know I should have done, but I didn't want Lily to know I'd hit the man she obviously loved.'

'But she knew – or guessed – what happened and later she accused you of killing him?' Chapman nodded.

'When was that?'

Chapman hesitated before saying, 'I can't remember exactly – maybe a day or two later.'

'What was your reaction to her accusation?'

'We had a rather heated argument and I'm afraid I lost my temper and not only admitted that I'd hit Rainbird but I was glad he was dead.'

'Where did this "rather heated" argument take place?'

'In our private sitting room.'

'Where presumably no one is likely to have overheard – unless
of course your voices were raised so that anyone happening to
pass your room might have been tempted to stop for a moment
and listen to what was being said.'

Chapman sat for almost a minute without speaking. Then he
said in a quiet but determined voice, 'I'm not going to answer
any more questions without advice from my solicitor.'

Chapman introduced his solicitor as Alec Peters. He was a clean-
shaven, fresh-faced man whom Sukey judged to be about fifty,
although he might have passed for several years younger. His
manner was brisk and professional.

'Inspector Rathbone, my client emphatically denies being
responsible for the death of Lance Rainbird, but he admits
attacking him on the evening in question. He is aware that this
renders him liable to prosecution, but I understand you have not
so far charged him with any offence.'

'That is correct,' said Rathbone.

'May I ask why not? My client assures me that he has nothing
to add to his previous statement.'

'The reason,' said Rathbone 'is that we are also investigating
the murder of one of the waiters at Dallington Manor, Reginald
Law, which occurred two days after the death of Lance Rainbird.
We believe that your client may be able to help us with our
enquiries into that death as well.' He turned to Chapman. 'If you
remember, sir, you admitted earlier today that you had what you
described as a rather heated argument with your wife Lily "a
day or two" after the death of her lover, Lance Rainbird. Is that
correct?' Chapman glanced at Peters, who nodded.

'Yes, that is correct,' said Chapman.

'What started the argument?'

'It was Lily – she'd obviously been churning things over in
her mind and suddenly accused me of deliberately murdering
Rainbird because of their affair. I kept repeating that all I did
was give him a punch that knocked him over and that he was
alive and on his feet when I left him. In the end she accepted
my account of what happened.'

'What did you do then?'

'I switched on the television and left her to sit and watch that while I checked the arrangements for the refreshments for Mr Freeman's party.'

'That would be about what time?'

'They came down at about half-past three.'

'But you would have got there a bit earlier, to make sure everything was under control?'

'Of course.'

'Was Law one of the waiters on duty that afternoon?'

'He may have been. I can't tell you without checking the duty rotas.'

'I can save you the trouble,' said Rainbird. 'Detective Constable Reynolds has already checked with a member of your staff, who confirms that Law was on duty that afternoon and finished about eight o'clock. And when he came off duty, as was his habit, he went out into the grounds to have a cigarette.'

'Really, Inspector,' said Peters, 'I see no point in these questions. Surely you aren't suggesting that my client should be aware of the individual habits of every member of his staff?'

'You are right, I'm not suggesting anything of the kind,' said Rathbone. He turned back to Chapman. 'Our enquiries have revealed that Reginald Law informed a member of the local press that he could offer what he described as a tasty titbit in exchange for some payment.'

'So how does that concern my client?'

'It concerns your client because shortly after he had that heated argument with his wife he overheard Reginald Law making a further telephone call on his mobile phone – a call which told him immediately that their argument had been overheard and that what had been said was in danger of being made public.' He turned back to Chapman. 'I put it to you that on hearing that call you saw your marriage, your reputation and your business being ruined, that you followed Law into the garden and silenced him by taking him by the throat and throttling him.'

Chapman shook his head and cast a despairing glance at Peters, who said, 'Before I advise my client how to answer, may I know what evidence – if any – you have to support this accusation?'

'A perfectly reasonable request,' Rathbone said calmly. He laid on the table a transparent envelope containing a pair of white cotton gloves. 'Do you recognize these, Mr Chapman?'

Chapman stared at the gloves for a moment as if mesmerized. Then he said, 'They look like a pair of waiter's gloves.'

'Have you seen them before?'

'I've seen plenty like them. I can't possibly say if I've ever seen that particular pair.'

'We believe these gloves were worn by Reginald Law's killer. Are you sure you've never seen them before?'

'Really, Inspector,' said Peters, 'how can you possibly expect my client to identify this particular pair?'

'I admit that identification is not possible just by looking at them,' said Rathbone, 'but our enquiries have shown that DNA tests have proved not only that these gloves were worn at some time by your client, but also that they were worn by Reginald Law's killer.'

Chapman said nothing. Peters said, 'Inspector, I should like a few moments to confer with my client.'

'Fifteen minutes,' said Rathbone. 'Interview suspended at eleven thirty.' He switched off the recorder and left the room, accompanied by Vicky and Sukey.

'It looks as if we've really got our man this time, Guv,' said Vicky.

'Let's see what he comes up with before we start counting our chickens,' said Rathbone. 'We've got time for a quick coffee.' He headed for the machine. When they returned to the interview room he switched on the recorder and sat down. 'Right, Mr Chapman, perhaps you can account for the presence of your DNA on both sides of these gloves?'

'I think I can answer that Inspector,' said Chapman. 'A couple of weeks ago we organized a dinner for a local business consortium and as it was a formal occasion we hired formal dress for our waiters. It so happened that we were unexpectedly a waiter short that evening so I put on a black tie and gloves and helped with the service.'

'What did you do with the gloves when the function was over?'

'As far as I know I sent them back with the rest of the clothing that we hired.'

'So how do you account for the fact that they were subsequently discovered in a rubbish bin behind the hotel?'

'I suppose they were overlooked and no one bothered to send them back.'

'But we know they are the gloves you wore because your DNA is on the inside and outside of both gloves. And,' Rathbone paused for effect and fixed Chapman with his characteristic steely gaze, 'DNA tests also prove that the hands that wore these gloves are the hands that throttled Reginald Law.' He stood up. 'Maurice Chapman, I charge you with carrying out a physical attack on Lance Rainbird, thereby causing his death, and with the deliberate murder of Reginald Law.' He recited the formal caution and then said, 'No doubt your solicitor will wish to apply for bail on your behalf, so you will be handed over to the custody sergeant while the application is being considered.'

TWENTY-EIGHT

After the arrest of Maurice Chapman, DCI Leach summoned the team to his office.

'Congratulations, Greg,' he said warmly. 'Your first case as a DI turned out to be one of the trickiest and most frustrating we've had in a long time. You and your team have done really well to bring about a result.'

'Thank you, sir,' said Rathbone. 'It was pretty tricky at times, chasing up what turned out to be blind alleys and so forth, but we got there in the end.'

'There's still quite a bit to do before we submit the case against Chapman to the CPS,' Leach went on. 'Bail has been granted, by the way, as Chapman isn't considered to be a threat to anyone else – unless to himself, of course, but no doubt the magistrate considered that possibility and rejected it.'

'I don't think for a moment that he'd top himself, sir, if for no other reason that it would cause further distress to his wife. He's absolutely devoted to her but, reading between the lines, it seems there's one rather significant way in which he can't express his love.'

'Yes, I gathered as much from your report and I've made a

note to check with his GP about that. He may have sought help.'

'It would certainly account for his wife seeking satisfaction elsewhere, I suppose,' said Rathbone, 'but the murder of Reg Law was only indirectly due to his marital problems; it was simply a matter of expedience. He was smart enough to use gloves, but not smart enough to understand about DNA.'

'So what's Chapman doing now, sir?' asked DC Mike Haskins.

'He was taken back to the hotel in an unmarked police car,' said Leach, 'and as far as we know he's carrying on with the business until a date is fixed for the trial. I'm calling a press conference first thing tomorrow, by the way. All I'll say is that a man has been charged with causing the deaths of Lance Rainbird and Reginald Law and released on bail pending further enquiries.'

'I don't suppose for a moment that will satisfy them,' said Rathbone. 'We took care that none of the paparazzi actually witnessed Chapman being arrested, and I've no intention of saying anything that might put them on his trail.'

'Quite right, and I want everyone to bear that in mind,' said Leach. 'We've got some work to do before we've got a strong enough case to submit to the CPS. As I'm sure you're all aware, the press are pretty cautious these days after an earlier experience when an innocent man who was questioned and then released without charge was hounded by the press for weeks. A lot of money was paid in compensation, but it took the poor chap a long time to rebuild his life. Just the same,' he went on, 'it only takes one rogue reporter and an irresponsible editor of one of the red tops who thinks he's got a scoop to set the cat among the pigeons, so be doubly careful.'

'How is Lily Chapman, sir?' asked Sukey. 'She was terribly distressed when I left her.'

'By all accounts she's a very brave lady,' said Leach. 'After a tot of brandy and a few minutes to pull herself together she said something like "Well, the show must go on", went to her private apartment to repair the damage to her make-up and has been carrying on since as if nothing had happened. She must have been delighted when her husband returned. I believe you took him home, Penny. How did she seem?'

'I didn't see her when I took her husband back, sir,' said Penny.

'I drove into a space in the car park and he just got out of the car and told me to leave right away. He seemed very anxious no one should see him in my company, probably in case someone happened to recognize me.'

'That makes sense,' said Leach. 'I've heard nothing so far to suggest that anyone apart from the office staff at the Manor actually witnessed the arrest. No doubt Lily's sworn them all to secrecy. You have a question, Sukey?' he said as she raised her hand.

While these exchanges were going on her thoughts had gone back to the scene in Lily's office when it had been obvious that despite the shortcomings in her marriage she was devoted to her husband. It was equally obvious to Sukey that he loved her very much and was a fundamentally good man overwhelmed by circumstances that had driven him to commit murder. 'It's such a sad situation,' she said. 'I'm wondering what will become of her, and to the business, if he's found guilty and sent to prison.'

Leach nodded. 'I agree, it is a tragedy for both of them and it's difficult to say what will happen. It's hard to see how she could carry on with the business on her own. Fortunately that isn't our problem.' He closed the file that lay open on his desk. 'Your next job is to look at the case from every angle, anticipate the sort of line a clever brief is likely to take, based on the evidence you've collected so far, and decide how best to deal with it. I'd like a further word with you, Greg; the rest of your team can go and get some lunch. They can then do some thinking on their own and I want everyone back here at three o'clock.'

'What do you reckon, Sukey?' asked Vicky as they sat down with their sandwiches at a table in the canteen. 'His account for his DNA being on the gloves is plausible, but he's going to have a job accounting for Law's being on them as well.'

'We don't know for certain that he did a waiter's job at the formal dinner,' Sukey pointed out. 'We should make a note to check that with the staff at the Manor.'

'Good point,' Vicky agreed. 'But if he didn't do the waiting job, he must have found the gloves lying around and put them in his pocket with the deliberate intention of putting them on to kill Law.'

'But the formal dinner when he claims to have done the waiting job was at least a couple of weeks before Law was killed,' Sukey objected. 'Chapman wouldn't have known until he overheard the phone call that Law had to be silenced.'

'You're saying he wore those gloves to do his stint serving at table and when he finished he put them in his pocket and forgot to send them back?'

'He might have done, but after he heard the telephone call he remembered he still had them and put them on to strangle Law.'

'It sounds reasonable,' said Vicky. 'But what about Rainbird's death? If Chapman was lying, and Law witnessed that attack, surely he'd have reported it to us right away. It's hardly the sort of thing he'd describe to Harry as a "tasty titbit".'

'That's true,' Sukey agreed. 'Perhaps he'd noticed what Chapman described as the chemistry between Rainbird and Lily, and that was what he was referring to when he called Harry. Maybe, as we thought might have happened, Rainbird was so dazed after his fall that he fell into the water after Chapman left him.'

'And no doubt a brief would think of that possibility too.' Vicky finished her sandwich and stood up. 'I'm going to get a coffee – shall I get one for you?'

'Thanks.'

When the team reassembled in DCI Leach's office after lunch he opened by saying, 'DI Rathbone and I have been discussing how best to present our case to the CPS, after consideration of possible counter-claims Chapman's brief might put to the court. Before we reveal our thoughts we'd like to hear yours. You first, Vicky.'

Vicky consulted her notes and repeated the points she and Sukey had agreed on. Leach nodded and said, 'That's a good start. You next, Mike.'

'Tim, Penny and I have been thinking on similar lines, sir. Then we remembered that Chapman insisted that Rainbird was alive and well when he left him, and that someone else must have come along and finished the job. That sounds feasible, so we tried to figure out how he could account for the fact that only his DNA was found in the gloves used to kill Law?'

'And have you come up with a solution?'

'It's a bit far-fetched, sir, but supposing the real killer was already wearing gloves thin enough for the waiter's gloves to put over them? Rubber or latex gloves for example?'

'You're thinking of someone like a cleaner, a member of the kitchen staff, or one of the chambermaids, for example?'

'Yes, sir.'

'I have my doubts about that, but I'm not going to dismiss it out of hand,' said Leach. 'We'd have to figure out a way he found the gloves, of course. What do you think, Greg?'

'It's certainly feasible, sir,' said Rathbone. 'That would mean that there's no connection between Law's murder and Rainbird's death. I admit that possibility had crossed my mind.'

'You're suggesting Rainbird's been shagging one of the staff when he already has the boss's wife on the go?'

'He can hardly have it off with Lily on her home territory. Maybe he needs it more often than he can have it with her.'

'That could mean that the woman concerned was either married or in some way involved with another man, who found out and killed Law out of jealousy,' said Leach thoughtfully. 'In which case, one would expect her to show signs of distress at Law's death. I'll leave you to look into that, Greg.'

'Right, sir.'

None of the members of the team, who had between them interviewed everyone who was present on the night of Rainbird's murder, could recall noticing any of the women appearing unduly distressed by his death. Further enquiries among those who were not on the premises at the time were equally fruitless. Eventually, after consultation with Superintendent Bradley, Leach informed the team that a case would be prepared for submission to the Crown Prosecution Service. Meanwhile, they would return to their normal duties.

The case was heard at Bristol Crown Court. As the team had anticipated, Chapman's counsel employed all the arguments they had considered, ending with an impassioned plea to the jury for Not Guilty verdicts on all charges. It took several nail-biting days before the foreman of the jury announced that on the first charge against Chapman, that of assaulting Laurence Rainbird causing actual bodily harm, the unanimous verdict was 'Guilty'. On the second charge of manslaughter, they found him 'Not Guilty'. It seemed that they accepted Counsel's argument that Rainbird, being unsteady on his feet after hitting his head on a heavy piece of timber, must have fallen into the lake by accident and drowned, as was shown by the post-mortem examination.

On the charge of murder of Reginald Law, the jury found him guilty by a majority of ten to one, and Chapman was remanded to await sentence.

EPILOGUE

'So, three years for punching Rainbird in the guts and twelve for the murder of Reg Law,' said Harry as he and Sukey sat down with Major Matthews and Lady Freddie to a sumptuous meal in the dining room in The Stables. 'That makes a round total of fifteen years. It seemed the only verdict in Rainbird's case as it was obvious the jury accepted his story. Anyway,' he raised his glass at Sukey, 'our top Detective Constable had already figured out what must have happened so really they had to come to that conclusion. By the way, you said something about applying for promotion to Detective Sergeant. Is that serious?'

'It was DI Rathbone who suggested it,' she said. 'I told him I'd think about it.'

'What about the poor man who died in that awful road accident?' said Lady Freddie. 'It doesn't seem as if anyone's going to be charged with causing that.'

'All the evidence points to the pipe coming adrift as a result of poor maintenance,' said Sukey.

'So the case is closed?'

'Not quite. Chapman's counsel is seeking leave to appeal, but we think it's unlikely it will be granted.'

'What do you suppose will happen at Dallington Manor?' said Major Matthews. 'Surely that poor woman can't carry on the business on her own?'

'Actually, there's some very promising news there,' said Sukey. 'Lily and the remaining staff, who have been incredibly loyal and supportive, are keeping the place ticking over until all the present guests have left – there's only a handful still there anyway. There'll be an announcement shortly that it's closing down for refurbishment. It's hoped the place will reopen in time for Christmas under new management.'

'Do you know who's taking it over?' asked Harry.

'Yes, and it's a really heart-warming story. Lily's

brother-in-law, Pansy's husband, is filthy rich and he's planning to do a substantial makeover before the reopening.'

'That's great news,' said Harry. 'I suppose Pansy is the sister Lily used as an alibi so she could sneak up to Richmond and spend time with Rainbird?'

'That's the one.'

'Well, all I can say is I wish them the very best of luck,' said Lady Freddie and they all raised their glasses in agreement.

One evening a week later, Harry called Sukey and said, 'I've got some good news and some other news. Can I come round and share it with you?'

'I've been wondering why I haven't heard from you,' she said. 'Yes of course, come now.'

When he arrived he opened a bottle of wine, poured two glasses and led her into the sitting room. 'This should really be champagne,' he said, 'but there wasn't time to chill it and I couldn't wait to give you the good news. My editor nominated me a few weeks ago for regional crime reporter of the year, and he's just told me I've got it.'

'Harry! That's wonderful – I'm so proud of you.'

They raised their glasses and drank the toast. Then he put his glass down, took hers from her, put his arms round her and held her close. After some moments he said, 'Would you like to hear the other news now?'

'Other news – oh yes, of course – I'd almost forgotten. What is it?'

'It's Dad and Freddie. They're getting married at Christmas.'

'How lovely!' said Sukey. 'I'm so happy for them. Will she move in with your Dad?'

'No, they're going to move into her place; it's bigger and quite a bit more luxurious.'

'You're going to miss him,' she said thoughtfully.

'That rather depends on you.'

Sukey eyed him warily. 'Go on.'

'Well, Dad's flat is a bit bigger and more convenient than yours . . . and remembering what we agreed when we spent that weekend at Greenings, I thought I'd mention that Dad never got rid of the double bed he shared with Mum for so many years.'

Sukey's head was telling her to play it cool; she knew it was a losing battle but she tried to hold out a little longer. 'I have a feeling,' she said, 'that you're asking me to move in with you.'

'Got it in one,' he said. 'I love you so much, Sukey,' he said gently. 'We make a great team, don't we?' He kissed her again, even more insistently than before. 'Well? What about it?'

Her head gave up the struggle. She drew a deep breath and whispered, 'The offer of a double bed is just too good to refuse.'